Amour Provence

A Novel

Constance Leisure

SIMON & SCHUSTER PAPERBACKS

New York London Toronto Sydney New Delhi

Simon & Schuster Paperbacks
An Imprint of Simon & Schuster
1230 Avenue of the Americas
New York, NY 10020

First Simon & Schuster paperback edition June 2016

SIMON & SCHUSTER PAPERBACKS and colophon are registered trademarks of Simon & Schuster, Inc.

For information about special discounts for bulk purchases, please contact Simon & Schuster Special Sales at 1-866-506-1949 or business@simonandschuster.com.

The Simon & Schuster Speakers Bureau can bring authors to your live event. For more information or to book an event, contact the Simon & Schuster Speakers Bureau at 1-866-248-3049 or visit our website at www.simonspeakers.com.

Book design by Ellen R. Sasahara

Manufactured in the United States of America

1 3 5 7 9 10 8 6 4 2

Library of Congress Cataloging-in-Publication Data

Names: Leisure, Constance.
Title: Amour Provence : a novel / Constance Leisure.
Description: First Simon & Schuster paperback edition. | New York : Simon & Schuster, 2016.
Identifiers: LCCN 2015036324
Subjects: LCSH: Man–woman relationships—France—Provence—Fiction. | GSAFD: Love stories
Classification: LCC PS3612.E35925 A84 2016 | DDC 813/.6—dc23
LC record available at http://lccn.loc.gov/2015036324

ISBN 978-1-5011-2228-6
ISBN 978-1-5011-2231-6 (ebook)

For Steven, Clémence, and Ivan.

La petite famille.

All love goes by as water to the sea
All love goes by
How slow life seems to me
How violent the hope of love can be

Let night come on bells end the day
The days go by me still I stay . . .

—GUILLAUME APOLLINAIRE,
"Le Pont Mirabeau"

1

Dirty Words

As the sun crested the dusky mountain, its golden rays
glazed the street-side houses. Didier Falque stood beneath a linden tree well apart from his friends Sébastien and
Eva, who held hands in the tumbledown lean-to that served
as a bus shelter. A third boy, Jeannot Pierrefeu, was busy
kicking pebbles down the road. Jeannot could never be still
or watchful like Didier. Instead he was always moving,
causing small disruptions even when they were in class, and
now he began to do a wild dance with his own elongated
shadow as the sun's curve rose atop the crenellated peaks
like a scoop of apricot sorbet delivered in a fancy dish.

From the bus stop, their little village of Serret resembled
a king's crown inserted into the mountainside. A great stone
rampart encircled houses perched like jewels one on top of
the other. Above it all, a ruined garrison of white limestone
shone opalescent in the early light.

Didier could smell the fresh scent of buds that had recently appeared in the trees. Even a few daggerlike swards of iris now poked through the rough soil by the roadside. They all wore T-shirts that spring morning and had the same long hair in shaggy disarray that was so fashionable in the 1970s. Only Didier's hair, wiry as steel wool, sat on his head like a helmet instead of lying smooth and flat. He pressed it with his callused fingers, hoping to coax it into place.

"Didi, have you considered ironing that bush?" Jeannot twirled annoyingly close, his big feet flipping another pebble over the gritty road. "That's what all the girls with frizzy hair do." Didier threw out a muscular arm, his knuckles just grazing Jeannot's bouncing shoulder. Unlike his friend, Didier was slow on his feet and that morning the big farm boots he wore felt like they were weighted by stones.

"Stop with your little jokes, Jeannot," Eva called from her seat in the shelter. But she smiled as she said it, knowing that it would be futile to try to stop the flow of Jeannot's words or to quash his brimming energy. She merely wanted to spare Didier, who, though he showed a façade of brash masculine insouciance, had a sensitive side.

But Didier barely heard Eva's plaint. Berti Perra was rounding the hill below, toting her heavy book bag, Berti whose perfect girl's body generally left him overwhelmed with the desire to say something, anything that would make her notice him. That morning her ebony hair glowed in the sun, giving her head a golden aura like the halos on the gilded saints in the village church. She was two years younger than Didier and, like him, born into a family of vintners, but they were from different worlds. Berti's par-

ents, Liliane and Clément Perra, were respected, even re-
vered, because their well-known appellations of Côtes du
Rhône wines were exported all over the world. Didier's
family barely eked out a living, though their vineyards, dotted over the hillsides in separate parcels, added up to a fairly
important landholding. But their wine was considered a
mere *vin de table* in comparison with the vintages from Domaine Petitjean, the Perras' vineyard.

When Jeannot skipped down the road and landed directly in front of Berti, an angry flush crept up the sides of
Didier's face. He had hoped to greet her first, but Jeannot
beat him to it.

"*Salut, ma belle,*" Jeannot said to her with a smile. "You're
late this morning."

"We had a crisis."

"A crisis! Was it exciting?"

"Pati appeared at breakfast with a black eye."

"Did Philippe slug her?"

"Neither of my brothers would ever touch us!" Berti exclaimed.

Didier listened, silently wishing that he had a large family of five siblings like Berti. Perhaps the fact that he was an
only child was the reason he often felt so uncomfortable
with others.

"So what happened?" Jeannot asked.

"Pati says she walked into a door, but her eye was swollen closed. *Maman* took her to the doctor."

Jeannot waved his hand. "This bears further investiga-
tion!" And then he put his arm around Berti's shoulders and
walked her up the hill.

Didier stood heavily in place, wishing he could enter into the conversation, but his mind went blank with the pressure of trying to think. Though all of them had known each other since they were small children, Didier was no longer interested in Berti as a schoolyard acquaintance. Whenever he had occasion to speak to her in the courtyard of the lycée, he got so excited that his voice grew louder and louder until finally he felt as if he was shouting. He knew each time that everything had come out exactly wrong when, after regarding him politely for several moments, she would give him a kind smile before turning away to join a group of friends.

Of the three boys there that morning, Didier would have been considered the handsomest if they had been lined up and compared. He was better built than willowy Sébastien and had a strong, conventionally handsome face, unlike Jeannot, whose rubbery, clownish visage went along with his buoyant spirit. For an adolescent, Didier had the demeanor of someone much older. His family, the Falques, were all dark-haired and Semitic-looking despite the fact that their forebears had been powerful bishops when Avignon and the surrounding Comtat Venaissin had belonged to the pope. Though the Falques remained important landowners, they were in reality no more than simple farmers, his parents working daily in their vineyards and small orchards like most of the other village folk. Didier had inherited the Falque family traits, coarse dark hair and a beard already thick enough that he had to shave every day. He had the high, rounded chest of a young steed and his shoulders stood out like wooden portmanteaux, broad and well defined. To Didier's chagrin, that manly aspect put off many of the girls at school, who seemed more attracted to the soft-skinned, fair boys like Sébastien, whose downy face and thin arms didn't implicitly demand anything. Didier's muscles and his shadowed jaw seemed to cry out that he would expect more from a young woman than she might be willing to give, so the girls in his class tended to behave skittishly when he was around and kept their distance.

Didier sometimes felt a little flutter of jealousy when he watched the amorous Sébastien and Eva, who had been going steady since grade school, but the two more often reminded him of simple barnyard animals the way they rubbed their faces together, emitting soft, unintelligible noises. His friend Jeannot had an easy way with girls, but they rarely took him seriously because of his unrestrained joking. Didier only cracked jokes out of frustration, generally when the afternoon mathematics course with Madame Morin had become incomprehensible. But he didn't have the ability or desire to keep up the flow of wordplay that Jeannot so easily employed, always just on the edge of going too far. It was unfair that Jeannot so effortlessly got good grades and seemed to always have the teachers on his side despite his irreverence, while Didier was accused of laziness and inattention, especially in trigonometry class, ruled over by the exacting Madame Morin. But being called lazy was better than being accused of being slow, something of which he had a horror because in his young heart he knew it was probably true, at least as far as school was concerned. Even if he had wanted to, he couldn't have spent more time at his books because he had chores on the farm and his afternoons and evenings were spent outside in the vineyards, spraying, trimming, pruning, or harvesting, depending on the season. More than anything he loved his father's tractor, loved the noise of the gears shifting, the big tires crushing rock and stone into the clay of the rough roads and field tracks. He adored noise and enjoyed the booming of his own voice that he exercised by hollering loudly above the sound of the tractor as if he was in competition with the roaring engine itself.

With the exception of the gang on the morning bus, Didier didn't have many friends. Boys his age didn't particularly interest him. The girls in his class, however, and the others at school, older or younger, held a definite fascination. He preferred dark-haired girls, and above all, Berti Perra, whose shining black waves fell beneath her shoulders. His youthful ardor kept him interested in the goings-on of most of the girls, but he knew he was wasting his life at school and wished to be out in the real world, where real things might happen to him.

That morning when the bus arrived, Jeannot pulled Berti next to him and Didier groaned softly as he slid by himself into a seat by the window. Blooming apple trees lined the route to school, and in the distance Didier saw the mother of a former schoolmate wheeling a bicycle by the side of the road as she made her way up a steep hill. She was wearing a skirt, and through the school-bus window Didier noticed that she had nice legs in addition to a wild twist of black hair, thick as a pony's mane, unsuccessfully bound by a loose cotton scarf. When she stepped back to watch the bus go by, her eyes met Didier's. She raised her hand in a wave and gave him a dazzling, openmouthed smile that revealed pointy white teeth like those of a fox. Sabine Dombasle. Surprised by her warm greeting, Didier inadvertently lifted his own arm in response, but then quickly lowered it, hoping that no one had seen.

Sabine Dombasle's son, Manu, had dropped out of the lycée two years before and now worked in his father's vineyard, just the way Didier would work full-time for his father after he graduated. But the families, both winegrowers, weren't friends due to a land dispute several years before.

"Bruno Dombasle has gone and planted half a hectare of vines on that little *bout* of land we own by the forest on the Plaine du Diable," Didier's father, Guillaume, had told the town's notary, who acted as the local lawyer when property was involved. But after carefully going through the necessary deeds and documents, the notary admitted he couldn't be truly sure of the actual boundary that marked the edge of each family's terrain. There had been an unfriendly back-and-forth for several years, and finally, after a bitter wrangle, Didier's father had grudgingly ceded the land to Dombasle.

Nearly seven years later, the families still didn't speak. But Didier would nod when he saw Manu or his parents. The Dombasles had well-located vineyards that were, for the first time, bringing in real money. Because of his expanding sales, the paterfamilias, Bruno, suddenly found himself able to indulge his passions. Leaving Manu in charge, he had begun to travel to central France to fish, and in game season he visited various places in Eastern Europe where deer and other wildlife were plentiful. Still, the

Dombasles lived like most farmers in a ramshackle stone house beneath the village rampart. Manu had recently moved into the family's grange, located in a copse of live-oak trees on the plain. In front of his parents' house, a morning-glory vine twisted up a drainpipe, the sole floral ornament, as Sabine was not a gardener and didn't care for flowers. Every spring, the same plant reseeded with no one's help and covered the façade with a generous array of dark indigo blooms.

Getting off the bus that day, Didier couldn't understand the feeling of happiness that pervaded him. Maybe it was just the beautiful morning, the warm sun beating on his shoulders, the girls who made their way through the enclosed courtyard dressed in their light cottons. But when Jeannot came up behind him and, in the high, squeaky voice of a mewling baby, said, *"Maman! Maman!"* Didier realized that he must have witnessed Sabine Dombasle's wave and his own impulsive response. In a rush of shame, the truth came to him; it had been Sabine's gesture that had been the reason for his nebulous thrill and now it had all been destroyed, trampled beneath the feet of the joker, Jeannot, who would henceforth give him no peace. But Jeannot didn't mention it again that day and Didier felt relieved, hoping his friend had forgotten the incident.

It was odd that in the days that followed, Sabine Dombasle, whom he'd never noticed in particular, seemed to be constantly out and about in the village. One afternoon he saw her sitting at the door of the tea shop near the central fountain, whose grotesque heads spouted forth water fed by mountain springs. Sabine's white legs were crossed and Didier saw a flash of pale thigh as he passed on the way to his father's field just beyond the town.

"Didi, how do you manage to work so hard and go to school too?" she asked him. "My son, Manu, never could!" Didier shrugged, not sure what to say. "Why don't you sit down a minute. Here, have a piece of cake." Sabine held out her plate to him. He shook his head, and mumbled something about no time. She smiled and tilted her face up at him, revealing her sharp foxy teeth, and Didier felt he'd made a mistake, as he would have enjoyed eating the cake and passing a few moments with her. But he'd missed the opportunity and it was too late to say yes.

When he was working, especially on weekends, he often saw Sabine in her garden above, hanging up laundry or slashing back spring flowers and blooming bushes with a small scythe. Sometimes she simply leaned over the parapet, gazing into the distance, but Didier had the feeling that her eyes were often directed right at him.

Toward the end of April, Didier spent all of Saturday morning in the vineyards. There was spraying to be done and his father helped him to fill the enormous metal container attached to the back of the tractor that dispensed what was needed to treat the newly budded grapes. By midday, he'd completed about a third of the work to be done, so at lunchtime he parked the tractor at the edge of their property just below the village. He decided to walk up through town and then descend the cobbled streets through the ancient Porte de la Bise. In the old days, the arched stone gateway had not only been closed and locked at night to keep out marauders, it also helped to block the fierce mistral, the buffeting wind of the north that threatened to sweep away everything in its path. The mistral was called *la bise*, the kiss, and the old, north-facing gate had been named after it. That day, his mother, Patou, had told him that she would leave his lunch in the oven since she and his father would be out. As he mounted the steep hill, Didier guessed the meal would be the cassoulet made with beans and preserved goose they'd eaten the night before, and his empty stomach twisted in anticipation.

He passed by the Dombasles' long stone farmhouse. The dried-up stems of last year's morning glory would soon be replaced by a new young vine that had already sprouted and was twisting up the base of the metal drainpipe. As he made his way up the dirt track, the farmhouse door opened and Sabine appeared in the dark rectangle of the embrasure.

"*Salut*, Didier," she said to him.

"*Salut*," he replied. Sabine's hair, bound by no scarf that day, was loose and wild. She wore a light white shift that in the shadow could have been a nightgown or even an underthing. As he slowed, his shoulders seemed to turn of their own accord toward her and he noticed her feet shod in lavender espadrilles. His eyes rose up her nicely shaped legs, over the luminous shift, and then to the pale face surrounded by the lion's mane of pitch-black hair.

"I've been watching you," she said. "You always work so hard."

"There's a lot to do," Didier replied.

"I've made strawberry tartlettes. Come in for a second and have some," she said, stepping back. "You must be hungry."

He jerked his head, indicating the uphill climb. "I'm on my way home for lunch."

"All right, then, I'll give you one to take with you." She opened her mouth and her teeth were once again revealed in that dazzling, eager smile. Sabine stepped back to make room for him as he walked through the doorway. When she closed the door behind him, only a gray, filtered light came through the shuttered windows, the air thick with an aroma of warm fruit and honey. Sabine turned and put her hands on his shoulders. "You've turned into a real man, Didier," she said. "The girls must all be after you." He shook his head, trying to think of how he might respond, but nothing came. She ran her hands slowly down his chest, still smiling.

Didier stepped back and stammered, "Where is your husband . . . Monsieur Dombasle?"

"Bruno? He's fishing in the Morvan. He comes back Wednesday." She again approached, letting her hands glide over Didier's chest. Though he felt a swell of desire, Didier turned away and in two steps found himself in front of the doorway, his hand already on the iron latch.

"I better go," he told her.

"All right," said Sabine. "But come back later for your dessert. It will be even better when it's cool." Sabine again gave him her strange smile and Didier opened the heavy timbered door and let himself out onto the street.

When he returned to the field that afternoon, Didier kept glancing up at the Dombasle house. His work made him breathe deep and he smelled the earth release a living scent as he broke up clods of clayey soil with his heavy-soled boots while moving down the rows of vines. He became aware of the wild thyme that plunged long roots into the dry earth and now, blooming a delicate purple, released its perfume along with that of rosemary and other herbs that grew hither and thither on the rough ground. In late afternoon when the sun was low, a breeze blew up over the plain and there came a chilly bite, but Didier didn't notice it. He felt only the exiguous rays of the sun that pulsed around him, over the vines, up onto the hillside and the house on the hill where the shutters remained shut tight.

The innate politeness of a child made Didier wonder for a moment if he should stop at Sabine's on the way home to pick up the dessert she had offered. But then his body, which still felt the sensation of her hands upon his chest, told him that it was prudent to stay away. When he passed near the old grange where Manu now lived, he realized that his former schoolmate was just two years older than he was, and the pleasant flicker of desire that had flamed for a moment sputtered with the thought that Sabine was old enough to be his own mother. As twilight descended he took the long way around through vineyards and olive groves, then up the dirt path that ran beneath the ramparts so as not to pass before her door.

The following Saturday, Didier found himself in a different patch of vines. He'd been put to work attaching young stems to wire leads that his father had installed that week. He was bent over the lowest rung when, along with a rustle, there came a glimpse of something pink and he stood to find Sabine next to him. This time her black hair was pulled back and twisted in a shiny clip and she was dressed in rosy cotton with a print of tiny flowers. Her white throat looked like the pale breast of a wild bird and he felt that he could see the flutter of her pulse upon it.

"You never came to eat the dessert I made," she said. "I had to eat it myself."

"I'm sorry. I forgot."

"Never mind. It's funny, I hate to cook, but I enjoy making pastry. And with Bruno away so often, I don't have to make dinner for anyone, so I eat pâtisserie instead. I suppose I'm just an indolent housewife. Here." She lifted a package wrapped in white linen out of her satchel. "I brought you a *petit goûter*. Just a little snack." She unfolded the linen and held out a square of chocolate cake. "I thought maybe you didn't care for tarts, so I decided to tempt you with something else."

He took it from her, feeling strangely exposed alone with her there in the field. Then he lifted it and took a bite. At first, his mouth was very dry and he wondered if he could manage to swallow, but quickly the unctuousness of the rich chocolate made his salivary juices flow and he smiled with pleasure.

"*Bon,*" she said before she turned away. "I just wanted to be sure that I hadn't lost my touch."

"Thank you," said Didier politely, his mouth still full of cake. But by then she was at the end of the row of vines where a red rosebush was covered with just-opening buds, and she didn't look back.

In May came the long weekends celebrating the various religious holidays, but he never saw Sabine. Perhaps she had gone off with her husband somewhere. He often spied Manu working in distant fields. School was still on for another month, but it felt like summer and Didier had trouble concentrating.

"Monsieur Falque, are you dreaming or are you completing those mathematical exercises?" asked Madame Morin one hot afternoon when everyone couldn't help but gaze out the window at the pure blue sky rather than keeping their heads down and grinding away at the quiz she'd given them. His friend Jeannot snickered. Didier made a few marks by the equations, but the numbers seemed to him nothing more than garbled nonsense.

One night when he'd finished his homework and there was nothing to do, he noticed that even though it was nearly nine o'clock, it was still light, so he went for a walk. He took the gravelly, zigzag path up the mountainside to the ruined garrison at the top of the town. Beneath a half-moon, the white stone edifice looked gaunt as a haggard face, making for an eerie feeling way up there in the deserted wastes where no grass grew. Didier careened down the slippery slope of the opposite path and found himself in the church square where egg-shaped river stones embedded in the sidewalk were arranged in a fan shape that resembled the half-moon in the sky above. He descended a steep alleyway until he was on the curving road that looked over several hectares of his family's vineyards, the ones that abutted the Dombasles'. There he leaned against the stone wall and gazed down into the valley. No one was out. The church bell tolled the hour and Didier noticed a sliver of light coming from the terraced garden that extended from the side of the Dombasle house. A door thrown open to the night. He sauntered down the street to take a closer look, telling himself that it was nothing more than idle curiosity that led him to see if someone was out and about. But when he reached the edge of the garden, the door made a creaking sound as it was pushed wide open.

"Why, Didi, what are you doing out so late?" Sabine's voice was deep, as if she hadn't spoken in a while. She emerged slowly from the doorway, once again dressed in something pale that skimmed close to her body. Her pile of dark hair blended in with the vines and bushes that grew in the garden behind her.

"Just taking a walk," he said. He put his hands into the pockets of his blue jeans and closed them into fists, ashamed of his rough workingman's fingers.

"Well then, come in for a moment," she said. "Climb over the wall there into the garden." At the end of the garden the wall wasn't high, but it was still a drop of a few feet, so he swung his legs over and jumped. A thorned quince tree grazed his arm, leaving several razor-thin scratches, but he ignored them.

"Come," said Sabine. She cupped her hand and motioned for him, and he entered through the door into a cellar.

It was dark and he tripped going down a step he hadn't seen, bumping into Sabine. A wisp of her wild hair brushed against his face, but she pushed him away as if he was a nuisance. Then she went up a flight of stone steps and he followed, wondering all the while if he should turn around and exit through the garden the way he had come. But seeing a dim light through a doorway above, he passed into what looked like a hallway. Then she turned.

"I don't think you should be here at all," she said. "I don't know why you came." She put her hand on his chest as if to push him again, but her touch was electric. In an automatic motion, his arms went around her, lifting her up, and they were moving down the hallway into the kitchen, she up against the kitchen table making small cries and then sighing deeply. At first, he thought he'd made a mess of things, he'd been so excited. But he kept kissing her and she helped them both undress, and then she took her time and directed him and he did his best to follow.

It was close to midnight when he came to his senses.

"Your parents might ask where you've been," Sabine told him as he pulled on his clothes. "I think you should tell them you ran into a friend. Who could that be?" She tapped the table with the flat of her hand. "Maybe Jeannot Pierrefeu. Your parents aren't particular friends with his parents, so that should be a safe little lie."

But that night he didn't see his parents when he got home. Didier couldn't sleep from pure excitement and wonder as to how this remarkable thing had happened to him.

After that, he never got through his work in the fields without certain prescribed delays, and thanks to Sabine's suggestions, he always had a credible excuse. He amazed himself as the false tales slipped off his tongue. His parents never questioned him at all.

But the two of them had to be careful, more than careful. Sabine impressed that upon him. There was her husband, Bruno, who, above all, must be kept in the dark, and that also included her son, Manu, and all the villagers who spent their days looking for the slightest thing out of the ordinary that might be interesting to pass on as gossip.

At the edge of a stand of live-oak trees perched on a cliff about a kilometer from the village stood an abandoned *cabanon*, really just a stone shack with a door. They began to meet there, each taking a separate route through the woods so no one would see them coming or going together. Sabine brought a thick comforter that Didier hid up in the rafters. The *cabanon* had no lights and no window and they didn't dare leave the door ajar, so Didier supplied a small flashlight that they tilted up against the rough wall when they were together. Sometimes Sabine would grab it and move the spotlight over her body or dance, slowly swirling it over her belly, her breasts, her hungry mouth. Standing over him, she would open her legs so he could glimpse the pink madder of her sex that glistened like a budding rose under rainfall. In his overwhelming desire, Didier would have liked to crush her to him, to squeeze her and kiss her hard, his natural inclination, but he learned to be gentle because they couldn't risk the tiniest bruise or mark, anything that might give them away. The gentleness was intoxicating, Sabine a perishable flower in his hands. Her breasts were soft and white with translucent marks like pale veins. She'd had a son, after all. Sometimes he playfully swung them back and forth when she leaned over on top of him, but she didn't like that. "Don't mock me, Didi," she'd say. "Am I just an old woman to you?" And Didier would pull her to him and tell her she was everything he had ever imagined a woman could be.

During their meetings, her teeth and lips were like a

drug for him. He stuck his fingers into her mouth and rubbed the sharp white points of her canines. He couldn't stop kissing her. And that mouth called him all sorts of things. At first, it was just *mon petit trésor* or silly nicknames she made up. But then came other names, dirty names and epithets that bent him more than ever to her will. Her deep growling voice showered him with curses. The foulest language, combined in phrases he'd never even thought of, began to be a potent force that made him desire her all the more.

One afternoon, as Didier was leaving school, a woman dressed in a black hijab with a facial veil beckoned to him. He turned expecting someone behind him to react, one of the Arab kids, but she moved her hand quickly at him, indicating that he should come. She was carrying a basket of ripe cherries and he thought that maybe she wanted to sell them. But when he came closer he saw her eyes and knew that it was Sabine. He followed her to a parking lot across the way and they drove up into the hills on one of the rough fire trails where cars rarely went.

"You're taking a big chance," he said to her, uneasy at her boldness. "If anyone sees your car, they'll know it's you." She pulled off her veil and laughed at him. Her teeth glinted whitely in the bright sunshine and she nearly drove them both off the road when he threw his arms around her and kissed her neck in complete abandon.

Later, under cover of a huge pine tree whose long boughs brushed the ground, Didier said, "What are we going to do? It was you who warned me not to take chances and now you're the one being reckless."

"Bruno's away again. If we're careful it will be all right."

"But we're not careful," he said, indicating their half-naked bodies lying on the pine needles in full view of anyone who came close enough and had eyes to see.

And then she rolled toward him and out of that mouth came a song of the coarsest, most foul language. "*Putain, fils de merde*, stupid prick with your filthy scrub-brush hair." Despite the words, her voice sounded to him like mournful cajoling, like begging. And though a part of him was disgusted, making him wonder if he should think seriously about ending what was between them, he found himself completely subject to her.

"Our Didier has become a contemplative type. Have you noticed?" Jeannot remarked at the bus stop one morning. "He's always looking away, his nose up in the air, as if he's considering some grand subject. Or is he simply musing about driving tractors and pressing grapes, the banal concerns of a fledgling vintner?"

Berti smiled at him and said, "That's exactly what Didi should be thinking about!"

Didier bumped his shoulder against Jeannot's without taking his hands out of his pockets.

"What's your opinion, Sébastien?" Jeannot asked.

"Maybe he's sorry to see school end for the summer," Sébastien replied. "He's going to miss Madame Morin. She's given you how many detentions this semester, Didi? Maybe our math teacher has a perverse attraction to you."

At the word perverse, Didier's eyes darted from Sébastien to Jeannot. But they seemed intent on the discussion of Madame Morin, who didn't bother anymore to ask Didier if he understood the mathematical equations. Didier grinned guiltily at the boys, feeling relieved that his friends were off the scent.

"Maybe Didier is simply turning into a man," said Eva kindly. "Not like you two perpetual infants." The boys laughed, and Didier found himself scanning her face, afraid that maybe perceptive Eva might be the one to have guessed something. He was disturbed to find that he felt afraid.

The summer came and Didier spent all day in the fields. Even though there was a lot to do, he saw more of Sabine than ever. They met in the little *cabanon* even more frequently and Didier often had to lie about his whereabouts. On July 14, the celebration of the storming of the Bastille, there was the usual village fête. It was held in the main square that was surrounded by ancient sycamore trees whose leafy shade extended over the entire area. Everyone dined at long tables covered with strips of brown paper. A stage had been constructed for the *animateur*, who stood above the dancers and sometimes sang, but mostly played tapes that included everything from the paso doble and Edith Piaf to American rock and roll.

Before dinner that evening, everyone stood around drinking wine supplied by the local cooperative. Except for Didier's parents, who didn't enjoy dancing and never came to celebrate the Quatorze, most of the townspeople were there along with a smattering of tourists who had paid their twenty francs for the night's entertainment. Didier didn't drink except for a rare half glass of wine that his father offered when an exceptional vintage was opened for a special occasion. Instead he drank Cocas with Jeannot, Berti, and

Eva while standing off to the side of the stage where the music was loudest.

Didier spotted Sabine as soon as she appeared on the square. She wore white, the color that suited her best. That night, her hair swirled up into a knot of curls at the top of her head. She sat down on one of the folding chairs at the end of a table while her husband, Bruno, elbowed his way to the bar to get drinks. Sabine's eyes met Didier's, but she had warned him that if they looked at each other at a public gathering, it would be quickly obvious to any bystander that there was something between them, so Didier reluctantly broke eye contact and let his gaze wander over the crowd. At the bar, Bruno turned around, carrying a yellow pastis in one fist and a wineglass of rosé in the other. He surprised Didier not only by looking straight at him, but by advancing in his direction.

"Bonsoir," Bruno said when he reached Didier. Dombasle was on the corpulent side with a wide body, yet he was fit, tanned, and muscular. He had short gray hair and a direct gaze from the brown, slightly bloodshot eyes that were common among vintners who spent long days under the bright sun of the Midi.

"My wife tells me that you are always very polite to her despite that minor disagreement between our families over property. Manu likes you too." Bruno kept his eyes on Didier. "It seems stupid that there's an animus between us." Didier gave the man a half nod in return, fearing Dombasle might be aiming to ensnare him in some terrible trap, and he forced himself not to glance toward Sabine. "Maybe we can break the silence." Bruno smiled. *"D'accord?"*

Didier smiled back at the man, but felt it must look more like a grimace. So he asked, "Do you think that would be a good idea?"

"You'll spend your life here, a vintner like your father and me. There shouldn't be an unnatural rupture between us." Bruno raised the glass of pastis toward Didier, a gesture meant to end all hostility.

"What was that about?" asked Jeannot when Bruno made his way back to the table where Sabine sat waiting.

Didier shrugged, feigning calm, but his heart was pounding. He took a deep breath and kept his eyes on the stage, where the disc jockey was inviting people to dance a lively polka. Didier gulped down his soda and watched as an elderly couple cavorted across the floor.

As the summer progressed and the hot days concluded in long, lazy evenings, Sabine became even more demanding. Didier was often in view working in the fields beneath her kitchen window, and that seemed to provoke her boldness. Sometimes she'd even walk by when he was in the fields and signal for him to join her at the *cabanon*. Whenever her husband was away on one of his fishing trips, she insisted that Didier come to her house.

"I don't think this is safe," he told her one evening when they were naked together in the dark, shuttered salon. "What if Manu or anyone else saw me coming in? That would be hell for both of us." But Sabine seemed strangely oblivious.

"Do you love your husband?" Didier asked her.

Sabine shrugged. "I'm comfortable with him."

"What is that supposed to mean?" asked Didier.

"It means there are advantages to being his wife." Unlike many of the women in the village, Sabine didn't work and Didier wondered if that was what she meant. Bruno was quite a wealthy man. Didier knew how many hectares of vines he had and what that meant in terms of number of bottles sold, the best of his stock often shipped overseas. On the other hand, perhaps once the passion was gone, couples became pragmatic and were content to settle for something less than they'd originally hoped for. But for the first time Didier thought Sabine might have a hard, empty side to her that he had heretofore been unwilling to admit. He wondered if she repeated the same dirty phrases to Bruno that she said to him. Or perhaps it was Bruno who had taught those words to her.

"Are there advantages to being with me too?" he asked, hoping to get a word of affection from her.

She rolled toward him and ran her teeth over his chin as if to carve something there. Then she moved on top of him and said, "You are my enormous advantage." And she began to whisper to him, foul things that mixed up into something entirely new and exotic, like a strangely perfumed flower, and he was swept away by her as he always was.

In the autumn, school recommenced. It would be Didier's final year at the lycée, the grade called *terminale*. Unlike Jeannot, he wouldn't be continuing his education. There was no reason to. But sometimes he thought about getting away from Sabine. He still desired her more than ever, but he had a feeling their luck was running out. How much easier it would be if the following autumn he could simply go away to university in Montpellier or up to Grenoble like some of his fellow classmates. At times he couldn't believe he and Sabine hadn't already been caught. He imagined that some people might actually know about their liaison, but were keeping it to themselves. A word from just one of them could bring the whole world crashing down upon Sabine, her family, his parents, and himself.

One evening in late October, over the Toussaint holiday, when the Day of the Dead was remembered by visits to the cemetery, Didier was at Sabine's house. Bruno was away again, this time hunting in Romania, and Didier had told his parents he was spending the evening with Jeannot. He and Sabine would have hours together in rare tranquillity. Of course, they kept the lights off and the door locked so no one would know that Sabine was at home. She had made a *pain d'épices*, a seasonal treat, and the house smelled of honey and spice, reminding him of the first time he had entered it. He began to kiss her as soon as he came into the hallway. There was no reason to wait, so they went directly into the bedroom, though Sabine often preferred other shadowy places in which to fulfill her needs.

The shutters were closed, but the windows were open, letting in the sultry air of the mild October night. Sabine was more ardent that ever, perhaps encouraged in her abandon by the clement evening and Didier's obvious desire. She called him names and danced around him, she knelt on his chest and said every foul word he had ever heard plus others that mixed nonsense with filth, all said in that plaintive tone of hers, and Didier couldn't help but respond. She wouldn't have had to do anything to make him desirous. The way she moved, looked at him, touched him, was enough. But the words were part of her theater and she created a private place that enclosed just them with her whispered, low-spoken, sometimes cried-out gutter words that made her seem to be at once violated and the violator. But he didn't mind. She met demands that he hadn't even dreamed he had. He could make love to her for hours, which he did without restraint because Sabine always was ready to receive him.

Around midnight he left her. They had agreed that his exit would be through the wild, overgrown garden, as he was less likely to be seen there than if he slipped out the front door. Even though winter was on its way, the air still held its last breath of summer, and as he passed through the village there lingered the smell of old roses that hung down in profusion over the stony walls of gardens belonging to high village houses. Sabine had told Didier to come the next night, Saturday, after dark. "Don't forget," she said, caressing his chest. "Come through the garden."

In the morning, there was plenty of work for Didier even though the grapes had all been harvested. One last special collection was to be done, the *grapillage*. If there were enough grapes still left on the vines, his father would make a sweet wine from the slightly wrinkled, heavily sugared fruit. Didier stayed out all morning. The vineyard he was working in was on the other side of the village, not near Sabine's house, but on the slope below the cemetery, where a man was already selling pots of chrysanthemums that would be purchased by people visiting their family graves on the following day, the Feast of All Souls. His mother had given him a sandwich wrapped in paper for lunch. As he ate he wished he could drop by Sabine's, but it would be too risky. He thought about how long this could go on between the two of them. Sabine would be turning forty soon. That meant she was nearly an old lady and he worried she might not be so interested in him if her desire for sex waned with age. As for himself, he couldn't imagine not being completely enchanted by her and he hoped she would always respond to him when he lifted her up, her strong white calves tight around him and everything radiating pleasure.

That night his parents went to dinner with friends in the valley. Didier ate his meal alone and then waited until well past sundown. He took the low route around the town, down through the patches of vineyard that belonged to many neighbors who had owned the land for generations, the Viguiers, the Doumencs, the Roux, the Pelouzes, and finally, the large parcel that belonged to his family, the Falques. When he reached the curve in the road that revealed Sabine's farmhouse above, he saw with shock that the hulking mass was lit up like an ocean liner on a black sea. Every window blazed, even the ones upstairs, and the door to the garden, brightly illuminated by a spotlight he'd never noticed, was ajar. Didier quickly crossed the road into a low grove of olive trees and crouched amid them. He thought he saw Manu peering from the garden doorway, so he backed farther behind one of the thick olive trunks, but then the young man reentered the house and the door closed with a clack.

After waiting nearly an hour, but seeing nothing, Didier stood up. If he walked by the house it wouldn't be a crime. No one could accuse him of anything. Even if someone spotted him it wouldn't look strange, a young man out by himself on a Saturday night. Nothing unusual in that. So he began to slowly wend his way up the hill. When he arrived at the front of the house, the windows remained as brightly illuminated as ever and he surreptitiously glanced inside, trying to see if Sabine was there. The living room window was almost completely blocked by the morning glory that had twirled its way around the shutters, still alive even at the very end of the season. The flowers closed at nighttime and in the light that came from the interior they looked like shriveled insects. He saw no one. Neither was there a soul in the garden, nor anyone near the thorny quince. He continued on up the hill, remembering the day he'd first gone into Sabine's house and wondering what could possibly be happening at the Dombasles'. And then, coming down the steep path before him came his friend Jeannot's parents, Louis and Marie Rose Pierrefeu. Louis, who was the *garde champêtre*, the village policeman, had his arm linked with his wife's as they proceeded down the hill.

"Hello, Didi," said Madame Pierrefeu when they came abreast of him. "What are you doing up here so late?"

"Oh, I had something . . ." He made a vague gesture toward the vineyard below.

"Ah." She nodded.

And then Louis Pierrefeu said, "There's been some bad news. Have you heard?" When Didier shook his head, Louis abruptly blurted, "Bruno Dombasle has been killed."

"What?" asked Didier, hardly able to comprehend what Louis had told him.

"Yes, in Romania. Apparently he was shot while hunting. An accident."

"Does the family know?"

"A telegram was delivered earlier. It's a terrible thing. And can you imagine that all this is happening just at Toussaint!"

Didier stood there, his hands cold as rocks, his bare arms covered with goose bumps. He wanted to rush into the house to grab Sabine and run away with her forever. But instead he stood immobile in front of the Pierrefeus. Finally, Marie Rose patted him on the shoulder and told him to go home.

Unable to sleep that night, Didier fell into a deep doze just before dawn. When he came downstairs his parents were finishing their breakfast. His mother poured a splash of coffee into a bowl and then added hot milk before placing it in front of him.

"Have you heard about Bruno Dombasle?" his mother asked. When he nodded she said, "Poor Sabine. I'll visit her later today."

"Don't be sentimental, Patou," Didier's father said. "Dombasle probably deserved it." His father broke a baguette in two and divided it down the middle with his pocketknife.

"You hated him that much?" asked Didier, shocked to hear his father speak that way.

"Of course not. Even after the land dispute, I never hated him," said his father. "I simply did not respect him.

It's well known that he's been playing around with women for years. Apparently, one of the jealous husbands might have been along on this hunting trip in Romania. People are saying that it was no accident."

"You mean someone murdered him?"

"Could be," said his father, carefully smoothing butter onto the crust with the thick steel blade. "It wouldn't be the first time a thing like this has happened. Years ago Dominique de Laubry disappeared hunting up on Mont Ventoux. Some say he'd been having an affair with someone else's wife. Anyway, everyone knows Dombasle's been with a string of women."

Didier turned to his mother and abruptly asked, "What time are you going up to see them?" He didn't dare use Sabine's name.

"I thought about eleven o'clock."

"I'll come with you."

"There's no reason any Falque has to go pay his respects to the Dombasle family," said Didier's father.

Patou pulled out her chair and sat down with an angry grunt. "You're very wrong about that, Guillaume. We've known these people forever. They're our close neighbors. It's the correct thing to do."

Didier shaved, showered, and dressed in a jacket that he hadn't worn since the previous Easter. It pulled at his shoulders and his arms bulged awkwardly against the fabric. He and his mother walked up the hill, through the Porte de la Bise and down to the other side of the village together. At the Dombasles', Manu opened the door to them. In the main salon the windows were open and the shutters thrown wide. Didier hardly recognized the place in the glaring light, he was so used to the gloaming that Sabine preferred, the shutters closed to block out both night and day. There were a few people sitting in chairs against the wall— vintners, their wives, and some others from the nearby town of Beaucastel—muttering softly among themselves. Didier didn't see Sabine.

"Will your father be brought back to the house?" Patou asked Manu in a low voice. Manu looked at them both and then he blurted, "His head's practically shot off. They'll keep him at the funeral home until the burial." An anguished sigh escaped from Didier, who covered his mouth as bile rose into his throat.

"Is your mother resting?" asked Patou.

With a motion of his chin, Manu indicated she was upstairs. "She didn't sleep last night."

"That's understandable," said Patou. "Please let Sabine know that I'd like to help her in any way that I can. If you would like something to eat, I'm cooking a daube today. I can bring it up this evening."

Manu bowed his head and said, "That's kind of you, Madame Falque."

"Call me Patou," she said.

Didier glanced at his mother. She was tall and slender with her hair cut short so that it surrounded her head in a burst of mahogany curls. He realized that she was still pretty. Had Manu noticed? What if he found her attractive? Didier wondered with horror what would be the circumstances in which his mother might succumb to a man's attentions. As he turned away it occurred to him that Sabine was quite different from a gentle woman like his mother, and that, in truth, his lover was a mystery to him.

Didier wished he could sit down in a chair and loll against the wall like the other visitors. But the idea of seeing Sabine was unbearable. Still, he wished he could wait there all day, bide his time, breathe in the same air that she was breathing. Maybe he'd hear her footsteps, see her shapely calves on the staircase, her knees, the curve of her hip. How would her face look if she saw him there?

His mother put her hand through his arm and they walked to the door. Was it possible that she could have perceived his pain and desolation?

"It's a terrible thing, a violent death like that," Patou said when they were outside on the street. "It's a stigma that the family will have a time getting over."

"Does *Papa* really believe someone killed Dombasle out of jealousy?"

"That's what the rumors are in the village," said Patou.

"But who would know the truth?" asked Didier. Was it possible that everyone in their little village really knew the totality of everybody else's business; that the Dombasles, both Bruno and Sabine, were involved with other people? Did they know that he was one of those people? Didier felt a frosty rivulet of sweat run down his rib cage.

"Your father predicts that by tomorrow we will have some news," Patou continued. "That's when the other men on the hunting trip get back. They've been delayed by the Romanian police."

When they returned to their house, the streets were deserted. Didier sat outside on the fieldstone stoop. There was no one he wanted to see, but he didn't want to be inside, so he took his chances sitting in the shadow of the doorway. Anyone might walk by. It could be a painful encounter or it could be a pleasant diversion. That's the way it was in the village: you never knew who might stumble around the corner. Didier didn't care. But in his heart he wished that Sabine would appear in front of him wearing her lavender espadrilles, dressed in that light shift, with a smile on her face and her pretty teeth gleaming.

Bruno Dombasle was laid to rest in the village cemetery. The stone tombs, all aboveground because of the unbreakable mountain rock beneath, were covered with a profusion of violent colors, pots of magenta, gold, white, and orange chrysanthemums, the floral offering of choice for the Day of the Dead.

Didier had installed himself beside the wrought-iron gates at the entrance. He refused to attend the service in the small chapel into which his mother had slipped to pay her respects. He couldn't bear the idea of being crushed in with others to watch Sabine seated at the foot of her dead husband's coffin.

Soon enough, Manu came up the hill pushing a rolling catafalque along with a few family friends. Sabine walked just behind the simple oaken box that held Bruno Dombasle's remains. She wore a silvery dress that shimmered and reminded Didier of the defenseless belly of a fish. A black jacket covered her pale arms and shoulders, while her face, strained and bloodless, was bent forward. Was it sadness or the shame of facing everyone who knew that Bruno had been an unfaithful husband?

When the coffin turned upward and passed through the gates, the gravel shifted with a dry crunch beneath the skidding wheels of the cart and Sabine looked up. Her eyes zigged over Didier's face and her dry lips parted for an instant before she looked away. Didier felt his hands clench. He wanted to touch her, to stroke her arm, to grab her to him and make love to her until she forgot, until they both forgot about the horror of the situation in its entirety. But he suspected it would no longer be possible to make a connection, or even to extend a sympathetic hand, and certainly not possible to achieve any sort of abandon together.

One of the Dombasle cousins, a mason who lived on the other side of the Rhône, had already chiseled open the edges of the flat stone that held the blackened coffins of Bruno Dombasle's parents. The mortuary attendants slid in the casket next to the others, and after a few brief words from the priest, the mason began to cement the opening shut again.

Didier went up to the village each night, over the cobbled stones and down the long street to the ruined tower that loomed just above the Dombasle house. He could glimpse through the lit windows that people were there. He never saw Sabine, though once he spotted her speeding down the mountainside in Bruno's car. Sometimes in the evening he would perch in the field below looking up at the house and the darkened garden hoping for some sign. Once, when it was late and the air had turned wintery, he found the place in total darkness and imagined her shut up inside. He waited in the deep shadow of the stone wall and then jumped into the garden, where he dared to make a few bird-like calls, calls that had once made Sabine laugh when he'd practiced them while they were alone together. It was nearly eleven o'clock and there were no lights around him, either from the houses perched in the village above or from the valley below, and there was no response to his forlorn chirping. Didier hoisted himself over the wall and crept to Sabine's front door, where he listened. He thought he could make out the faintest sound of music, but it could have come from somewhere else. He gave a small, hesitant knock on the door and put his ear against it again. In a moment he heard light footsteps. But the door didn't open and there was no sound. After a moment Didier couldn't resist and gave a harsh whisper, calling her name. When the door abruptly opened he nearly fell over the sill. There was Sabine in the darkened vestibule, her face contorted, ugly as a reptile. "Leave me alone, you little creep. Don't come around here again! *Emmerdeur.*" And she slammed the door in his face.

Didier didn't try to see her again. But he still gazed up at her shuttered windows when he was working in the fields below. There were times when he remembered with longing how she had been with him, and though he felt an overwhelming desire to try to reignite something, he stayed away.

In the New Year there was a school dance and he asked Berti Perra to go with him. She said yes and an easy friendship developed between them. They began to meet and talk together in the courtyard after school. He managed to speak to her in a normal tone, not the nervous, dominating voice that had formerly been his mode. In February, the almond trees bloomed as usual and spring came early that year.

2

Le Toulourenc

It was imperative that Filou lie low for a few days like a fox in his den. He skirted the villages of Serret and Beaucastel in his white *camionnette*, and just before the wrought-iron gates of Domaine Petitjean he pulled the little truck onto a dirt track and parked where he wouldn't be seen. There was always a place at his friend Liliane Perra's that he could borrow in an emergency, though when he was a boy the hideout had been nothing more than a hut for a *troupeau* of goats. Filou had a key for the low door half blocked by the trunk of a gigantic fig tree that crawled its way over the roof. He remembered the taste of those figs in season when he would pluck them warm and meltingly honeyed right off the branch. But now, in early spring, the leaves were barely out.

The wooden door made a cracking noise as he pushed his way in, setting off eager howls from Clément Perra's hunting dogs penned at the back of the house. Filou carefully eased the door closed behind him, hoping they'd settle down. The small space had been renovated to lodge a hired hand some years before, when Liliane and Clément had expanded the domaine's wine production. A cement floor had been poured, the walls shored up, and a few amenities added, including a small gas heater, a kitchenette, and the sole decor, a circular mirror in a plastic pearlized frame. The view from the single window looked over a bank of aloe plants that pointed their fleshy, knife-tipped leaves upward as if indicating the direction to the turreted pink château that dominated the upper village of Beaucastel. Filou sat down on the lumpy mattress of the old iron bedstead and pulled from his knapsack a set of rose-dotted sheets and a carmine towel that he'd taken from the closet at home where Pierrette kept the household linens. Then he put his head in his hands, ready to berate himself for everything that had happened.

At forty-three, Félix Rabaute, known to everyone as Filou, still had the physique of a young man. Though not particularly tall, he was perfectly proportioned with a pleasant face made interesting by a strong, slightly prognathous jaw. During the days of his youth, he'd worn his thick russet hair to his shoulders, a length that he felt expressed his iconoclastic nature. But now that his hairline was beginning to recede, not wanting to display any signs that might signal a diminution of virility, he regularly shaved his head. His eyebrows, dark and glossy as bird's wings, made his green-eyed gaze alternately unsettling or attractively magnetic depending on who was at the receiving end. Above all, Filou was a man who possessed uncanny endurance, an attribute that had served him well in life. Many stories were told about Filou and his special abilities, especially in Beaucastel, where he'd been born, and where he still sometimes worked as a carpenter and jack-of-all-trades. A favorite was the tale of Filou's ski vacation when he'd carried a woman with a twisted ankle ten kilometers through the Alpine snow at night, delivering her to the local hospital and then staying out until dawn with three Swiss stewardesses he met at a chalet bar who invited him back to their hotel, where he further proved his legendary stamina.

In his youth, women behaved around Filou the way besotted honeybees might conduct themselves in a field of overblown roses. Perhaps it was the muscles that undulated just beneath the surface of his forearms that attracted them, or his legs, brawny enough to scale walls and jump from roof to roof, where he was often seen adjusting the red clay tiles that served to protect against what little rain was shed in Provence. If it wasn't his singular looks or his phenomenal strength, perhaps it was his love of adventure that did it—the camping trips through the wilds of Corsica, his enthusiasm for discovering isolated beaches in Slovenia, painted caves in Puglia, or white-water kayaking in the Ardèche. As soon as he scraped enough money to leave, he'd be off, and the girls would miraculously follow. That's how it had once been! But now there was Pierrette, whom he'd lived with for seven years and who had come to believe that, despite his nature, Filou should evolve into that most desirable of mates, a one-woman man.

A knocking brought him to his feet and his friend Liliane pushed through the ill-fitting door, causing the dogs to recommence their howling.

"I thought that might be you," she said. "What's going on?"

Filou sighed.

"Oh no," said Liliane. "What have you been up to?"

"Just taking life as it comes. *Carpe diem!*" he exclaimed with a desperate gesture of his hands.

"My dear Filou, when are you going to grow up!?" Liliane put her fists on her hips and gazed at him, a disappointed look on her face. "You're not a youngster anymore. It's 1980! Besides, Pierrette's an independent woman who doesn't have to put up with this kind of behavior. You're going to lose her!"

Liliane was still a handsome woman with a pleasing figure despite having had five children. Her fine chestnut hair that showed no gray was pulled back in a chignon. Of course, as Filou well knew, she wasn't what she'd been as an adolescent when she had whiled away summer days lying on a chaise longue in a miasma of perfumed suntan oil that had made her splendid body gleam like expensive quartz. Filou had been a mere boy then and the lovely Liliane the object of his devotion. He would drift over to Domaine Petitjean each day, deserting his classmates, who he felt frittered away their summers playing pointless games in Beaucastel's dusty square. Instead, he was eager to fulfill Liliane's every wish, mostly having to do with running to the town's *épicerie* in order to purchase cellophane bags of potato chips and select the frostiest bottles of Fanta from the rusty electric ice chest that stood out front. He and Liliane had shared this bounty together and talked until the sun descended behind the cypress trees, at which point Liliane would wrap a towel around her glorious form and bid him good-bye. "You're the most intelligent and interesting boy I know," she often told her adoring slave, and Filou had hoped she would feel that way forever.

By the time he was thirteen and she was eighteen, Liliane represented much more than the pleasure of a snack of salty chips and fizzy orange drink imbibed in female company. The daughter of vintners with a large landholding, Liliane came from quite a different background than Filou, whose own father had disappeared years before, leaving his mother to eke out a living selling produce in the nearby town of Saint-Maxence. For Filou, Liliane was the forbidden fruit, within reach, but never to be touched. And to his chagrin there were others who began to come around, older boys who seemed to have more of a claim on Liliane than he ever would. Finally, when Clément appeared on the scene, all was lost. Filou realized in his young heart that his love for Liliane had been hopeless, and he determined that this would be the last time that he would ever allow an unrequited passion to overtake him. His philosophy became to pursue and conquer, and if things didn't quickly work themselves out in the way he desired, he'd be off to something new before the undecided female could say, "Don't go!"

"Who was it this time?" Liliane asked him. "You haven't had to move into our little room for quite a while now. She must have been a bombshell!" Filou noticed that an amused smile flickered across his friend's face despite her accusing tone.

He shrugged. "I was working in Serret yesterday replacing some joists on Madame de Laubry's roof when *tiens*! I thought I recognized someone going into the place across the street. When a light came on in the upstairs window, I saw that it was her, Victorine Duruy! Someone I'd known years ago. I felt that I must at least say hello. She immediately recognized me and was more charming than ever, in fact, even better-looking than she'd been as a girl." Filou made a motion with his hands to show Liliane what he meant. "Then Victorine invited me in for a drink."

"And that was that," said Liliane.

"Well yes," said Filou. "I got home a bit later than usual. I don't know how Pierrette could possibly have guessed, but this morning before she left for work she told me to pack my things and get out!"

"*Ma foi*, Filou, what's going to happen now between you and Pierrette? And little Françoise and Gaspard! What's to become of them? Those children need you, Filou. You can't desert them!"

Filou rubbed his face with his callused hands and said, "I know, I know. I really am not sure what I'm going to do."

"Well, I can't advise you." Liliane shook her head. "But I do know that Pierrette deserves better than a man who can't resist any woman who happens to walk by with a friendly look on her face."

Filou's forehead creased and his lips turned down in a clownlike grimace. Liliane patted him on the shoulder. "Why don't you come into the house and we'll have a coffee. I'm busy making a cake for Berti to take on a picnic with her friends."

As they walked through Liliane's garden everything was the yellow-green of spring. Easter had been celebrated the Sunday before. Filou made a bonfire that day because the mistral was blowing, bringing a cold snap from the north, and he and his children had played horseshoes in the garden, Françoise in her red wool jacket and Gaspard, who was now a big boy of six, refusing to put on a coat because Filou never did. But that morning at Liliane's, it seemed that the warm days had finally arrived, even though Filou felt a particular chill that wasn't relieved by the glow of sunshine. He knew difficult days lay ahead and that he had brought them upon himself.

As the two drew close to the house, Liliane's daughter Berti appeared on the kitchen steps. "*Bonjour*, Filou," she said. The sight of the teenager broke Filou's somber mood. Berti was in her last year at lycée and looked like her mother when Liliane had been in her prime. They were both petite and voluptuous, but instead of Liliane's straight hair, Berti had a tousle of wild jet curls and she'd inherited the olive complexion of her father. If Berti hadn't been the Perras' daughter and if Filou had been just a bit younger . . . But these things didn't bear thinking about. He would never touch Berti Perra!

The sudden noise of a growling engine made them all turn, and Clément Perra's green Peugeot sped through the gate. As he braked, the car swerved, almost mowing the two of them down. Instead of apologizing, Clément shook his fist through the cranked-down window of the car and shouted, "Damn it, Liliane! Max Boyer says he's been telephoning the house all morning and getting no response. He finally got Bonfils to come get me. It's your job to answer the damned phone!" He threw open the car door, his gray hair a mass of tight waves close as a sheep's hide, and stomped toward them.

Filou was well aware that Clément Perra had a temper. He'd once seen him throw a punch at a fellow vintner at a village fête, and even in public Clément never hesitated to reach out and cuff his children if one of them displeased him. But Filou had never seen him behave this way with Liliane. After all, it was she who had inherited Domaine Petitjean from her parents, and she who had been in large part responsible for the improved fortunes of the family's business. Everyone knew that despite his skill as a wine-maker, Clément could be irrational and difficult. It was Liliane's charm and savoir faire in dealing with distributors, wine experts, and the public that had been the real key to their success. So it didn't surprise Filou when Liliane drew herself up and said, "Clément *chéri*, Berti and I have been here all morning and the phone hasn't rung once!"

"That's true," said Berti. Her hands clenched the stair banister as she stared at her father, wide-eyed as a frightened doe.

"Ah bon?" Clément leaned toward the women like a lizard about to bite. "It happens that the prefect of police in Marseille has arranged a wine tasting for his top-echelon people and he was given the name of Domaine Petitjean. Luckily I was able to contact the *préfecture* in time! The group arrives at five o'clock. I'll need you both here to receive them!" He pointed at Berti. "And not in those filthy blue jeans!"

"Berti's leaving for a picnic," said Liliane.

"Oh no she's not!" said Clément. Then he turned to Filou. "What the hell are you doing lurking around here?"

Filou smiled and replied, "And good morning to you too, Clément."

Without responding, Clément stormed into the house.

"As soon as I have my *bac* I'm leaving just like my sisters did!" Berti said, her voice quavering. "He drove them away and it will be the same for me!" When she began to cry quietly, Filou's heart flew out to her. He remembered that Berti's eldest sister, Marguerite, had left for Canada before she'd even finished lycée. The word was that except for a single letter to Liliane, Marguerite had never again been in touch with the family. The next daughter, Pati, hadn't let grass grow under her feet either and immediately found a job at a bank in Belgium after graduation.

Everyone wondered why Clément Perra was so strict and inflexible with his children, especially his daughters. Over the years, the same facts and conjectures about him had been endlessly repeated by his neighbors in an effort to figure him out. He'd come from a French family who, for generations, had owned a farm in Algeria, so long in fact that not one among them had ever visited mainland France. When the war for Algeria's independence ended, the family was forced to emigrate and begin all over again in Provence. Some said that Clément was not really rooted in the French way of life the way they were because he remained faithful to the antiquated customs of the Algerian countryside, where women were chained to the home, dominated first by their fathers, then their husbands, never free to do as they wished. But Clément was nearly as strict with his sons and his aggressive behavior remained a conundrum.

Liliane climbed the steps and took Berti in her arms. "Go on to your picnic. I'll handle your father. He'll be much too involved with his guests to pay attention to your absence." Then Liliane motioned to Filou. "You haven't been scared away, I hope? Let's go inside and have our coffee."

As soon as Liliane poured out three espresso cups and added a touch of cream to Berti's, the phone rang. "The *préfecture* is finally getting in touch." Liliane laughed.

"I'll get it," said Berti. There was only one telephone in the house, located in the salon. In a moment, Berti was back. "I guess I won't be going out today after all. Eva's Deux Chevaux won't start and her parents won't let her use their car."

"I'll be happy to drive you," said Filou, who had downed his coffee in one gulp. "I'm working at Madame de Laubry's today. She doesn't mind when I come and go. Later I'll bring you all home."

When Berti left the room to telephone Eva, Liliane said, "And after that, you'll go straight to Pierrette and beg forgiveness on your knees. Understood?"

Filou's brow creased again as he wondered how exactly that might be done with any success.

Liliane packed up the cake she'd made, and as she handed it to Berti, said, "Please be careful, the Toulourenc can get wild this time of year."

"You know I don't like deep water, *Maman*. Besides, the river is probably too cold to even put a toe in."

Outside, the sun was surrounded by a bright aureole in a slightly misty sky.

When they got to Filou's *camionnette*, Berti sighed. "I've really had enough. If it wasn't for my mother, I would have run away long ago the way Marguerite did."

Filou put his hand on the girl's shoulder. "You know, Berti, good things come with the bad. You have a lovely mother, and don't forget that together your parents have made the domaine successful. That means a great deal. I grew up with nothing—no father, no money, and I hardly ever saw my mother, who worked all the time. You're lucky, you know, even if Clément can be an ogre!"

The breeze blew through the open windows as they rolled over hills covered with rows and rows of budding grapevines.

"Will you be going to university when you finish up at school?" Filou asked.

"I'd flunk out in the first semester!"

"I hear Eva and Sébastien are going up to Grenoble. You're at least as smart as they are!"

"They know what they want to study. I don't."

"Why not take courses in viticulture? After all, you already know quite a bit about growing wine."

"And work for my father at the domaine? Never! I'm going to Scotland in June. *Maman* has a cousin there who will hire me, at least for the summer."

"Doing what?"

"He owns a restaurant."

When Filou spotted Eva with her boyfriend, Sébastien, he pulled over to the side of the road. Eva threw her backpack in behind him and gave Filou a kiss. "*Merci mille fois!* Seb and I had given up hope of going!"

"Yes, you saved the day!" Sébastien declared. Filou wished the saving of his own day would be so easy, but the youngsters' gaiety perked him up. Filou wasn't one to brood or stay unhappy for long.

"I made a pâté for the picnic," said Eva in her throaty voice. "It's absolutely the best thing I've ever cooked!" She was not a pretty girl, but she had a way about her, and that marvelous voice simply forced them all to smile.

They drove past the ruined château of Entrechaux and then into the neighboring region of the Drôme, where Mont Ventoux rose up nearly two kilometers into a sky the color of a pale sapphire flame. Going down into the valley Filou asked, "So who is going to be there today?"

"Oh, just some kids from school," Berti replied.

"She's not telling the whole truth." Eva brought her face close to Filou's and said sotto voce, "Berti has a date!"

"Please don't mention that to anyone, Filou!" Berti pleaded.

"Of course not. But who are you meeting? Is it your old friend Didier Falque?"

"No," said Berti. "I hardly ever see Didi anymore since he went to work in his father's vineyard."

"Then who is it?"

This time it was Sébastien who leaned forward and said, "Gautier Marcassin."

"Not the guy who plays music at the disco!" said Filou. "He's not your type, Berti."

"It's none of your business. Especially you, Seb!" Berti said, turning around to glare at her friend.

"Marcassin's too old for you! He must be thirty," said Filou. "And he doesn't have the best reputation."

"What do you mean?"

"Apart from working weekends at the discotheque, as far as I know the only thing he does is sell marijuana."

"But he's a *bel homme*— and so sexy!" Eva piped up. "Since he danced with Berti last Saturday, she's talked of nothing else!"

It wasn't lost on Filou that at one point in his life he might have been very happy to attract a pretty young thing like Berti. But he also knew that someone like Gautier Marcassin would stop at nothing once he had her in his clutches. Even Filou, who was at heart a gentle and sympathetic person, had at one time believed that under certain conditions a man had the right to take what he wanted from a woman whenever and however he could get it. He didn't want Berti to find herself in a bad situation.

As they drove toward the river, Berti turned to Filou and said, "Even if Gautier does come today, and I'm not sure he will, I'm afraid that I should really be home for that wine tasting this afternoon. I don't want *Maman* to have to take the blame if my father notices I'm not there."

"That's fine with me," said Filou, pleased that he'd so easily be able to rescue Berti. "I'll finish early today anyway. The work I have shouldn't take long."

The road became steep during the final descent into the river valley, and hairpin turns made it tough going. Filou jammed the clutch of his *camionnette* into second gear. When he turned off for the river, the route changed from rutted tarmac into packed earth, and the truck eventually bumped up onto a weedy patch overlooking the water. There was already a small group of kids milling around below. Most of them were from the lycée, but a few older boys were there too. Manu Dombasle, a husky young man in his twenties, stood apart, lobbing stones into the river. He'd become dull and thuggish since his father had been killed in a hunting accident two years before. Even their mother, the widow Sabine, didn't seem to pay much attention to her only son. But Filou forgot about Manu when Gautier Marcassin roared up on a black motorcycle and parked under a tree. Marcassin's long hair was pulled back in a ponytail, just the way Filou had once worn his own hair, and he had on a sleeveless shirt that revealed the tattoo of a scorpion on his upper arm. He was dressed in jeans and the usual heavy black boots of a biker.

Berti jumped out of the car and Marcassin came over and kissed her on both cheeks. Filou once again felt angry that a man that age would find it appropriate to associate with mere children. He looked at the young faces of the girls waiting by the riverside and wondered if anyone else would be prey to the good-looking ruffian. Marcassin was nothing but a transient, someone passing through, who would move on when he'd made too many mistakes, or too many enemies. Filou thought of things he could say to scare him off, but he knew it would be time wasted. The man would pay him no mind. Besides, he had the roof to finish and the problem of Pierrette that he must allow to percolate in his mind.

"Okay, *je me casse*. I'm going," Filou said in a loud voice so Gautier Marcassin would hear. "I'll see you later." Then he leaned over to Sébastien and whispered, "Keep an eye on Berti and that cretin!"

Standing next to Gautier, Berti watched Filou's truck make its way up the road. But when Gautier grabbed her hand, saying, "Why don't we take a walk upriver and find a nice spot. We'll lead the way," she felt an unaccountable shyness.

"I have to change my shoes first." She slipped out of his grasp, still surprised to be singled out by someone like Gautier, who had always gone for older girls, girls who were free to do as they pleased and didn't have parents who expected them home at a certain hour. He stood close to her as she pulled off her sandals, and she noticed his strong flat chest and the way his jeans hung around his hips. Her heart beat faster and she took her time lacing her sneakers, hoping he wouldn't notice the flush that she felt creeping up the sides of her face.

"Ready now?" Gautier asked. He held out his hand to her, a hand that felt dry, so different from the usual sweaty palms of the boys her age. They slid down the sandy embankment as if it were soft snow.

On the riverbank, Berti's school friends surrounded her, giving her the *bise*, which for adolescents meant several kisses on each cheek. Gautier must have grown impatient because he began to walk ahead. As he got farther away, Berti felt as if she'd lost an opportunity. He probably wasn't really interested in her after all. Well, it wasn't important, she told herself.

She continued on with her friends up a gentle rise, cleaving to the shallows, but the melting mountain springs had swelled the Toulourenc, causing it to overflow its banks. In places the river rushed so fast that the breaking waters looked like silvery fish leaping over the gray and white stones. Behind her, Manu Dombasle was again busy tossing rocks into the water. When a big one landed near enough to splash her, Berti turned and said, "Stop your silly games, Manu!"

"Just because you think you're such a big girl now, I can't have fun?" Manu shouted.

Berti let it pass and simply picked up her pace to get out of range. Ahead, she saw Gautier wading in the shallows, his boots off and backpack slung over his shoulder. The water skimmed just below his rolled-up jeans. When she caught up, he fell into step next to her.

"Do you like it here by the river, Gilberte?" She was surprised that he'd called her by her given name, since everyone, at least everyone her age, called her by her nickname. Maybe he was just being formal, or maybe he didn't realize she was called Berti. After all, they hardly knew each other.

The river flooded into her canvas sneakers as they veered into deeper water, and Berti replied, "It's too cold!" Gautier took her arm. The current eddied around her ankles and made them ache, but she ignored the discomfort, enjoying the feeling of his body close to hers. As they strode along together, a sort of excited weakness pervaded her. She regretted that she and Gautier were not alone and that the day was to be spent with her classmates.

Small stones rolled into her shoes and she tried to kick them out from between her toes, making the water splash. Gautier laughed as if he thought she was just having fun. For a long time they kept a steady pace, barely speaking, but when she began to limp, he said, "Are you getting tired? We'll stop soon." She turned and noticed that they had been moving along at such a clip that even Seb and Eva were out of sight. She'd never been this far upriver and didn't recognize anything, not the tall rocks that rose up beneath the silvery shadow of Mont Ventoux, or the dark swaths of conifers that grew up on either side of them. Gautier led her to an embankment where the ocher-red soil was soft with decayed pine needles. There he turned her toward him and she felt a wild thrill when he began to kiss her.

"Let's go," he finally said. "There are some places I want to show you."

Tiny pebbles filtered into her shoes again and the bottoms of her feet became abraded and sore, but she managed to keep up. At the next bend in the river they mounted the side of a waterfall and all at once Berti found herself standing at the edge of large, perfectly clear pool. Around the edges, white flowers on needle-thin stems were reflected like stars in the water. Beneath them small rainbows played faintly around the tumbling cascade. Gautier ran a hand through her hair. "What do you think?" he asked.

Berti could only nod, afraid he might suggest that they swim, but he surprised her and said, "There's something just ahead. Come on."

"Maybe we should wait until my friends come." Berti laid her satchel on the ground.

"It's just a few minutes away. If you like it, I'll take you back later." Berti knew there would be no later, since Filou was coming, so she acquiesced, and after dumping the pebbles out of her sneakers, let him lead her beyond the river and into the wood. They came upon a steep cliff face and Gautier scrambled up. Berti tried to stay close behind, but her wet sneakers kept slipping on the rocks. Sometimes he'd grab her arm and impatiently hoist her up.

Eventually, they found themselves on a landing where the abundant trees obscured any view of the Toulourenc below. Berti looked down over the cliff and felt a vertiginous pull, as if she might fall straight down. She wondered how she would manage to descend. Perhaps Gautier knew an easier route and he had been testing her to see if she was strong enough to make it up there.

Gautier heaved off his backpack and she saw a military insignia with his name sewn on the flap in block letters.

"Were you in the army?"

"At one point." Gautier came over to her and slid his hands over her shoulders. Then he began to play with her hair, twirling it around his fingers. He had a wry grin on his face as if he was well aware of the kinds of emotions he was causing each time he touched her.

She stepped away and said, "My father was in the cavalry when he lived in Algeria."

Gautier cocked his head. "Your father is Algerian?"

"No, his family was French."

"So after the war they all got thrown out. Not before he'd killed his share of Arabs, I'd wager."

"He never talks about that," said Berti. "But I know he feels that his family's land was stolen."

"What about the French who took the land from the people living there in the first place!"

Berti didn't want to get into an argument over something about which she knew little. Instead she asked, "Have you ever been there?"

"We were sent all over the place—Mali, Chad, Algeria. I was with the Foreign Legion."

Berti had heard that the Legion attracted desperate people and its recruits were considered nothing more than well-trained cannon fodder, shipped out to places too dangerous for the regular army.

"Why did you join?"

"I was forced to." Gautier scowled at her and Berti thought he wouldn't confess anything more. But after a moment he said, "When I was a kid I was always in trouble, mostly petty crimes. But then a friend of mine got a pistol and we were caught robbing someone. The judge gave me the choice of prison or joining the Legion. So I started over. They even gave me a new identity." Gautier stopped talking and stared at her. Finally he said, "I was born in France to a French mother, but my father was Algerian, so I had an Arab name. As you know, it's so much easier when people believe you are purely French."

"I thought you might be Spanish."

Gautier laughed. "I thought you were! I've seen your father and now it makes sense that he comes from Algeria. Perhaps with his dark skin he's a mixture like me."

Berti said nothing, wondering if that could be possible. Her father rarely talked about his family. But he had always had an animus toward North African immigrants and never hired them to work at the vineyard. Even during the harvest, when many hands were needed and there were truckloads of Arab workers who lived in the region, her father always chose the Spanish or Portuguese migrants who crossed the border for the sole purpose of picking grapes.

Gautier came close to her again. "I don't usually tell anyone about myself. Somehow with you it's different." He wrapped his arms around her and she felt his lips run along her cheek.

Berti stepped away, suspicious of the effect he had on her, particularly the strange feeling that there was something already dangerously intimate between them.

"I know when a woman is something special," Gautier said. And then he made a leap up onto a rocky outcropping and twirled exuberantly around in front of her, his man's body looking like a picture out of a book, a bounding Bacchus in a tale of goats and talking foxes. All he needed were the vine leaves entwined in his hair and Pan piping away in the background. And then, several thin high notes of a flute burst from above. The hair on Berti's arms stood up.

"What was that?" she asked.

Gautier shouted, "Who's there?" The flute stopped, but there was no response. "It's probably just a bored shepherd spouting his music."

"But there are no sheep on the mountain. There's nothing to graze on," Berti told him.

She wondered who might be lurking there on the ledge

above them. Maybe it was Manu Dombasle playing a trick. It would be just the kind of juvenile thing he would find amusing.

Gautier put his arm around her waist and pulled her forward on the narrow path. The mountain air smelled like pine with the sweet undercurrent of woodland flowers and the sun reflected pink off the burnished cliff above them. She could feel Gautier's thigh move against hers as they walked in tandem. The air seemed to vibrate as the sun appeared and disappeared behind the branches overhead, and she felt a dreamy drunkenness, as if she'd had a glass of wine on an empty stomach. She wondered what it would be like to make love to Gautier. She'd only gone that far once with a boy she'd met on a camping trip the previous summer. He'd been sweet, but was as inexperienced as she, and she'd known there would be no commitment because she'd never see him again. It would be quite different with Gautier, who lived just on the other side of Beaucastel. She didn't have to imagine how her father would react if he knew she was seeing an older man, a man with Arab blood.

Soon they stopped and Gautier pointed up at the rocky face of the mountain, where there was a circular opening about a meter high. "This is the place," he said. He pulled her up onto the ledge. When she hesitated he said, "Don't be afraid!" She let him help her jump down after him. As soon as she landed, damp humid air surrounded her like clammy hands, and the springtime heat that she had been enjoying quickly dissipated. As her eyes adjusted to the darkness, she saw that they were inside an immense domed chamber, but as Gautier led her farther in, the light dimmed.

A sickly odor of the sort that she'd smelled in their base-ment when her father laid out mousetraps and neglected to collect the cadavers pervaded the place. Gautier pulled her along and she found herself passing through a doorway into a cold and uninviting blackness.

"It's so dark," she said, wishing to break away and re-turn to the warm sunlight outside. Gautier began to stroke the inside of her forearm as if she were a cat who needed calming. Then he leaned back against the cave wall and pulled her against him, his legs splayed on either side of her. For a moment she fell into a dream, enjoying his touch, but when she felt him start to undress her, she said, "I don't like this place. Let's go outside again."

She tried to move away, but Gautier gripped her arms and held her in place. She raised her voice and told him no, but his hands tightened painfully. Tears sprang to her eyes, not because of fear, but because there was something all too familiar about the struggle. Her father held her in pre-cisely the same manner when he was angry. She always felt that somehow she deserved Clément's punishments, even if she'd done nothing, and his violence expiated whatever deep sin of hers might have provoked him. Now she blamed herself again. She'd been an idiot not to have known that this was what Gautier had led her up there for, not friendship or affection, just sex pure and simple. She should never have left her friends and she cursed her own stupidity.

When Gautier pressed her hard against the wall, Berti screamed and it seemed that the prolonged cry that rever-berated throughout the caverns originated from some other place. Gautier immediately put his hand over her mouth. As she struggled against him, her body became slick in the clammy air. And then, within the surrounding darkness, there came a subtle change of atmosphere, as if the hot breath of some enormous primitive god had wafted through the chambers. In a great convulsive motion, the area overhead came alive as a wave of what at first felt like dry leaves blew over them in a roiling tide. Berti perceived the touch of sinewy wings, the tiny furry bodies of a horde that must be exiting through some opening quite near them as the bats moved en masse through the air, dipping and rising and finally exiting the cave in one long, hot stream that coursed just over their heads.

Gautier deflated like a balloon. He flailed his arms at the teeming, darting bats, a futile effort, as they kept coming. Berti crouched and began to run back through the cavern over the uneven rock floor, keeping her eyes on the circle of light. She hoisted herself through the hole and was well along the path when Gautier stumbled out of the cavern's entrance. He was covered in a grayish powder and had a nasty snarl on his lip as he turned toward her. As she started to run again, a voice came from the overhang above. "Eh-oh! Who disturbed the chiroptera? It's against nature to bother them when it's their bedtime!" A man with thick white hair embedded with straw like a farm animal's pelt peered over the ledge.

"What the hell?" Gautier shouted.

Berti recognized that singular face. It was the eccentric that everyone called Lapin, who lived on a tiny farm above Serret where he grew just enough to earn a living selling vegetables and mountain sausage at the weekly market. Some said he was a madman, but Berti had known him since she was a child and he'd always been kind to her whenever they crossed paths. With Lapin there, Gautier wouldn't dare come after her.

As soon as Berti reached the cliff edge she felt like one of the surefooted chamois she'd seen on the high mountain as she managed to jump from rock to rock with ease, not missing a step. She had never been so well coordinated. Perhaps it was just adrenaline, but she flew through the air as if suspended from a trapeze. The sun was still shining, though part of the valley was already in the deep shadow of Ventoux. When she could see a glimmer of the Toulourenc and hear the waterfall, she jumped down even faster, hoping to find Seb and Eva waiting for her below.

In Serret, Filou used the ladders he had placed the day before to ascend to Euphémie de Laubry's roof. The middle-aged widow was rarely around because she spent her days wandering in the mountains like a wood nymph, arriving at dusk with an armful of wildflowers or a basket of leeks that grew willy-nilly on the hillsides. The previous week, she'd pressed a clutch of skinny wild asparagus into his hands. From his perch by the chimney, he could see into the ravine that ran behind the de Laubry mansion. It might be fun to go down there one day, he thought. As a child, he'd explored the stream that ran beneath, all but hidden by the tall cypress trees that grew on the high banks. But for now, he had to finish up and not be tempted by other amusements.

Still, he couldn't help but glance from time to time across the way at Victorine's window, relieved to see that the place was dark.

As the afternoon light slowly began to change, he thought of Pierrette, who would still be at the lab where she worked as a technician. Later, she'd pick up Françoise and Gaspard at the *garderie* at school. He wondered if the children would ask why he wasn't at dinner that evening and what Pierrette might say. Suddenly Filou realized he'd have to hurry to return to the Toulourenc in time. It was not only necessary to get Berti away from Gautier Marcassin, but if Clément got into one of his furies, it could adversely affect the security of his temporary lodgings. It was important to have the little dwelling to himself for a few days, as he was sure that Pierrette wouldn't be convinced of his contrition until she'd had some time to cool off.

As he was about to descend the ladder, Victorine suddenly leaned out her window wearing a décolleté blouse that revealed an abundance of soft white skin.

"Filou," she said with a smile. "If you've finished, why not come over and see me."

"I can't today," he replied, giving her a sad shrug. He made certain to keep his head down as he hefted his equipment, not daring to look up again for fear that he wouldn't be able to resist all that attractively swelling flesh.

When he arrived at the Toulourenc, there was no sign of anyone and he wondered if they'd all left. He decided to walk upstream to see if the kids were still there. It was late afternoon and Filou felt his stomach contort, as he hadn't had anything to eat or drink all day except the coffee that

Liliane had prepared for him that morning. Usually he brought along a sandwich or a slice of vegetable *tian* left over from the night before. Pierrette was an excellent cook and always made sure there was something good that he could bring for lunch. At the thought of her, his feeling of hunger disappeared and he felt that he was just a sad specimen who had brought unnecessary unhappiness down on them both.

Filou had never seen the river so wide and deep. In places it made great curves and swirling eddies along the usually dry swaths of piled-up stones. Along the way, he spotted some papers fluttering by the riverside, probably where Berti's classmates had stopped to picnic. He continued on, trying to stay in the shallows, but at times he found himself jumping from rock to rock, and soon icy water began to work its way inside his boots. There was no sign of anyone and he wondered if he should continue. But the thought of Berti and Gautier Marcassin alone together made him press forward. Filou felt his mood lighten briefly when he remembered how desirous Pierrette had been when they'd first met, chasing him around, jumping into his arms in an enthusiastic embrace, and making love to him wherever she could. He'd never met a woman quite like her and that had kept him more faithful to her than he had ever been with anyone else. But he had occasionally made mistakes, and this time he was afraid that he might have definitively extinguished whatever passion Pierrette still felt for him.

Filou heard the sound of a waterfall, and then around the bend came the hulking figure of Manu Dombasle.

"Filou!" he shouted. "Thank God it's you! Berti's hurt and we didn't know how to get her down. Eva and Seb sent me to get help."

"What happened?"

"She fell on the rocks and her head's all bloody," said Manu. "Eva wrapped her wounds up in Seb's shirt, but she hasn't woken up." Filou started to run, pushing the young man ahead of him to speed him up.

It was a long hike down for Filou with Berti in his arms. After he'd ascertained that she had no broken bones, he'd lifted her up, but the unconscious girl was a deadweight. A deep twilight had already set in, making it hard to see. Filou's feet lost all feeling from being constantly immersed in the river's flow. The kids followed along, Eva holding on to Seb and Manu trailing behind. Filou thought of Pierrette and what she would do if either Gaspard or Françoise had been hurt. Suddenly the idea of no longer living beneath the same roof with the mother of his children made him shiver with pain as he made his way down through the treacherous waters.

When they reached his *camionnette*, Filou's hands shook with exhaustion as he gripped the steering wheel. Manu gave him an odd look when for a moment his frozen feet forgot the sense memory of clutch and gas, so when he started up the engine, the car jerked and stalled. Eva and Seb cradled Berti in their arms in the backseat. When they got to the hospital, various parents were telephoned. Liliane was the first to arrive. She was alone, without her husband, Clément, who, she explained, was still entertaining the group from the *préfecture*. Filou explained things and waited with her until a doctor came to tell them that Berti had a concussion, but that she'd briefly awakened, which was good news. Still, they planned to hold her for observation until the morning. Liliane arranged to have a cot set up next to her daughter so she could spend the night.

Outside in the calm dark, Filou had a great desire for a smoke, though he hadn't had a cigarette in years. The illuminated sign of the *tabac* indicated that it was still open on the square below. He decided on a pack of Gitanes, the brand he'd smoked as a teenager, and as he lit up he thought of going to Gautier Marcassin's house to beat him to a pulp. The cigarette tasted acrid, but he puffed it anyway, wishing he could just go home. Then he walked back up the hill to the hospital entrance, marked URGENCES, where his truck was parked. The night sky appeared dark as espresso with a thin edge of pale cream at the horizon. On the square below, he saw a car turn up the street toward the hospital. It was an Opel like the one Pierrette drove. He let the cigarette fall and crushed it with the heel of his boot. The car pulled up in front of him. Gaspard and Françoise were kneeling in the backseat, their hands pressed like starfish against the window. Pierrette leaned toward him, and without saying a word, she reached over and opened the front door.

3

The Golden Chain

For her birthday Mohammed gave her a necklace made of gold. After fastening it beneath the tumble of her dark hair, he stepped back to look at his young wife, still amazed that he'd had the good luck to marry a gentle beauty like Rachida, with her smooth almond-scented hair and skin light as café crème. Since her arrival in France three years before, Mohammed had made an effort to help Rachida fit in as he had, still aware of their Moroccan roots but eager to make the best of life in a new country.

"You should have the same things Frenchwomen do," he told her.

Rachida hesitated before touching the slender links that moved like the scales of a serpent beneath her fingers.

"But this is too much, Hamidou," she exclaimed. Rachida called Mohammed by his pet name, Hamidou, but she was the only one. He was chief of field hands at a large vineyard, and everyone there, his employer and fellow workers alike, called him Mohammed as a sign of respect.

The gift came as a shock because Rachida and Mohammed were always careful about money. He'd often told her he hoped to save enough to one day build them a home back in Morocco for when he retired, a promise that seemed to Rachida impossibly distant. Instead, she wished that they could simply move out of the lean-to shack in the tiny village of Beaucastel where they now lived and into some other, nicer place. Even in Morocco, a hut like theirs was fit only for livestock. But Mohammed told her that it was hard for Arabs to find acceptable places to live because the French didn't want to rent to them, and for anything decent the prices were far too high. Still, he promised Rachida that soon they would find something better.

She touched the necklace again and wondered what Mohammed had spent on it. In her hometown near Fez, women wore only silver jewelry because Islam taught that gold was too luxurious for personal adornment. Rachida felt a pang of guilt as she examined herself in the mirror and saw the way the lustrous chain drew attention to itself like a living thing against her throat.

Mohammed embraced her, then placed his hands on her shoulders, gazing down into her face. At twenty, Rachida was quite a few years his junior. He was in his late thirties, tall and slender, with an elongated face that he knew no one would call handsome. But Rachida didn't seem to mind. She told him that she was happy because he was always considerate with her, and never lost his temper, unlike her father, who had ruled her family by fear. When Rachida stood on her toes to kiss him, Mohammed felt his eyes burn, but he managed to hold in check the grateful feeling that welled up in his chest. It wasn't the custom for a man to show too much emotion. But Rachida must have seen the change in his face and she took his hand and caressed it, feeling with her soft fingers the roughness of his palm put there by hard work.

Mohammed had come to France as a teenager following the death of both of his parents. Through an uncle who lived in Toulon, he was able to obtain a visa and, upon his arrival, find a job picking grapes with a team of itinerant workers, mostly Arabs originally from Morocco, Tunisia, or Algeria. Later, he'd been employed as a field hand at the domaine where he was now foreman.

Rachida's own life had changed dramatically when, in 1993, she married Mohammed and immediately returned with him to France. In this new country, she was no longer obliged to conceal herself beneath long robes, or wrap carefully arranged veils around her head to cover her hair, as had been the custom in the small village where she'd grown up. At her job cleaning house twice a week, she dressed in loose black pants and a long blouse that billowed modestly over her hips. And each day she simply twisted her long hair up into a plastic clip without any sort of head covering at all. Her employer, Corinne Chave, owned the vineyard where Mohammed worked, and Rachida walked to her house, just a few kilometers down the weedy river road. Corinne's field hands were mostly Arabs from the North African Maghreb, all longtime expatriates who had lived and worked in France for a good part of their lives.

Rachida was now a part of that workforce, a free and equal woman, she reminded herself each time she saw the words engraved in stone above the entrance to the town hall proclaiming: LIBERTÉ! ÉGALITÉ! FRATERNITÉ! But Mohammed was against too much liberty for his young wife and didn't want her out and about like Amina, Rachida's closest friend, who had multiple jobs and was always on the run. He felt Amina had been coarsened by the experiences she'd had working in places where she wasn't always treated with respect, and he didn't want that for Rachida. "I make a good living so you don't have to work like a dog for others," Mohammed had told her more than once.

But Rachida admired the way Amina had arranged her life. She'd raised two sons, and her husband, Tariq, worked in the same vineyard as Mohammed. Amina was free to do as she pleased, and because of her various jobs, she had plenty of money to spend. As for herself, Rachida was often alone and idle, increasingly aware that there were plenty of people ready to hire an energetic young Moroccan woman to do a variety of chores. But whenever she discussed her desire to get a full-time job, Mohammed always replied, "You hope to conceive a child. We both want that, Rachida. Please be patient and wait a little longer before you make any decisions."

Rachida had never mentioned to her husband that she secretly worried about the fact that after nearly three years of marriage she had not become pregnant. Her sister had waited even longer before conceiving and now had four children, so Rachida comforted herself with that fact and hoped it would be the same for her. But recently, in addition to the normal monthly discomfort that was always a bother, she had begun to experience new sorts of pain. She sometimes found herself doubled over, pressing her belly, hoping to assuage the unpleasant feeling. But these symptoms were things she kept to herself, not even telling her friend Amina. She hadn't considered seeing a doctor because she'd heard that French doctors often treated Muslim women as if they were ignorant animals and prescribed medicines that did more harm than good.

Even with Mohammed's attentiveness, not everything had been as smooth for Rachida as he might have wished. When she first began working at Corinne Chave's house, Rachida had been surprised that there was no man in residence, a fact that would have been considered an oddity in Morocco, where women in the countryside never lived alone. There was always a brother, a cousin, or an uncle to step in as head of the household in the absence of a husband or a father. More confusingly, Corinne had a roommate named Sophie d'Aigouze, a small woman with thick rough hair, white as a baby goat, who worked as an accountant in the nearby town of Fenosque. One morning, while Rachida was ironing, she'd glanced out the window as the two women were leaving for work and saw them in the driveway embracing, not a simple *bisou* on the cheek, but lips upon lips like man and wife! At first, Rachida had been so shocked that she had hidden behind the curtain, wondering if she should sneak away and never come back. But then she thought it better to wait to see what Mohammed would say. After all, he'd known Corinne for fifteen years and was bound to know more than Rachida concerning his employer's life. Still, a part of Rachida felt that such behavior was *haraam*, forbidden in the same way eating pork or drinking alcohol was prohibited for Muslims.

That night as she tended the couscous they would eat with dinner, her words began to erupt like the steam from beneath the cover of the *couscousière*. "Hamidou, do you know that Corinne Chave and her friend Sophie live together like a married couple!"

"That's not your business," Mohammed replied. "Corinne has always been fair to me, probably better than a man would be. Her private life is none of my concern. Remember, Rachida, France isn't Morocco and we can't judge people by the same standards that we would if we were home."

That was her husband's answer to the majority of her questions about the differences between the two countries. "You can't compare them as if they were loaves of bread," he often told her. "It's much more complicated. You will come upon many things that surprise you, and then you must make your own judgment about what you accept and what you don't."

So that's what Rachida tried to do, simply accept that Sophie and Corinne were Frenchwomen free to live life the way they saw fit in accordance with the words on the town hall that proclaimed their liberty.

When Rachida had first arrived in France three years before, even the air had felt different. As she and Mohammed drove from the port of Algeciras up through Spain and arrived at France's Mediterranean coast, she'd smelled the briny sea along with the aroma of wild herbs and a hint of pungent fruit from the grapevines that stretched in ordered rows off into the distance. Those aromas had been quite a change from her parents' farm with its sharp odor of donkey and camel dung, and the musky scent of sand and desert brought by hot, dry winds. Yet there was always a place of repose in her father's shady orange grove and in season the sweetest scent of blossom imaginable. Rachida looked for orange trees along the highway, but saw none.

Upon arriving in her new home in Beaucastel, a Provençal village of four hundred people, Rachida had been so shy that she'd spent her first days sitting in Mohammed's car parked beside Corinne Chave's vineyard. During that time, she would listen to the radio and try to make out the strange sequences of words repeated over and over in a continuing cycle on *France Info*, a news station that Mohammed turned on for her. But after nearly three years, though her language ability had improved, she had still not gotten used to being alone in the little house built into the rocky hillside where there was no garden to tend or animals to care for, and no friends and family with whom she might pass her days. She had accepted her husband's will that for now they would continue to live in the simple place whose back wall was rough rock face long ago carved out by troglodytes, the cave dwellers who had once inhabited the steep hillside. She used the hollow indentations as shelves to store food and arrange her few cooking utensils, an earthenware tagine, a steamer, and a flat pan for the morning's bread that she made fresh each day. A single spigot jutted over a stone sink, the only water source except for a closet that hid a toilet. The double burner fueled by a propane tank and a minuscule refrigerator were her sole appliances. Even for a person who had been raised in the Moroccan countryside, the place was primitive.

One hot July day, shortly after Rachida's birthday, her friend Amina arrived at her door with an excited look on her face.

"The man who just bought the château at the top of the village is interested in hiring you," she announced. Rachida thought of the splendid castle that stood at the town's crest surrounded by a verdant park filled with trees. "I cooked for him on Saturday," Amina continued. "His name is Monsieur Descoing. He pays well and wishes to hire another woman. I told him you would be perfect!"

Rachida had always wanted to see the inside of the pink-turreted château that had been an object of fascination for her since she'd first arrived in France, but she knew that Mohammed wouldn't allow her to meet with a strange man, much less work for him. Amina cajoled her. "Come, Rachida! At least speak to him. Then if you're interested you can discuss it later with Mohammed!"

The temptation to see the grand house was overwhelming. Rachida put Mohammed's objections out of her mind and agreed to meet her friend there later that day. She dressed in her very best clothes, a perfectly pressed abaya the color of apricots that fell from her shoulders to her toes and a light veil that draped over her head. The veil was just a token that completed the ensemble, not a required covering as it had been at home, and her gleaming black hair was fully visible. Rachida removed the golden chain Mohammed had given her, fearing it might appear ostentatious to the eye of her potential employer. Then she folded everything away in a drawer of the small bureau that contained her meager possessions, a heavy djellaba for winter, a few extra blouses and pants for work, and some plain abayas that her husband enjoyed seeing her wear around the house.

"You always keep the place so neat," he had told her many times. There wasn't room to fit a folded spiderweb, as her mother would have laughingly said if she had ever seen their home. Neither of her parents, nor her brothers and sister, had visited, and Rachida had not yet returned home to Morocco to see them. She hoped she and Mohammed would be able to go during the winter of the following year.

That afternoon, as the sun beat down upon the thin layer of clay tiles that served as their roof, Rachida found herself perspiring beneath her light cotton robe. She powdered her underarms knowing that it wasn't just the heat that was bothering her. Since their marriage, she had never done anything to displease Mohammed. As she smoothed the bedcover one last time before leaving, she tried to convince herself that if the house was left in perfect order she could ignore the painful fact that she was going against her husband's wishes. Mohammed was a reasonable person and she hoped to be able to change his mind if she decided she was interested in a job at the château. As a young woman, Rachida's hours had been filled by a multitude of chores completed under the eyes of her observant parents. If she'd married someone from her home village, her life would have been even more constrained. "In Morocco, a woman needs her husband's permission even to laugh!" was how

Amina put it. But there, her days would have been full of activity surrounded by people who had known her all her life, quite a change from the lonely hours she often spent waiting in the tiny house for Mohammed to return from his day at work.

Rachida opened the front door and felt the metallic pain in her belly that had begun to trouble her. She sat down for a moment until it subsided and then she rose and locked the door behind her. It was a steep climb to the top of the village, and as she made her way past the houses piled like a disorderly jumble of sugar cubes, her sandals sank into half-melted tarmac. She kept to the narrow backstreet, glancing here and there, hoping not to encounter anyone. Even in the bright afternoon light, it was as if a protective blanket had fallen around her and she feared anyone penetrating it. When she'd first arrived, she hadn't understood the things that were said to her on the street, but now she comprehended the unfriendly words and rude gestures all too easily. Her black hair and tanned complexion were a red flag to certain of her neighbors. They didn't care who she was, they just knew she was from North Africa, the Maghreb, and they didn't want her, or anyone like her, living nearby. She was especially careful to avoid the center of town, where villagers lingered on benches beneath the shady sycamore trees or stood around chatting with their neighbors at the butcher shop or the newspaper stand.

Just after her arrival in Beaucastel, she had eagerly explored the little village that Mohammed said was to be her new home. In the market square she'd spied a wicker basket in front of the *épicerie* filled to the brim with oranges. Their fresh green stems and shiny leaves reminded her of her father's citrus grove and she'd run forward to buy some. When she'd chosen two and entered the dusky interior of the shop, the woman behind the counter had flicked her fingers at Rachida as if she was a dirty cat, motioning at her to leave. Outside she'd tried to replace the fruit, but the woman ran after her, shaking her hands and shouting. When Rachida got home she stood staring out her lone window wishing she had never left her family and her quiet village. Even though she'd grown up in simple circumstances, she'd never experienced such treatment. She peeled and ate both oranges for her lunch that day, even though the effort not to cry tightened her throat and made it difficult to swallow the bittersweet morsels.

That evening, Mohammed had kissed her hair, annoyed that he hadn't been able to protect his wife from the thoughtless cruelty of others. As he pressed her to him, he tried to explain in a sensible way why things were the way they were. "You know that France ruled most of North Africa for over a hundred years," he told her. "In Algeria, there was war for independence and much violence. After many deaths on both sides, the French colonists were finally forced to leave and they lost everything—land, homes, businesses. Some had lived in the Maghreb for generations! When they look at an Arab face, it reminds them of all they've lost."

As Rachida mounted the path to the château that day, the church spire jutted against the cobalt sky, reminding her of the minarets that sprang from the domed mosque near the place where she'd been born. And then, turning onto the path just above, she saw Monsieur Le Lièvre, the one Frenchman who had been friendly to her right from the start. Even when she'd understood not a word of the language, he'd always passed her with a smile and spoken in a soft and gracious way so that she knew what he expressed was meant to be kind. He was a very pale man, unusual for the Midi, and especially unusual for a farmer, which she knew he was since he always carried a burlap sack of potatoes or onions on his back that he sold at the outdoor markets in surrounding villages. In addition to his white skin, he had a shock of snowy hair that fell in tufts over his forehead, making him look like a schoolboy even though he must already be an old man.

"*Salut, ma belle,*" he said to Rachida as they neared each other. "You look ravishing in that beautiful robe!"

"*Merci, monsieur,*" Rachida replied. She knew that everyone called the man "Lapin," a name that meant rabbit. But she didn't know why and felt it might be rude to use a nickname, so she always addressed him formally.

"Terrible heat today," he said. Despite the temperature, he was wearing a flannel shirt and a thick denim overcoat along with a large black beret, wide as a tart pan, that he wore flat on his head. "I hope you're going someplace nice and cool!" he said, giving her a nod. She smiled at him and continued on.

At the top of the hill, her friend Amina stood waiting at the iron gates of the château. She was dressed in a gray djellaba trimmed with gleaming embroidery. The robe made her look bigger and much older than her thirty-eight years, since it accentuated her large bosom. But she looked distin-

guished, her chin held high, and her eyes, elongated with
kohl, glinted with pleasure as Rachida approached. Their
very first meeting had been at the town's *lavoir*, where most
of the Arab women gathered in the morning to wash their
laundry. Mohammed had brought Rachida there early on,
knowing she'd be well looked after, since, like her, most of
the women had come to France as young wives with little
knowledge of the culture in which they would be living.
Standing at the basin where water gushed from a metal
spout, Amina and the other women had taught Rachida her
first French words: *L'eau. Savon. Soleil!* But it had been
Amina who had taken Rachida under her wing, and despite
the fact that Amina was nearly her own mother's age, they'd
quickly become close.

Amina lived in a cinderblock house at the edge of town
where she'd raised her two boys, Fahmy and Mustapha,
with her husband, Tariq. In the garden were the same pots
of peppers that Rachida's mother grew, fiery red and green
capsicum shaped like squiggling snakes, along with purple
aubergines and heavily fruited tomato vines held in place
with twine just like at home. The first time Rachida saw it,
she'd had to cover her face to hide her emotion. Amina had
made a pot of steaming mint tea that they drank together at
a low table outside. "Don't worry," Amina had told her.
"You'll see. It's better here. A woman can earn her own
living!"

Amina had showed Rachida the resident's permit that
allowed her to work, along with the card that gave her free
medical care, and most astonishing, a driver's license, a
thing almost inconceivable in the Moroccan countryside,

where one almost never saw a woman behind the wheel of a car. Rachida hoped that someday she too would have the special papers that granted so many privileges.

Once a week, the friends went together to the outdoor Arab market to buy vegetables and halal meat from the butcher there. Amina lent her the French cahiers that she'd saved from her children's schooling and spoke to Rachida only in French so she would learn. But Amina was often out at her various jobs and most days Rachida found herself striding over deserted paths, up through woods and vineyards, and quite often lingering at the chained and padlocked gates of the rose-colored château whose towers poked like the sharp horns of some mysterious beast squatting beyond the clustered leaves of a grove of live-oak trees. Mohammed told her that the place had originally been built by crusaders, men who fought the Arabs centuries ago. "They say a treasure might be buried somewhere up there," he'd said, and Rachida thought of the tales she'd heard as a child of wealthy sultans and casks of gold.

That afternoon, the château gates were open. When Amina kissed her, Rachida recognized the familiar perfume of oil-of-argan soap. "You're right on time," Amina said. "That's good because Monsieur Descoing is always in a rush. You'll see. He constantly checks his watch!" Rachida's heart, already beating from the climb, pumped even more strongly and she whisked away a drop of perspiration that was coursing down her cheek.

Amina took her arm and said, "I know he's going to like you."

Together their feet crunched over the graveled driveway where rosemary hedges bristled along the length of a
stone wall.

"They say that where rosemary grows well a strong
woman is in residence," said Amina. "But Monsieur Descoing is a bachelor. I don't know if he's looking for a wife."

They went through an arched doorway into a garden
where a fountain in the shape of a child's face spouted water
into a moss-covered basin. Rachida breathed in the moist
air, remembering the shaded gardens of Morocco where
there was always a fountain or pool exalting the luxury of
pure flowing water. Here there were neither mosaics nor
marble inlays like they had in her country, just the natural
world gone wild. It was obvious that the garden had been
untended for years. Dead bushes protruded from flattened
beds invaded by weeds, while across the lawn sea-colored
ivy wrapped its strangler grip around the few specimen
trees that still graced the hillside. But the savage riot of the
living and the dead only made Rachida long to plunge her
fingers into the rich brown earth, so different from the hard
blanched clay in the vineyards, where clods broke and
crumbled like loose cement beneath one's feet.

As they crossed the stone terrace, the white peak of
Mont Ventoux rose through distant cloud cover. The land
beyond the garden sloped gradually downward to a vineyard of dried-up and broken grapevines overgrown with
tall grasses. Rachida's robe billowed and she felt chilled by
the sudden breeze. She shivered, thinking she shouldn't be
in this place at all, betraying Mohammed's trust. A part of

her wished that she could fly away with the wind and disappear into the clutch of trees below, but she kept pace with her friend.

"Come on, don't be nervous," Amina whispered.

Rachida turned toward the fortified towers whose massive stone bases were splayed like giant elephant feet. The two women climbed low steps to a wooden portal that had been left ajar. From there they passed through a hallway into a vast, light-filled room where a pair of French doors opened onto a balcony facing west. A smallish man with black hair slicked into place with pomade lounged shoeless on a white velvet couch. Monsieur Descoing. On the ground next to him sat a large black telephone that looked like an outsized toad. The only other furnishing was a marble dining table the size of a ship with a dozen or so chairs around it. Except for an enormous stone fireplace, all was light and air with high ceilings decorated with entwined plaster leaves painted white. Tall windows on three sides let in the blazing afternoon sunshine.

Descoing glanced over as if surprised to see them and then looked at his watch. Out of the corner of her eye, Rachida saw Amina smile, and her nervousness and guilt were momentarily dispelled. The man had full lips like the clowns depicted on posters advertising traveling circuses, and as he turned to Rachida his marine-blue eyes rapidly traced their way over her, obviously deciding things before she'd even had a chance to speak. He did not get up and Rachida felt grateful, fearing the idea of shaking hands with a strange man.

"This is my friend Rachida," Amina introduced her.

"I didn't expect you to be so young!" Descoing said. He crossed his leg and drew it toward him with soft, manicured hands. "But you look intelligent. Amina told me you are. I like that because I want to hire only the best people to work for me. It will just be a few hours a week at the beginning, but later I will need full-time employees. I'm beginning renovations on the château soon. In the meantime, I want some things planted in the garden before I begin landscaping next year. Do you know anything about gardens, Rachida?"

"My father grows oranges and my mother has every sort of vegetable."

"I don't want fruits or vegetables, but I do want flowers and lots of them."

Without waiting for her response, Descoing abruptly offered Rachida an hourly wage that was several times what she was presently earning. Her surprise must have shown because he lifted his hand in warning and said, "I'm happy to pay you nicely, but everything will be in cash. It's up to you what you do with your money. You can hide it under your pillow if you wish, that's your business. Eventually, if you work for me full-time, perhaps we'll see about getting you the proper papers." Then he stood up and from his back pocket pulled a packet of bills fastened with a gold clip. He peeled off two five-hundred-franc notes and held them out to her. "Consider this an advance. We can settle things once you begin here."

The golden clip shimmered and Rachida was reminded of the crusaders' treasure. But she looked at Descoing and shook her head. "I'll have to speak to my husband first."

"Aren't you free to make your own decisions?" he asked. Rachida didn't respond and Descoing continued, "Well, I hope you will be able to come and help Amina this Saturday. I've invited people for dinner."

He slid the money back into his pocket and turned to Amina. "Why don't you show Rachida the kitchen and pantry. Perhaps you can help convince her husband to let her work for me." Rachida felt the tips of her fingers grow cold as she imagined what Mohammed might say.

When the phone at Descoing's feet rang, he answered and began to speak in an unrecognizable language. He looked at his watch again and then turned away. The interview was over. Rachida followed Amina through the hallway to the other side of the château.

"He wasn't speaking French," Rachida said.

"No, he speaks many different languages." She chuckled. "He's a foreigner like us!" When they reached the kitchen, Rachida felt she'd never been in a more beautiful room. The floors covered in dark ocher tiles were mirrored in the vaulted ceilings that arched upward like the interior of the little town church into which Rachida had once slyly entered. On the kitchen wall an old-fashioned bread oven yawned. Two doors with handles in the shape of swans led to a newly dug kitchen garden, the earth a rich umber. Rachida gazed out at the view.

"That's the old grange." Amina pointed to a long stone building at the end of the driveway. "Monsieur Descoing told me he's going to build apartments above it for the people who will work here." Rachida imagined a room overlooking the trees that were silhouetted against the radiant sky. Maybe they would all live there one day, she and Mohammed along with Amina and Tariq, and perhaps there would be a third couple or, maybe someday, children. Rachida closed her eyes and told herself that nothing that she imagined was likely to come to pass, as her desire for a new life had led her to go against the wishes of her beloved husband. A sigh escaped her and Amina said, "Shall I ask Tariq to speak to Mohammed about you working here?"

Rachida shook her head. She didn't want Amina's husband to get involved. Mohammed was Tariq's boss, and even though Tariq was older, he wouldn't have the right to give advice to someone like Mohammed. She would have to make the plea on her own.

Though the sun was still high in the sky, it was already late when Rachida returned to her house. She was surprised to see Mohammed already there, sitting outside on a wooden stool. He lifted a cigarette to his lips and took a deep puff, unaware of her presence. Rachida didn't like to see him smoke. Sometimes Mohammed did the same things that the French did, things forbidden to Muslims, like drinking wine and other sorts of alcohol on the evenings when he played cards with friends at the Ace of Hearts, a café on the river road. Though Mohammed wasn't a strict observer of the faith, they still went regularly to the small, unadorned mosque, really a converted warehouse, in the nearby town of Saint-Maxence, and she knew her husband was still attached to the old ways even though he'd lived so long in France. But none of that mattered now. She wouldn't dare complain to him about his habits when it was she who was at fault.

"Where have you been?" Mohammed asked. He snuffed the cigarette out beneath his shoe.

Rachida folded her hands into her sleeves and remembered her habit of doing the same thing when as a girl she had confronted her formidable father. She bowed her head, chagrined that she'd automatically made that same gesture with her husband.

"I met Amina up at the château." She was surprised that her voice sounded calm when inside she was quaking. "She introduced me to the new owner, Monsieur Descoing. Hamidou, he wants me to work part-time for him up there. I'd be with Amina, of course."

Mohammed's yellowish-brown eyes flashed and his forehead became a mass of dark lines. "You went up there without telling me?"

Beneath her sleeves, Rachida squeezed her forearms.

"I was afraid to tell you," she said.

"You were afraid because you knew I wouldn't like it. And I *don't* like it. Who is this man?"

"Amina knows him. She works for him already and she brought me because she needs a helper in the kitchen. He pays generously and in cash."

Mohammed stood up and shook his head. "Have you thought about Corinne, who counts on you?"

"I can still work for Corinne. I'll only be at the château on weekends. And I might do some work in the garden."

"He wants you to dig his earth like a common laborer? You will do that for no one, Rachida!"

"But, Hamidou, you told me that we were saving for the future. If I work more we can save more. And then I could get my papers. That would mean many benefits!" Though Rachida's hidden fingers tensed even further, her face remained impassive.

"We don't know anything about this Monsieur Descoing!" Her husband's mouth turned down and he pointed at her naked throat. "Where is your necklace?"

"I took it off before going to the château."

Rachida stood before Mohammed, a straight column in her long robe. It had been a while since he'd seen her dressed so elaborately and she looked to him suddenly foreign, not remotely French, as she sometimes appeared when she wore her black pants and golden necklace. He reminded himself that she was still his to protect and care for. Of course they'd all heard of the man who had bought the grand château at the top of the village. He was very rich, but that only made things worse as far as Mohammed was concerned. The rich could do as they pleased and he didn't want Rachida exposed to that kind of world. He was all too aware that in France men considered the seduction of women a sport and a young woman like Rachida would be looked upon as fair game. Even this so-called *châtelain* might see Rachida as a potential plaything. There were limits that a husband needed to place on his wife; otherwise he'd lose control of her.

After a moment Mohammed said, "Don't make supper for me. I'll be back later." As he strode into town, he noticed that Rachida was still standing in the narrow alley watching him go. But he didn't turn around, afraid that if he saw her eyes he would weaken and return to her.

The afternoon waned and the sky became fiery red.

When the sun set, the air transformed into a pale lavender haze that descended over the clay rooftops. Rachida waited. She turned in rounds in her tiny house, drinking cup after cup of mint tea that served to assuage her hunger. Every once in a while she peered longingly out the door. When it began to get late, she removed her abaya and folded it to preserve the crisp lines of her careful ironing. As she undressed, she found spots of blood on her underthings. She lay down on the bed, pulled a pillow on top of her aching belly, and pressed down with both hands, deciding that she would confide in Amina as soon as the opportunity presented itself. And then her thoughts turned to what she might say to Mohammed to convince him to let her work for Monsieur Descoing.

When she'd lived with her parents, several times Rachida had dared to stand up to her strict and demanding father, a fact that had stunned the entire family. Her elder sister, Fatima, had always been perfectly obedient no matter what the issue. But Rachida wasn't Fatima. As a girl of ten, she'd told her father that she wanted to finish grade school and not quit the way most of the other country girls did.

"Why do you want to be different?" he had asked her. "You should be home learning things from your mother now." Her parents had little education and didn't value it, but she'd managed to persist.

"You're going to need someone who knows how to write and do figures so you can be fairly paid when you sell your oranges at harvest." She'd tucked her hands inside her sleeves to hide her nervous fingers. The prized orchard that her father had planted several years before was just coming to fruition. That time he had reluctantly granted her request to remain at school, as he'd later done when she would beg small freedoms, shaking his head at what he considered her willfulness. But when she turned sixteen and her father told her she would be marrying a man more than twice her age, a man who had lived in France for as long as she'd been alive, she'd argued that she'd prefer to stay in Morocco. She was thinking of the neighbor's boy, her childhood friend Jamel, who had a high smooth forehead and light hazel eyes like hers, unusual for Moroccans. They were both tall with long, slender legs and arms. When they were children, people in the town had said the two of them were mirror images. However, as teenagers they were no longer allowed to mingle, as was the custom, but Rachida sometimes felt Jamel's eyes upon her when he drove his herd of goats by their orchard and she knew that he had not forgotten her.

Three times she'd gone to her father to argue for her freedom as her planned wedding to Mohammed drew closer. The last time, when the festivities were imminent, she'd come alone into the darkened room where her father rested after his midday meal. He was sitting on a pillow drinking tea by the open window that looked over his tethered camels and the pens of goats and chickens that the family kept. She was well aware of the laws to which he adhered, the mores of the old world that were still the dominating force in the countryside of the Maghreb, a force that encompassed his family as well as all of his neighbors, who considered women to be property even more valuable than the camels whose fancy harness ornaments jingled in the same way that the stack of silver bracelets jingled on her own arm.

This time her father raised his voice. "We've already discussed this, daughter!" She stopped herself from shaking by holding firm to her wrists, hidden by the long sleeves of her abaya. Her father had gazed out the single window that looked northward, saying, "There is nothing more to say. It is finished!" Rachida knew herself to be a reasonable person, but her father could turn things upside down, making her look obstinate and pigheaded. Though she knew Mohammed was a good man, a responsible man with a job, unlike so many in Morocco, where gainful employment was hard to come by, Rachida couldn't help but be unquiet. Her sister had also been married to someone chosen by their father, but Fatima lived nearby, so she could see her family, and in particular Rachida, whenever she cared to. It wouldn't be that way for Rachida if she married Mohammed. She'd be far away in a strange land.

"The world is changing. I will be able to provide for myself," she said at last.

Her father unfolded his long limbs and rose, a dramatic sign of his anger, as generally nothing could disturb him when he rested tranquilly after the noon meal. "A woman does what she is told." He advanced toward her. "Do you think you can go off on your own? Well, you cannot! You are under my protection until you have a husband. If you leave you will no longer be a part of this family and it will be certain to be a miserable decision. Look me in the eyes and believe me." Rachida looked. She'd heard of girls who had run away, girls who had chosen badly and become pariahs on the loose, but never free. Rachida had given her father a last imploring glance then bowed her head in acceptance.

That night when the church bell tolled ten o'clock, Mohammed was still not home. Rachida emptied the darkened mint leaves from the teapot and got into to bed. Before the quarter hour chimed, the door lock clicked and Mohammed entered. As he drew near, she could smell cigarettes and a pungent odor that she recognized as pastis, the evil spirit many locals made in their bathtubs, using family recipes and grain alcohol obtained illegally. It was said that homemade pastis could cause insanity and even death.

In the darkness, she heard the stool scrape and fall to the floor. She remained silent as Mohammed righted it and slowly undressed. When he put out his hand and touched her hip, she sat up.

"Mohammed, you want me to be an obedient wife, but you don't live the good life. I smell alcohol! That is *haraam!* I know that in your heart you are a fine man, but you aren't living like one!"

"And you, Rachida! What kind of wife runs behind her husband's back to a strange man's house!" He sat down beside her on the bed.

Rachida touched his arm. "I'm sorry. I shouldn't have gone there without asking you. But, Mohammed, I don't want to stay home all day doing nothing. I want to be out in the world!"

"We'll talk about this in the morning, Rachida."

"Will you remember?"

"Of course! I had one glass of pastis!"

"One is too much!"

"Don't worry." He laughed. "I'll remember."

The next morning, as Mohammed washed himself in the small closet using a bucket of cold water that he'd filled from the kitchen tap, he thought about what he would do about Rachida working at the château. One thing was certain: he would insist on meeting this Monsieur Descoing before he would allow his wife to do anything there.

Rachida stood flipping flattened bread dough over a low fire as she did every morning, toasting it brown on both sides. Several loaves were already on the table for their breakfast, while others cooled on a rack. Before Mohammed left for work, they would be folded neatly into a package along with cooked aubergine and salad for his lunch. She slipped her hands into the ends of her sleeves when Mohammed sat down.

"Is that to warn me that you are ready for a fight?" He pointed at her hidden hands.

"No, I thought we were going to talk."

"All right. Let's begin again. Tell me what you want to do."

Rachida took a deep breath. "I'd like to go up with Amina on Saturday and work for one night. Then we can decide together what I will do."

Mohammed passed his hand over his face. Then he nodded his head in the sideways manner he had that meant yes and no at once. "All right. One night," he finally said. "But first I want to meet this Monsieur Descoing."

The meeting was arranged, and as Mohammed towered over the slighter man, Descoing seemed sincere as he explained that he always treated his employees fairly, that he employed people of all races and religions without distinction, and that he had enormous respect for Muslims. "I'm not originally from France," he told Mohammed. "So believe me, I am no stranger to prejudice and hatred. I promise you that your wife will be respected and well treated here." And so it was agreed that Rachida could help Amina.

But the next day, when Mohammed had already left for work, Rachida heard her husband's car pull back into the gravel inlet off the side of the road where he parked when he returned home.

"What's the matter?" she asked, leaning out of the doorway as he trotted up the hill toward her.

"A bomb exploded on the *métro* in Paris. Many people have been killed and wounded. They're saying Arabs were responsible."

Rachida heard his words but didn't understand. "What do they mean Arabs?"

"Algerians probably."

"Why Algerians?"

"They are fighting a civil war with a lot of killing. Maybe the French are involved. We'll never know. But this is going to make problems. The police are going to be looking to arrest people. We must be careful."

"But it happened all the way up in Paris!"

"It doesn't matter. This is going to make a lot of people believe once again that Arabs are the enemies of the French.

Things are going to be harder for us all. I want you to stay in the house today, Rachida. Understood?"

She nodded and he told her to lock the door. Then he got back in his car and drove down the hill to work.

The following Saturday, as Rachida was getting ready to go up to the château, Amina came to fetch her. She was breathless as if she'd run from her own house to Rachida's. "Let's go. We have a lot to do," Amina said. Her flesh was the color of yellowed plaster and her round cheeks drawn.

"What's the matter?" Rachida asked. Amina's face crumpled into something unrecognizable. "My son Fahmy was fired from his mechanic's job in Marseille," she sobbed. "His boss says he doesn't want him around because Arabs make his customers nervous."

"Because of the bombing?"

"What do you think?! Tariq says there will be roundups."

"Of Muslims?"

"Yes," said Amina. "Fahmy was born here and is a French citizen, but they automatically treat him like he's an illegal immigrant—or a criminal! I'm praying to Allah that he finds a new job soon. I don't like the idea of him wandering the streets in times like these."

As they mounted to the château, Rachida could see that Amina was trying get a hold on her emotions. She held her head high and said no more about her worries. It would be undignified to show how upset she was in front of Monsieur Descoing.

Together they set the dining table, something Rachida had never done before. In addition to the regular utensils, there were dessert forks and spoons placed at the top of each setting along with extra knives and forks for the first course. Rachida thought of her own country, where no cutlery was used and food was served in communal dishes and eaten with small pieces of bread, so simple and so neat.

In the kitchen, Rachida stayed silent, listening to Amina's occasional sighs and mutterings as they chopped vegetables and grated onions to make sauce for a special Moroccan lamb dinner. Rachida didn't know what to say to her friend. How could anyone truthfully tell another that things would turn out for the best? One could only trust in Allah.

Soon the enormous clay tagines with their glazed covers were in the oven. Rachida opened the glass doors with a view of the hill that led down to the huge stone grange. She imagined herself and Mohammed living there together one day. As she stepped outside there came the scent of freshly cut grass. Monsieur Descoing had told them he'd consulted with a local vintner named Didier Falque to help restore the badly neglected hectare of vines planted on the hillside. "I'm going to have the best wine in the region with the help of young Monsieur Falque," he told her. "Even though he's only in his thirties, he's the most innovative winemaker down here!" In the meantime, the vintner had sent one of his hired hands, a young Tunisian named Musa, to do the rough work of cutting back the dead trees and mowing the grass. It was clear that Monsieur Descoing was a man who enjoyed new projects. He was even planting a grove of olive trees, though they wouldn't bear fruit for years. And he'd told Rachida, "I still want flowers planted on the terrace when the things I've ordered from the Côte d'Azur arrive. I have a lady friend coming to visit and I know you'll give it that special female touch!" She'd nodded, but thought with anxiety of Mohammed, who had objected to the idea of her working in Descoing's garden.

That evening, as the sun hovered above the distant peak of Mont Ventoux, casting long shadows, the terrace filled with guests. Jacques Descoing poured champagne into a dozen slender glasses and regaled his friends with stories about the château, boasting that it had once been a *commanderie* of the Knights Templar. "The original owners of this place were not just crusaders," said Descoing. "The Templiers became landowners, farmers, and above all bankers, who amassed so much wealth that Philip the Fourth, the so-called king at the time, got nervous and had most of them burned at the stake!"

Mohammed had been right, Rachida thought as she passed around plates of hors d'oeuvres. The wealthy Knights Templar might have hidden their gold somewhere right there, especially if they were aware that the king was plotting against them.

When Rachida discreetly whispered to Monsieur Descoing that dinner was served, he held his hand out toward her and said in a loud voice, "This is my newest employee, who I hope will become a permanent fixture here. She's Moroccan and her name is Rachida. I'm pleased she will be working for me."

"You might not say that if you had been on the *métro* this week, Jacques," said a woman dressed in white silk.

"I'm very sorry about the bombing," said Descoing. "But every time something like this happens, people start saying, 'France is for the French! Foreigners go home!' I'm a naturalized citizen, but people dare to tell me I don't deserve what I've earned and that I'm a dirty so-and-so because I wasn't born here. Meantime, I'm one of your most valuable citizens," he declared. "I pay enough taxes to merit the Légion d'honneur!"

Everyone laughed. But Rachida heard a woman near her whisper, "Rich as he is, Jacques makes sure to hire the cheapest labor—Arabs!"

Rachida stepped back and as she did a light hand fell upon her shoulder. When she turned, a man with dark eyes stared into hers. "Don't pay any attention to her, Rachida," he said. "Some people are simply ignorant." Despite words meant to be kind, the idea of being touched and spoken to by a strange man made Rachida look away in embarrassment. She inadvertently reached up to her throat and was surprised when her fingers glided over her gold necklace. She hadn't meant to wear it that night and she was ashamed at the thought that perhaps it was the glitter and extravagance of the serpentine chain that had attracted the unwanted attention. She moved backward into the shadows of the corridor that led to the kitchen.

"Well, Jacques, now you have your own bit of French patrimony," said an older man standing next to Descoing and raising his glass in a toast. "A real fortified *commanderie*. That guarantees you're one of us!"

At dinner, the guests drank bottle after bottle of red wine. Their laughter grew raucous and Rachida wondered what the imam at the mosque would say if he could see her there. Would he chide her for continuing to bring more wine to the table? She must remember to ask his advice the next time she and Mohammed went to the mosque together.

At the end of the evening, the guests wandered out onto the terrace to drink demitasses of coffee while Monsieur Descoing passed around glasses of cognac from what he called his private stock. Rachida cleared the table. The double doors of the entrance were opened to the warm night, and as she passed with a stack of plates, the man who had spoken to her stood in the doorway smoking a cigarette, a glass of amber liquid in his hand. She hurried by him, suddenly feeling the same constricting pain that she'd been plagued with for several days. As she entered the kitchen, she released the plates on the nearest countertop with a loud clatter.

Amina turned from the sink. "What's the matter?"

"Nothing. I'm just not used to so many people."

"Come here, my sweet bird, and dry these things while I bring in what's left. You've done too much."

As she polished the glasses with a linen towel, Rachida couldn't help turning to look behind, fearing that the dark-eyed stranger might reappear.

It was well past midnight when the two women finished their work. As they walked down the driveway Rachida took another look at the grange. She knew that Monsieur Descoing would soon begin renovations there and that with luck the apartments for his servants would be ready sometime the following spring.

"I think Monsieur Descoing was pleased," said Amina. He had given them each a three-hundred-franc tip in addition to their salaries. "Tonight was a fine evening. And I feel better about Fahmy too. My son's a good boy who can take care of himself. I shouldn't let myself imagine terrible things." As Amina kissed her and disappeared behind the church, Rachida wished that she didn't have to walk home alone on such a dark night. There was only a tiny fingernail of a moon and no lights coming from any of the houses below. As she arrived at the top of the alley that led to her house, she saw the red coal of a cigarette in the darkness of the churchyard and she felt herself grow faint with fear. But when the person stepped forward, she saw it was her beloved Hamidou come to take her home.

"You're very late," he said.

"There was a lot to do." Rachida put her hand in his.

"Your fingers are so cold!" Mohammed squeezed her hand and Rachida looked up at him knowing she couldn't mention the drunken guests, or the rude remark the woman had made, or the strange man who had touched her. When Mohammed asked about the evening, she told him with a nervous lilt that it had gone just fine and that Monsieur Descoing had asked her to plant some flowers for him. Mohammed shook his head in that yes-no fashion of his, but he didn't object, so she took it to mean that she was free to do as she pleased.

Rachida lay awake that night knowing that what she had communicated to Mohammed was as evil as a lie and that her father had been right when he'd called her a willful girl. She had never before come close to telling her husband the smallest untruth and she felt she had not only brought a terrible curse down upon herself but that something between her and Mohammed had been irreparably shattered.

The following Monday, Didier Falque's field hand Musa dropped by Rachida's house to announce that the plants and flowers had been delivered to the château. He was a nice-looking young man who put his hands on his hips and told her, "It's crazy of Monsieur Descoing to order such fragile things. They don't have a chance of surviving a summer in the Midi."

"What if they are watered every day?"

Musa shook his head. "They're simply not made for this climate." He cocked his head and gazed at her, a friendly grin on his face. "Listen, it's hot. No fun to be working up there. I'd be happy to plant everything for you and then I'll take the blame when they shrivel up."

Rachida was grateful for his offer, but it wouldn't be honest to let Musa do the work. She colored slightly, realizing that honesty hadn't been her chief virtue during the past few days. "I was hired to do the planting," she told him. "I must fulfill my promise."

She went immediately up to the château. Monsieur Descoing had given her a large steel key to the front gate, and when she arrived on the terrace she saw that Musa had already planted the larger bushes and plants, many of which already looked parched and fragile under the midday sun. There were bushes clipped into the shape of singing birds, begonias whose delicate flowers drooped over the sides of basins, and azaleas, forced into bloom in greenhouses, whose flowers were already wilting despite the patches of damp earth indicating that Musa had given them a good soaking with the hose. She found several dozen thin-slatted wooden boxes filled with small flowering things sitting in the shade of the terrace. A case full of low-growing succulents, the one thing that could survive well in a dry climate, had a scent like the perfumed sand of Morocco, and she bent happily to remove the little celluloid pots.

The birds fluttered in the trees and all was calm, but even though it was still early, the heat pounded unrelentingly and Rachida was aware of the dull ache in her lower abdomen and a new soreness in her breasts. She was pleased to see that Musa had considerately filled the stone basins with rich, dark topsoil that had come in heavy, hundred-liter bags.

It was a pleasure to plunge the trowel into the soft earth and sift it between her fingers. She dug the new plants into the stone basins, and when she had nearly finished planting everything, she turned on the hose and drank deeply. The summer heat was at its worst in July, and the air shimmered in the distance like water trembling in a glass. Rachida's shirt was plastered to her back and she wished she had worn a veil to shield herself from the sun. As she moved into a shady patch, she felt herself seized by dizziness and a bouncing, starry light flashed before her eyes. She made her way to the fountain, where the stone baby's head dribbled a constant stream of cool water into the basin. She sat down heavily on its edge. Cicadas kept up their primitive chant, harking back to a time when there had been nothing there, no château or *commanderie*, no garden, just the crest of a hill that dominated the valley where the Ouvèze River, the color of molten metal, flowed in the distance.

When Rachida stood again her head whirled and her body felt cold and slimy as a frog. Several drops of sweat ran into her eyes, burning them, and she felt a strong painful twist in her belly. She breathed deep, wishing she had mentioned her problem to Amina, or to Mohammed, who might have insisted she see a doctor. With a shock Rachida thought she saw her mother standing next to one of the leggy fig trees now stripped of the strangling ivy. She closed her eyes and then looked again, but her mother had disappeared. The shovel leaned against the low stone wall and she imagined gravediggers in the dry, sandy cemetery at home, whose stones and walls were whitewashed, always gleaming so bright and clean under the scorching sun. A wave of nausea and weakness rolled over her and she fell to the ground in a slow painless tumble, like a child's ball that bounces softly and easily onto the grass. And she dreamed a deep dream that she was digging a great hole in the garden. She felt the rough wood of the handle and heard the scrape as the metal blade was driven into the earth. She kept at it until the shovel's edge clinked against something in the obscurity of the earth. At once, a clod sprang out and landed at her feet. As she picked it up, she felt herself surrounded with a cool essence, like air coming from a deep cavern. Something shone dully beneath the earthen thing that she held in her hands and she rubbed at it with her thumbs. A shiny metal began to appear as the soil crumbled away and she found herself holding a large ring made for a man's hand. The ring was old and slightly dented. Perhaps it had once belonged to one of the Templiers. As she turned it around in her fingers something moved against her palm and the head of a snake, triangular and golden, slid through the center of the ring. It opened its mouth and hissed, showing its forked tongue. She could see its sharp milk-white teeth as it moved close to the thin veins in her wrist and she felt that she must rush home and find Mohammed. And yet, she feared that when he saw the serpent her beloved Hamidou would automatically know everything about her lies of omission and her unworthy desires, and that would cause him to abandon her forever. She called out, but no sound came, and she tried to raise her hand to grab away the serpent, but there was no movement.

When Musa found the pretty Moroccan girl lying crumpled in the grass, he grabbed the hose and splashed water onto her face, rubbing her cheeks and neck with his hands. When she didn't react, he took her by her shoulders and pulled her up into a sitting position. Her head lolled to the side, her eyelashes black crescents against pale, yellow flesh. He pressed his fingers beneath her jaw, searching for a pulse, and felt a thready vibration as from the body of a weak and frightened animal. The château was locked, so there was no access to a telephone. He sat for a moment with the girl in his arms, and then he laid her down very gently in the shade of a fig tree and ran down through the gates to a house he knew where he demanded to make a call, explaining it was an emergency.

The *sapeurs-pompiers* arrived in their enormous screaming van, red lights flashing. Men in blue uniforms gave the young woman oxygen. For a moment Musa thought of accompanying her in the ambulance, but then realized it was more important to find her husband, who he knew worked at a nearby vineyard. When the firemen lifted the stretcher and slid it into the ambulance, Musa could just make out her pale face as the doors slammed shut. The vehicle crunched down the gravel drive and through the château gates, the *wa-wa* call of the siren loud and brash as the van descended through the village and onto the rural route, where the sound eventually faded until, once again, silence pervaded the empty garden, and all that was left was the pure light of high summer.

4

The Wanderer

Euphémie awoke feeling the pressure of hard fingers against her chest. A nurse peered down at her and she stared back from her pillow, all at once remembering her dream. She'd been a girl again, hiding by the stream while rifle fire banged in the distance and a strange chemical odor infused the air. The sounds and smells of wartime.

"Everything all right?" the nurse asked. She poked the tips of her fingers against Euphémie's breastbone again, neither a friendly nor reassuring gesture, and Euphémie smelled that familiar resinous odor of carbolic soap once more. The nurse must wash her hands with it! The scent brought back memories of the last days of the war, her father, her childhood friend Lapin, and the wounded pilot who had appeared by the flowing stream. They'd been with her during sleep for several nights now. She prayed the nurse wouldn't notice her galloping pulse. It didn't do to show any sort of *bouleversement* or upset in this place.

"I'm fine," Euphémie replied. "Why do you ask?"

"There was a disturbance down the hall, one of the patients making a commotion. It didn't wake you?"

"You woke me."

Euphémie no longer tried to communicate in any real way with the nurses. When she'd first arrived at the place several months before, she'd told them that she was just fine, never better, and ready to go home, away from the locked ward where most of the patients were unable even to speak. At first, the staff repeated the same information her daughter, Florence, had given her regarding the incurable malady that would soon rage through her brain, leaving her a feeble, worthless remnant of her former self. They were all so polite about it, just the way the first wave of invading German soldiers had been polite in order to make people believe that theirs would be a benevolent occupation and to induce her countrymen to behave and obey orders. Yet one evening Euphémie had made the mistake of having an altercation with the nurse in charge regarding this so-called illness diagnosed by a doctor she'd never met before. When Euphémie defended her health and sanity, perhaps a little too vociferously, the nurses had suddenly surrounded her and she'd found herself carried bodily to her room and buckled to her bed with belts of canvas until morning. After that, she'd learned not to make a fuss. Maybe that's what had happened tonight, a chair overturned in protest, a door slammed in fear, attendants arriving to quell the outburst. Perhaps it was those noises that had evoked the distant rifle fire of her dream!

The nurse's synthetic uniform rustled like a plastic bag as she exited, the door closing behind her with an efficient click.

Florence had told the doctor that Euphémie didn't sleep in a proper bed, but on a pile of straw, and that she foraged for food in the town garbage bins. It was true that cooking and housekeeping had become a terrible chore. Euphémie preferred long walks up into the mountains, where she'd gather wild leeks and asparagus the way her father had taught her when she was a child. She'd make soups with what she collected or simply eat her harvest raw. And yes, at night she often left her cavernous bedroom that faced the road, not for a bed of straw, but to sleep on the horsehair sofa in the *grand salon* or the little *canapé* by the window, where she could hear the stream that gushed through the deep ravine behind. It was so much nicer to be within earshot of soughing branches, rushing water, the trill of birdsong. And Florence was wrong about the garbage. Euphémie had only gone through the town bins once or twice. It was amazing the things people threw away! Boxes of cookies and galettes, and perfectly good cheese in unopened packages. That foraging took place well before she had met her dear friend Hamidou, a Muslim man whom she'd first encountered near her favorite spot on the mountain, La Fontaine des Fées, where a spring used to flow in the days of her girlhood. When they'd gotten to know each other, Hamidou began to bring her lunch each day at that special meeting place. He always arrived with the food in a basket, a linen napkin folded neatly over the top. They ate together on a stone bench where a line of poplars stole up the hill to a crumbled ruin that had once been a military garrison. Her friend always wore a suit with a freshly pressed white shirt and a red woolen hat, the Moroccan chechia, tilted back on his head. He had no family in Provence and no one to whom he could return in his native country. She gathered that he'd once had a young wife who had died due to complications of pregnancy. Now he made a modest living as an assistant to the imam at the local mosque, where he was considered something of a sage and was called *alhaji* because he'd been to Mecca twice. An unlikely acquaintance, this man who had spent most of his life as a foreman laboring in a local vineyard, but Euphémie had grown to appreciate his kindness and polite reserve. His name was Mohammed, but he asked her to call him by his childhood sobriquet, Hamidou.

She sat up in bed and slipped her legs over the side. Euphémie had been lithe as a youth. Now, as an elderly person, she remained slender with sinewy muscles developed from her long mountain treks. The regular meals in this so-called *maison de retraite* were making her stronger and she never felt hungry anymore. Her cheeks were round as plums and her blue eyes shone with health and vigor. Even though the food wasn't to her taste, she could always find something to eat, but she never touched the meat, gray and stringy with a putrid smell of old blood.

Yet the thought of not being able to continue life in her little village of Serret weighed upon her. Now that she had outlived most of her neighbors, she didn't have many friends, but occasionally she'd be invited to dine with one of the old families; Liliane Perra of Domaine Petitjean was always particularly kind. But her favorites were the more patrician Prosts, who had been in residence in a grand old house for generations, though now they spent most of their time in Paris. Gaston, the head of the family, whom she'd known throughout his boyhood, was now a charming and cultivated middle-aged man with children of his own. How quickly life flew by! But it was true that for a long time Euphémie had been leading a solitary life, her long walks in the hills being her chief joy and comfort.

She slid from the bed and moved to the window, where she lifted the sash to better hear the river's loud rush. Her elbows pressed down on the sill and she propped her face in her hands and gazed out at a night enshrouded in darkness except for one solitary light gleaming in someone's window across the way. In the morning, a white heron always perched on a cantilevered rock at the center of the river, the huge stone pushed nearly upright by the force of the flow. The heron spent his days on the rock availing himself of darting fish and the turquoise frogs that skimmed to and fro beneath the reedy banks. Euphémie knew the heron's movements by heart, but he wouldn't appear until after sunrise.

In the darkness, the water gleamed the muted color of gunmetal with foamy whitecaps that appeared and disappeared as the river hurled itself downstream. It had been a wet spring and the Ouvèze was wilder than usual. She had always enjoyed walking close to the untamed current, watching the water birds and smelling the combination of fresh, newly growing things along with the odor of rotting reeds and undergrowth, so typical of those murky banks. It was her long sojourns spent in the mountains and down in the valley, out of doors all day, that she longed for. The only other time that her freedom had been so drastically impinged upon was during the war, when it was too dangerous to traverse the balsam paths or walk by graveled streamlets. There was something about being in this locked place that caused her to recall those days with an unusual lucidity. During the long afternoons spent sitting with the other occupants in the common room, memories of her teenage years rose in her mind like spectral illuminations in a dark garden. Under Nazi occupation, she had been sensitive to the violence that pervaded everything, giving off its own special scent of decay and destruction. It was the same in this rest home, the putrid smells that occasionally wafted down the hallways coming from the vegetative patients who passed their time in wheelchairs banked up in windowless corridors, or the ambulant ones whose screams were quickly stifled with a needle. Looking at them, Euphémie sometimes felt that her own breath might be sucked right out of her unless she was careful. She had to be terribly careful.

She spent her days alone, walking around the glass-enclosed terrace that, like a cuckoo's nest, jutted out from the top floor of the building. To the south was a view of the town's cathedral, whose monumental Corinthian capitals, now used as cornerstones, had once decorated a Roman temple. Nearby spread a plowed field as yet unplanted. On the opposite side was a parking lot, and to the right of that, a garage run by a group of young mechanics where there was generally quite a bit of coming and going. Euphémie's face was so often poised behind the glass enclosure that when one of the men spotted her he would salute, holding up a wrench or waving a grease-covered hand. When there were church services, she peered down into the crowd hoping to recognize someone, anyone, who might have the wherewithal to come up and explain to the doctors and nurses that Euphémie was a healthy woman in body and in mind, and should be immediately released! Round and round she went, pretending she was climbing up rocky roads to high crests, and she imagined the familiar view over the patchwork valley of orchards and vineyards and the sound of the ubiquitous magpies that populated the environs of the small village of Serret. Even during the war, though it was too dangerous to take mountain walks, she had still tried to capture some time to herself in the natural world she loved so well.

Euphémie placed her withered hands flat against the windowsill. In the past, whenever people had asked about her experiences under the occupation, she always said the German soldiers had been perfectly respectful even though they had taken over the small château that belonged to her family, the d'Estangs. During wakeful nights in her room in the rest home, she'd come to realize how elaborate a barricade she'd created to prevent any thoughts of the Nazis, who had felt free to run their cold eyes over her, or of the American pilot who might possibly have become a friend. And then there was Lapin, noble Lapin, whose real name was Charles-Henri Le Lièvre, an aristocratic name, though he was the motherless son of a strange man who made a meager living as a farmer. Once a classmate, Lapin had fallen on hard times, but by the end of the war he had been transformed in her eyes from a lowly *paysan* into a hero.

Afterward, she'd hardly acknowledged him, passing him in the cobbled streets with only a nod. She could face nothing concerning those chilling days and there was no looking back. Thus silence became a habit. She couldn't risk even a short conversation with Lapin because that precious sealed coffer of memory might snap open like Pandora's box and she'd be forced to face what had happened in its dreadful totality.

As Euphémie stood there that night she thought that someone as old as she should be capable of mustering the courage to stare the past in the face without flinching. Don't people remember everything before they die, flashes of a whole life appearing like photographs in just a few seconds? In the darkness, her body shook in a spasm of anxiety (or was it elation?) as she breathed in and told herself that there was no longer anything to fear.

At fifteen, Euphémie was an early riser, up before dawn to collect eggs from the brown and yellow hens kept in the stone barn at the back of their château. That morning, she emerged from the warren of downstairs rooms where she and her father and their cook, Agnes, now resided, the Nazi officers having commandeered the better quarters, including the reception rooms and master bedrooms on the upper floors. She crept cautiously outside through the pantry door, her arms folded across her chest, though it wasn't cold. The walled-in courtyard between the château and the grange, once filled with geraniums in orange terre cuite *pots and roses that climbed in a tangled riot over whitewashed trellises, had been transformed into a dank*

and uninviting place. Anything green and growing had long ago been stomped away. Most of the flagstones were displaced and the pebbled path crushed into the mud, creating soggy gullies where jeeps and other vehicles drove incessantly in and out of what had become a military depot.

At dawn, Euphémie had been awakened by the thunder of antiaircraft artillery. A new troop of German soldiers had recently arrived to replace the first wave of officers, who, though they had been coldly efficient and not particularly friendly, had at least evinced a semblance of manners. That group had nicknamed her Mademoiselle Poulet, appreciative of the fresh eggs she delivered each morning for breakfast. But the latest arrivals lacked even a thin veneer of civilization. They entered the château scowling and shouting, obviously from a much lower rank of the military, invading her home as if they were on a search-and-destroy mission. One of the soldiers, a teenager not much older than she, had approached her in the wood-paneled entryway, his glittering eyes so pale that they looked like raw egg whites in a pan. She'd hunched her shoulders, embarrassed that despite her painful thinness, her rounded chest was suddenly becoming more visible, soft and vulnerable like the plump breasts of her hens. His bold gaze forced her to turn her back to him, hoping to hide the fact that she was no longer a child.

That morning when she dressed, she'd wrapped a strip of cotton sheeting tightly around her chest and pinned it at the back to disguise her figure. She still had the round freckled face of a girl, but she had been aware for some time that even a touch of lipstick would cause a risky transformation. It was safer to camouflage herself than to look like what she was, a person rushing unstoppably to womanhood.

Outside in the crepuscular shadow, the courtyard smelled of mud and chicken droppings. Euphémie felt that she was safe, or at least less likely to be interfered with by anyone at such an early hour. Her father had spent the night at the town hall, where he presided as mayor of their village. She knew that he found it increasingly important to spend long hours at the mairie so that he might have a chance of mitigating any trouble that occurred between the occupiers and any French person who ran afoul of them. Excepting the soldiers, it was only Euphémie and Agnes in the house. She picked up the tin pan of kitchen scraps, mostly rutabaga, potato peelings, and the crumble of old biscuits that Agnes always left for her on the sideboard for the chickens. Agnes said that here in the country they didn't have it as bad as the Parisians, who were literally starving to death. That's the way it had been in the first war too. Here people still had their potagers *of leeks and cabbage, their animals, and if they were lucky, a cache of preserves and legumes stored in the dark cellars beneath their homes.*

Euphémie scattered the feed onto the ground and then entered the barn, where she heard the mild avian cheeping of sleepy birds in their roosts that quickly changed to squawks when they became aware of her presence and flocked to the wire doorway of the cage. She could make them out in the dim light of the back window, where the glass panes had already turned from charcoal to pale violet. When she lifted the wooden hasp, the birds gushed forth into the yard. Momo, her biggest and best layer, was at the head of the flock. And then, as she closed the henhouse and was about to pass back into the courtyard, she sensed a disturbance. Through the half-open door, Euphémie saw a dun-colored uniform and dark boots kicking and tramping over the birds. When the soldier spun around, she recognized the ice-cold eyes that stared at her in challenge.

In a flash, he sank his bayonet into one of the hens. Euphémie clamped her hands over her mouth to stifle a scream, and with a laugh the soldier cut off the bird's head lickety-split and threw it to the ground. To her horror the other birds surrounded the head in a frenzy of pecking while the soldier twirled the carcass over his head, splattering blood as if it were a game.

Forgetting her usual timidity, Euphémie leaped through the doorway and tore what was left of her hen from the soldier's hands. Momo, her favorite! When she ran toward the pantry door, the soldier jammed the butt of his rifle against her back as if warning her to be aware that he had ownership of the bird, or perhaps something more.

Euphémie ground her teeth so she wouldn't cry. But when she entered the kitchen and saw Agnes with her soft cheeks and swirl of white hair knotted at the top of her head, she couldn't help but let out a sob. Agnes had worked for her family since Euphémie's father was a boy, and Euphémie had come to rely on her for nearly everything since her mother, Huguette, had died of tuberculosis at the beginning of the war.

"Oh, mon Dieu!" A look of anger and pain crossed Agnes's face. She took the hen and laid it carefully on the sideboard before hugging Euphémie to her. "Filthy barbarians!" she said. Then she sighed and softly rocked Euphémie until a sudden blast from a bullhorn began to issue incomprehensible orders in a loud roar. They heard running soldiers and the revving of trucks. After a few minutes the sounds ebbed as the vehicles departed and the engines faded to a distant drone.

"*Those were American planes that flew over so early, did you hear? That's making the Boche nervous!*" Agnes used the rude term for Germans. She lifted Euphémie's chin with two fingers and stated with certainty, "*We'll soon be quit of them.*"

"Is Papa *home?*" Euphémie asked.

"*Not yet.*"

As usual, her father would be left to deal as best he could with the occupiers, who behaved like angry hornets when things did not go right. The month before, when a German truck was blown up in a neighboring village, three innocent villagers had been hung in reprisal, their bodies left at the end of the ropes for days until the priest, whose brother was among the dead, had arranged to cut them down. Euphémie hoped nothing like that would ever happen in Serret. Her father might easily be blamed for the smallest thing, and be made to suffer the consequences. It was like having a poisonous viper loose in the house—a constant anxiety that sapped the pleasure from everything.

Outside, there were no sounds except for the clucking of hens oblivious to the violence that had so recently occurred in their midst. Euphémie clenched her hands, imagining being strong enough to wring the life out of that soldier, his pale eyes blearing into gray obliteration. She'd seen people murdered and knew how someone looked when they'd suffered a violent death. She shook her head, aware that anger and desire for revenge could engender savagery itself. Instead, she called up thoughts of the still place by the stream that she hadn't visited in weeks, and she skirted the barn, carefully looking around to be sure there was no one near. Beyond lay the field where Agnes's neat garden plot had been planted with the seeds she'd conserved from the previous summer. A bit farther on was the ravine filled with a steady flow of water that trickled down from mountain streams. Several immense cypresses towered at the edge. She knew the main source of the water, a place in the mountains called La Fontaine des Fées, where a spring gushed from a rocky outcropping. From there the waters descended through underground channels, filling cisterns and basins used for livestock, eventually tumbling from a precipice and forming the deep ravine behind their château. Euphémie placed her feet carefully on the ancient steps that jutted like an old man's displaced teeth, remnants of a stairway constructed by peasants in medieval times.

It was a warm Provençal morning with the sun already casting its splendid rays. She knew that a marten lived in the cypress tree just above her, but she hadn't seen him in a long while, as he only ventured out at dusk and she no longer dared visit the stream then. Blue and yellow wildflowers listed softly back and forth at the stream's edge. She bent to follow a tunneled path of tangled undergrowth that led to a mossy area obscured from view by low-hanging branches. The silvery water gave off a smell of iced apples. Above her the dappled tops of trees shuddered in the light breeze as the sun crested the rocky crags of the mountain. Euphémie sat down beside the undulating bank of moss that thrust up a host of starlike flowers on hard little stalks. She flattened her hand and let the spiky buds run across her palm. Warm air coursed over her throat and the swift-flowing water sounded the same as the wind passing through the trees. The strip of fabric that bound her chest pressed uncomfortably and she shifted it off her bosom and then made a little pillow out of fresh grass. When she eased herself down, everything felt perfect, the warmth of the air, the occasional silky scrape of bird wing, the aroma of the fresh-pulled grass beneath her head. But she knew better than to hope it would last. A regret at what the war had done burned within her. It had taken her mother first and then made them all prisoners, definitively ending Euphémie's free wanderings up into mountains where dark woods harbored deer and wild boar that had once ventured forth from their secret hollows, showing no fear.

A movement in the leaves across the way abruptly broke her reverie. She jerked up and quickly adjusted the binding cotton band around her. She had a good eye, easily spotting birds and other animals even at considerable distance. There had been barely a flicker, but she knew for certain something was there.

A sort of white heat coursed through her that made it difficult to breathe but at the same time filled her with energy. She remained perfectly still, reminding herself that the only person she'd ever seen across the ravine was the boy Lapin. They had been in école primaire together in the one-room schoolhouse located in the lower village that still served a dozen or so children each year. Lapin, a farmer's son, had been a talkative and intelligent boy. When he clattered on his wooden clogs into the schoolyard in the morning, he always slicked back his long blond hair with a comb made of horn that he wetted in the basin at the entrance. This hairstyle would last until the end of the first period, when it would again flop forward, a glasslike curtain hiding his eyes. In those days Lapin would frequently accompany Euphémie home for lunch, having been invited by her father. Because he was mayor, Augustin d'Éstang knew everyone in the village and had immediately taken a shine to *the young Charles-Henri Le Lièvre, whose gaiety illuminated his round child's face.*

"Why do you find that strange little boy so interesting?" Euphémie's mother, Huguette, had asked her husband. After all, Lapin was nothing more than a paysan despite his noble name.

"He's not strange; in fact, he's the most interesting boy in the class," her father replied. "Besides, Euphémie could use a friend."

Huguette had spoiled both children with small cakes and the local sweet, pâté de coing, *a delicacy that she made in huge batches in late autumn when the quinces were harvested. She insisted on calling Lapin by his given name, Charles-Henri, even though everyone else called him Lapin because of his prominent, slightly crossed front teeth, and because his family name, Le Lièvre, meant hare.*

"Come, boy," her father said to Lapin when he was eight. "It's time you perused things other than those lugubrious schoolbooks." And Augustin had taken him and Euphémie into his library and chosen a volume for each of them, old favorites that had pleased him as a child. Euphémie liked to read, but she didn't devour books the way Lapin did. He finished each one within days and returned what he'd been lent for something new, always chosen by her father.

"He's precocious, your friend Lapin," Augustin said to her one evening when she and her father were lounging together on the Récamier sofa he kept in his study. "If he can manage to stay in school and get an education, he'll do well. But his father's an odd sort. I don't know what he expects for the boy, if anything."

And then, at the end of summer vacation, just as Euphémie's class was about to enter the larger middle school in the neighboring town, Lapin had an accident. No one was sure what happened, but he wound up in the hospital with a cast up to his waist. Euphémie and her father visited him several times in his hospital room, where for months he lay in his girdle of plaster of paris. Augustin tried to arrange to have Lapin transported to their home, but a misunderstanding ensued between him and Lapin's father, so the transfer was never achieved.

When school began that September, Lapin did not appear in Euphémie's class. She thought he might simply have needed more time to recuperate and would rejoin them later in the year, but he did not, and without proximity their friendship fell away as easily as the autumn leaf.

It had to be Lapin across the stream. He'd once come sliding down the ravine right in front of her. Even so, they hadn't said a word to each other. The war didn't facilitate communication among villagers. In fact, distrust had arisen between formerly friendly neighbors when denunciations were made over petty things like an extra scrap of meat here or a bicycle tire there. People had become fearful under the occupiers since anyone could be accused of the smallest infraction and shipped off to a labor camp or simply executed. Besides, Lapin had changed. Like so many isolated farm people, his grinding life had obliterated the garrulous, clever boy she'd once known. He saw no one except his father, who made a tenuous living keeping a few pigs and growing a crop of potatoes that Lapin would bring to the tiny Thursday market in the neighboring town of Beaucastel.

When the foliage stirred slightly, Euphémie scrambled to her feet. "Lapin?" she peeped, but there was no answer. A kind of sickness came over her when she made out the silhouette of a uniformed man squatting in the deep undergrowth. For a long, groaning moment she believed that it must be the young Nazi come back to harm her. But almost immediately she realized that the color of the cloth was different. It couldn't be a German. And then the person stood, raising a hand in greeting and she saw him clearly. His jacket was stained a dangerously fresh red at the shoulder and he'd rigged some sort of tourniquet. A belt kept his arm suspended across his chest. Perhaps he was one of the Americans that Agnes had said were on their way! Euphémie knew that she couldn't possibly respond or help him. Instead, she bent low and scampered through the undergrowth to the stairs, not wanting to bring further trouble to her household. But as she dashed up the steps, the soldier bolted across the water and grabbed hold of her ankle. His was a gentle grip and she knew she could easily break away. But she halted and gazed down at him.

"Je suis un ami!" He had a soft voice, and as he explained that he was a pilot who had been shot down only an hour or so ago, he used an old-fashioned French vocabulary that reminded her of the novels of Balzac or Zola. His face looked as if it had been carefully sculpted by someone aiming for a masculine ideal: fine cheekbones in a thin face, a strong but not too prominent chin, and a clean beardless jaw. He must be very young. His brown eyes seemed to be carefully taking her and everything around her in. Finally he said, "Je m'appelle Harry." When he slumped down on the lowest of the steps, Euphémie realized he was at the end of his tether. She was well aware that a person who looked like he'd been superficially wounded could actually be at death's door. Perhaps he'd already lost too much blood, or had sustained other injuries that weren't visible.

"I can't hide you," she told him in a firm voice. "Our house is full of German soldiers. They're everywhere!"

He nodded and leaned his head against his good arm as if he might go instantly to sleep. For a long time Euphémie had convinced herself that she was a girl who was incapable of doing anything against the great force of the enemy. But as she stood over the wounded aviator she felt for the first time something within her of which she'd heretofore been unaware. She reached down and touched him on the head to make sure he was awake and could hear her. He lifted his face, eyes perfectly alert. Perhaps it was his training that made him seem in control and in command even though he very likely wasn't.

*"I'll think of something," she told him. "Go! Hide yourself there." She pointed into the grassy tunnel from where she'd come. "*Je reviendrai! I'll come back when I can!*" The soldier nodded and then disappeared into the green maze of reeds and twisting vines.*

Euphémie flew across the field, knees high, and then slowed, knowing that if one of the Germans saw her in an all-out sprint, she risked being shot. But there was still a blessed silence, uninterrupted by motor sounds or the shouting of rough voices. On the way, an idea came to her of where she might hide the pilot Harry.

At home, all was silent. Agnes must have gone to the mairie *to deliver something to eat to her father. Through him, they were often privy to confidential information, information with which it was becoming increasingly hard to cope as the violence and brutality of the German army increased. It was certain that the Germans knew an American plane had crashed, and Euphémie wondered if there was more than one plane downed and more than one airman seeking shelter.*

In the ground-floor hallway, she searched through her father's desk until she found the key to the house where old Mon-

sieur Painlevé had died over the winter. The key had been turned over to her father by the town notary, who was well aware that it was unlikely that any distant family member would come to claim the Painlevé property while the area remained occupied. In a hallway cabinet Euphémie found a bottle of disinfectant and wrapped it in a clean linen towel that she tucked into her pocket.

It was a stroke of luck that the Nazis had left so abruptly. The morning's bread sat uneaten on top of the pétrin in the pantry. Agnes usually made several large loaves, but that day there was an extra. Two small ones had been pressed together and baked in the form of a heart. She tucked the loaf under her arm and was searching for a bottle to fill with water when she heard Agnes's feet scuffing down the stairs in the fleece-lined pantoufles she always wore.

"What are you doing, mon enfant?*" Her clean, checkered apron reminded Euphémie of summer meals eaten in the courtyard before the place had become an army barracks, and their beautiful, wrought-iron dining table had been shipped to Germany as scrap metal. She didn't know what to say to Agnes, who eyed her and suddenly lifted her plump fingers to her mouth before exclaiming, "The plane crashes! You haven't found someone, have you?"*

Euphémie clutched the bread against her rib cage and said, "He's wounded!"

Agnes dragged her into the kitchen, where the southern sun streamed through the wavy panes of the small window, and said in a low voice, "How badly?"

"I don't know. I'm bringing bandages and disinfectant."

"Well, let's give him something to build up his force." From a covered bin beneath the table Agnes took out a half bottle of

red wine, perhaps hidden there for medicinal purposes or to contribute to Agnes's own fortitude. How she had come by it Euphémie didn't know, as the Germans had purloined every bottle in her father's cellar within a month of their arrival. Agnes uncorked the wine and picked up a jug of water, filling it the rest of the way. "We want him revivified, not inebriated." She chuckled. "And what else?" She turned around. "Ah!" From a low cupboard she removed some empty canning jars and, getting to her knees, withdrew a small pot that she held up as if it were a just-caught, prize fish. Puffing as she got back to her feet, Agnes handed Euphémie the last rillettes de porc that she'd made when precious meats like that were still available. She piled everything into a burlap bag and handed it to Euphémie with a smile. When Agnes asked, "Where are you hiding him?" the girl pressed her lips together. Euphémie knew instinctively that she shouldn't tell. For the first time it occurred to her that since she was no longer a child cowering in her chicken coop, but an individual who had sided with the Allied forces, she could be a casualty of war as others had been. She must remain silent to protect Agnes in case she was questioned.

"You deliver that and come right back!" Agnes commanded without asking for further explanation. Euphémie nodded in her docile way and cast her eyes down so Agnes wouldn't notice the gleam of determination that she felt must now be obvious.

Carefully clutching the sack, she went through the barn. At the back window, she unhooked the piece of fabric that bound her breasts and stuffed it into her pocket. She could use it as an extra bandage if need be. Then she opened the window and made her way across the field before descending the steps into the ravine.

She found Harry asleep in her special place, his head on the little mound of grass, but he awakened as soon as she was within several meters of him. "You must be hungry and thirsty," she said, kneeling. He immediately drank a third of the watered wine and then broke off a morsel of bread. A hint of color came into his face as he ate. Euphémie pulled out the linens and disinfectant and asked if she could make him a new bandage. He shook his head; instead he took the antiseptic, soaked the fabric, and with a wince, shoved the whole thing beneath the bloody uniform and onto his wounded shoulder. When he'd eaten a bit more, she told him about the abandoned house. He nodded as if he was willing and she packed up what was left of the food. Before leaving, he told her she had "du courage." She shook her head no, but it was true that she felt a new sensation that seemed to exclude fear.

They crossed the stream, and as they climbed up the rocky embankment, she noticed that the pilot was breathing heavily. She wondered if he was in pain. Maybe pilots were trained to ignore injury or suffering, just as she'd learned to hide the signs of her developing body.

"Is it much farther?" Harry asked after they had skirted several fields, staying at the edge where ditches of canebrake grew.

"Another kilometer or so," she told him. But as they ascended through an apricot orchard, Euphémie realized that his strength was flagging. The mistral had begun to blow, leaving the sky cloudless, but it made walking harder, pushing them back at every step with its wild gusts. She clenched the key in her pocket and wished the little house was closer.

"Do you need to rest?" she asked Harry when she saw his face had gone completely white.

"Ça va!" he said. And then, at the edge of a field, a figure appeared wearing the blue overalls and clumsy wooden clogs of a paysan. Euphémie pulled the pilot back into the shadow of the tree line. You never knew whom you could trust, and whom you couldn't. But then she saw the curtain of straight yellow hair blow across his forehead and she realized who it was.

"It's my old school friend Charles-Henri," she told the pilot, who had turned quite rigid at the sight of this new person. She thought Lapin might run away when he saw the soldier, but instead he approached steadily, with only the smallest evidence of a limp. And when he arrived next to them he offered his hand for the pilot to shake, just like a grown man would.

"They're looking for you," he said.

"I don't doubt it," the pilot replied.

"He's one of several shot down early this morning," Lapin told Euphémie.

"Yes," she replied. "I'm taking him to Monsieur Painlevé's old house."

Lapin stared at her with a serious look on his face. "I'll take him, Euphémie. No need for you to go any farther. You shouldn't be seen up here."

Then he pulled her aside and whispered, "I don't like the looks of that bloody bandage. He looks worn out."

But Harry overheard and said, "Ne vous préoccupez pas," in his strangely old-fashioned French. "I'm fine and grateful for your help. But I agree, we should let Euphémie go home now." He reached forward to softly stroke her hair and gave her a smile that made her cheeks even redder than they already were from the sun and the exertion of the climb. What *a lovely face Harry had, if only . . . but it was absurd to think those things, and she began to back away.*

When the pilot staggered, Lapin reached out and put his arm around his waist. "Don't worry," he said. "You'll soon be safe." And then, turning to Euphémie, he told her, "I'll try to get you a message. We both know that he can't stay up here indefinitely."

No, Euphémie thought, the Nazis would go house to house if they knew that anyone had survived the crash. They were good at finding people. They'd recently found two German-Jewish refugees in a root cellar in Beaucastel hiding beneath piles of old newspapers. No one had dared say anything when the couple was hustled away.

That night her father came home late. Euphémie was at her bedroom window watching for any sign of Lapin. She didn't want to burden her father with the news and was back in her bed, eyes closed, when he opened the door to look in on her. Perhaps Lapin had tended to Harry's wound and been able to stop the bleeding. Lapin would know what to do, as most farmers like him were experts in caring for injured or ill farm animals. If Harry could recover his strength, then perhaps they might manage to get him to one of the Resistance groups up near Mont Ventoux. Those people would be experts at hiding an Allied pilot from the enemy.

In the early hours, a commotion began as some of the Germans returned to the house and settled themselves down for the night. She wondered what they'd been doing all day after the morning roust. Searching for downed aviators, no doubt. At first light, her thought was of Lapin. She threw on her clothes and for a moment thought of binding her chest again, but it would just add to her discomfort during the trek. In the court-yard an empty convoy truck took up most of the space. Sneak-ing through the barn again, she inadvertently woke the chickens and the flock began to cluck with pleasure. She tried to hush them, but it just made them noisier, so she simply climbed through the back window out into the field and then moved quickly toward the ravine and beyond.

Without the pilot Harry as a burden, she soon traversed the fields and spotted the old man's abandoned house at the edge of a line of sycamore trees that had once marked a road. She circled around, keeping close to the trees. The red roof tiles of the little stone cabin shone mauve in the early light. There was no mistral and the sun already felt hot. The rough wooden door, the only entrance, was shut. Except for a quince bush, there was no cover, so she crouched behind the nearest syca-more and watched. She hesitated in her approach. She didn't know if the young pilot had concealed a weapon. He might fire if she came near without announcing herself. Perhaps it would be prudent to wait. Maybe Lapin would arrive. Or Harry might notice her and reveal himself.

After a few minutes, her legs began to cramp, and when she straightened up, her hands resting against the smooth bark of the tree, something slammed into her side, knocking the breath out of her, and she found herself flat on the earth. A heavy boot flipped her onto her back and the pallid eyes of the soldier who had killed her chicken peered into hers. He bent and jammed his hand over her mouth, pushing her skull into the ground until she felt that her jawbone would snap if he pressed any harder. Then she found herself pulled up and the soldier twisted her arm behind her. When she gasped, something hard smacked against her head. He pushed her forward, twisting her arm painfully and growling the same brutal-sounding words over and over that must mean, Shut up, shut up, shut up!

They hadn't yet reached the cabin when the door opened and Harry emerged with his unwounded arm held high in the bright clean rays of the sun. He shouted something to the German, who let go of her. Then the soldier pushed her to the ground again, kicking her to make certain she wouldn't be capable of interfering. Euphémie's eyes streamed tears but stayed wide open as the German shouted and pointed his rifle at Harry, who walked slowly forward. The German got behind and pushed him with the barrel of his gun. At the edge of the clearing, he shoved Harry against a sycamore, abruptly took a step backward, and fired a shot into the pilot's head. Euphémie screamed and the young German threw himself upon her in a frenzy, ripping her clothing, suffocating her, his big hands around her neck. In the sky there were no clouds.

When she felt that she would never take another breath, her persecutor's body suddenly turned into a rock-heavy weight on top of her, but his grip loosened. All at once Euphémie saw Lapin's round head silhouetted against the sky. He grabbed her hand to pull her up, hurling a blood-clotted hoe behind him. The German rolled off her and onto the ground, his neck cloven open, a gush of blood inundating the rough weeds.

"Are you all right?" Lapin asked.

"Yes," she replied, but she felt her face was wet, and when she rubbed it saw that she was bleeding. Lapin took her face in his hand and examined the cut. "It's not deep. Can you make it home? I have to get rid of the Boche's body. But I'll have to

leave poor Harry to be discovered by the Nazis. They threat-
ened to kill your father and ten other villagers if the pilot wasn't
turned in by midnight tonight."

"Father!"

"Yes, he received an ultimatum yesterday. We heard about
it then."

Euphémie began to cry softly and Lapin took her arm.

"Come on, I'll take you part of the way. But we have to
hurry. And you have to make sure you get home without being
seen. And never say a word about this! Do you think you can
do that?"

Euphémie nodded, but it was hard to focus. She just tried
to keep up as best she could with Lapin as he led her back down
through the fields.

Euphémie stood stock-still at the window, remembering.
Lapin had hidden the German's body so that it was never
found, even after the war was over. When the Nazi command came looking, they were pleased to see that the
American flier had been shot with a German bullet. They
listed their missing soldier as a deserter, not connecting his
disappearance with the pilot's death.

Euphémie and Lapin never spoke about what had happened. While the war dragged on, it wouldn't do to have
anyone know that the two had been involved in what had
gone on up there. And even after the war, on the occasions
when they would cross paths at a village fête or simply run
across each other on the road, the silence between them had
become too solid to break. As with so many, any mention of

the long-kept secrets, the horrors and bad blood that had
risen up between people during the war, became a sort of
taboo and those things lay forever concealed in people's
hearts.

And since then, who had Euphémie been close to? Everyone was gone—her kind and loving father, Agnes, who
had raised her, even her few friends in the village had mostly
died or moved away. There was only her dear Hamidou and
he probably had no idea where she had gone. And even if
he was able to find out, what could an Arab man do for an
old lady who had been legally committed to an asylum by
her own daughter? Euphémie let out a deep sigh. As the sun
came up on the other side of the Ouvèze, she had the small
but comforting pleasure of watching the white heron whirl
down onto his private spot atop the protruding river rock.

The Peanut Roaster's Woman

hroughout the town of Serret, from the vaulted medieval portal beneath which a cobblestoned lane mounted to the village fountain all the way down to the main square shaded by centenary *platane* trees, artisans were setting up stands. It was the *fête du village*, the summer fair, when everyone who had something to sell put out their wares and the little town found itself in full party mode, crammed with visitors for two days of festivities.

Didier Falque came out of his house at the base of the village ramparts early that Saturday morning breathing in air perfumed by a rose-covered trellis that extended over his doorway. At the age of forty-two, fit and muscular from his work in the vineyards, Didier retained all the vitality he'd had as a youth. As he looked around he saw his friend Jeannot Pierrefeu's wife, Mathilde, already setting up a stand near the stone balustrade. Her pale arms adjusted a red-

and-yellow-flowered tablecloth over the table where she would display her faience bowls and plates.

"Is Jeannot coming to sell his things today?" asked Didier. Mathilde and Jeannot were both potters, though Jeannot made monumental sculptures out of clay. He was still the same free spirit he'd been as a boy, an artist who knew how to do just about anything. Still, Didier felt proud that he made a better living as a vintner than his clever friend Jeannot ever would.

"He's up in Geneva," Mathilde replied. "He and Thierry are showing their work at a gallery there."

"Good for them. The Swiss have plenty of money to spend!"

Mathilde nodded, pretty in an ethereal way with her translucent skin and white-blond hair that she still wore long. Only her hands were flawed, prematurely aged by the chemicals and glazes that were intrinsic to a potter's work. Still, Didier could see why his old friend Jeannot had remained enthralled by a woman like Mathilde. As a student just arrived in Provence from Brittany nearly twenty years before, she had been a living angel. Didier remembered the first time he'd seen her at the Tuesday market, her pottery arranged in shimmering clusters around her. How his heart had pounded as he'd approached, irresistibly drawn to her. He knew he'd amused her that morning with his resonant voice and wide grin, but he'd been too late. Mathilde had already met Jeannot, Jeannot who had been to university and could speak eloquently about any subject. Poetry rolled easily off his lips and his jokes acted like charms on the laughing girls who seemed to always surround him. Didier hadn't stood a chance. He could never have come up with the fine phrases that would impress a girl like Mathilde. Still, there were compensations. His own wife, Christine, was attractive too, with her enormous doe eyes and thick chestnut hair, though often she and their two daughters, Mimi and Amélie, seemed to live a separate female existence that had little to do with him. Still, he was lucky to have married Christine, lucky that her wealthy father had given them the village house with a wide terrace overlooking the valley, its unobstructed view dominated by the ever-changing clouds that hovered above the mighty Rhône. Didier could sometimes make out the glinting silver thread of water that traversed the distant valley. In the evening, the clouds turned red-gold, or sometimes to glittering coal, as the sun descended behind them. That morning, when he'd awakened at first light, misty lavender wisps sat like roosting birds in the dawning sky, but Christine was already up and gone.

The sun soaked into the paving stones around him and Didier could feel the streets and houses already radiating their special summer heat. The *canicule*, they called it, the dog days named after the constellation Canis Major that was a bright glow in the night skies during the hottest part of the summer. But Didier didn't mind the heat; after all he'd been born and raised in the Midi. He gazed at Mathilde, dressed in a checkered skirt and a red top, and imagined her long pale body beneath. The intriguing mystery of the female sex was always of particular interest. He wasn't a ladies' man, but he was still curious, especially when he went off to the salons where he presented his vintages up in Lyon, or at the great convention halls in Paris, where there was always a crush of people buying, tasting, looking. Didier looked too. But seduction didn't come easily to him. He didn't have the subtlety that women appreciated, especially those desirable women who might have been available to him if he'd had Jeannot's way with words. It was a particular type of women who sought him out, the bold, impudent ones, and Didier generally found nothing mysterious or alluring about that sort of person.

He took the steps two at a time up the cavernous staircase that traversed the rampart wall and led to the maze of medieval streets upon which no cars could pass. Some of the other vintners, those with cellars in the village, already had their cases of wine stacked and ready. Tasting glasses emblazoned with the town crest of a tower with crossed keys were lined up next to bottles containing whites, reds, and summery-pink rosés. Christine would take charge of selling Didier's wine. She was on vacation from her job as an administrator at the local lycée, the same school that his daughters attended. They had promised to help their mother that day, leaving Didier free to do what he liked. He didn't need to promote or sell his wine at small fairs like this. Distributers handled most of his production for him, so the only vintage he would be offering that day was his simplest Côtes du Rhône.

At the top of the stairway, the town weaver already had her handmade woolens and multicolored jackets hung neatly from wooden racks. The white-haired old lady had lived in the village for most of her life, though she was originally from a neighboring town. Like many Provençal who have had deep roots in one place for generations, Didier considered her a stranger. But he greeted her politely. After all, they'd known each other since he was a small boy.

At the village fountain, small chairs and tables from the tea shop were arranged near the moss-covered stone heads that spouted water into the circular basin. Thérèse, the lanky brunette who owned the place, already had an assortment of cakes arranged on golden doilies. She was ten years younger than Didier and he gave her an appreciative grin. Like many southern women, she was dark-complexioned with almond eyes that gleamed like varnished oak. He could easily imagine Thérèse without her clothes because she resembled his wife.

"Here, Didi, have a piece of *quatre-quarts*." She held out a platter to him. "On the house!" Didier thanked her and put the entire half-cut slice of pound cake into his mouth. He would have enjoyed sitting down with Thérèse, but it didn't do to be seen too often with any of the village women. It could be dangerous if a husband got wind of something, whether or not it happened to be true. "Look but don't touch" had become his motto. He didn't want any trouble.

He continued down the cobbled streets, striding along over the sharp stones in his heavy work boots. Each cobble beneath his feet had been hand-chipped into its cubed shape hundreds of years before and fit exactly into its particular spot in the narrow alley. The perfection of the stonework always amazed him. The whole town was made in this way, each stone cut in accordance with the one next to it and placed just so, like a complicated puzzle. And then there were the very special, round *galets*, egg-shaped river stones that paved the esplanade in front of the village church, the place where he and Christine had been married. Noble stones like those were barely obtainable anymore since it took hundreds of years of flowing water to create the smooth, river-polished ovoids that now graced only the most ancient cloisters or the entrances to wealthy people's châteaux. Didier had seen Serret's church entrance photographed in tourist guidebooks. Seven hundred years ago those stones had been hauled out of the river one by one and brought up to the top of the village in wooden-wheeled donkey carts to be laid by hand.

As he descended the main street, he nodded to the various merchants. In the shady niche of her doorway sat his friend Jeannot's mother, Marie Rose Pierrefeu. As she always did, Marie Rose had made several trays of *oreillettes* for the fête, delicate, fried sugar cookies that would stay crisp and fresh for only a matter of hours. Didier bought a sachet of them and his booming voice could be heard praising Marie Rose's confections up and down the narrow alley.

When he got to the café the double doors were open to the bright morning light. Didier didn't intend to continue any farther, definitely not down through the lower gate that led to the opposite end of town. For him that remained an uninviting neighborhood, and even though his vines covered several of the sloped hectares located just below the village there, he avoided the road. His old schoolmate Manu Dombasle lived down on the plain. There was no particular rancor between them, but Manu wasn't a vintner the way Didier was. After his father's death, he'd sold the most valuable property and now he simply delivered his production of grapes to the cooperative, not even bothering to vinify it himself. The co-op wine was mediocre pinard as far as Didier was concerned and he didn't respect growers who didn't care enough to create their own vintages. Manu, who was unmarried, was naturally taciturn like so many *paysans*, but the truth was that he was an unkempt, lazy man who generally appeared as if he'd slouched out of a barnyard. Beneath the medieval tower at the end of the rampart, still in residence in the long rambling farmhouse, Manu's mother, Sabine, passed her days behind closed doors. She was old now, a widow who lived quietly, seeing practically no one. When he passed through his fields at night, Didier sometimes glimpsed the flicker of a lamp through her shuttered window and remembered all too clearly what she'd been like when she was young and desirable, and what she'd meant to him. But Sabine was more than twenty years older than Didier and ever since their affair had ended, he'd gone out of his way to avoid her. A month previously, he'd glimpsed her from a distance clothed in one of those shapeless dresses that snapped up the front with wide sleeves to cover old-crone arms. He'd felt a strange despair, as if seeing his own grave opened up before him, but was quick to harden himself. Sabine was nothing to him other than a fleeting reminder of the grim reaper's hourglass, the inevitability of the *croque-morts* who would come to take you away when the spirit departed, leaving nothing behind but a shrunken cadaver with stiff feet.

Standing at the zinc counter of the café, Didier downed his espresso in one gulp as the bartender Michel set up chairs and tables outside on the graveled terrace. Today visitors would fill the tables, consuming wine, sodas, and the ubiquitous glasses of yellow pastis served with a jug of water alongside to temper the strong alcohol. Already people lined the bar as others pulled up chairs to the Formica-topped tables. The song floating from the jukebox was Jacques Brel's *"Ne me quitte pas."* Then a couple stumbled together into the bar.

Didier had seen the two around since the winter. They lived in a trailer camp at the edge of the river in a dilapidated van hoisted onto cement blocks. The man made what living they earned by selling sugared peanuts at outdoor markets. Didier supposed he'd be setting up somewhere in the village that day with his hot pans of caramelized *cacahuètes* that he scooped into paper cones. But now he was with his woman. That was the only way to describe her. She probably wasn't his wife or girlfriend, nothing as respectable as that. She was the scarecrow he lived with, her hair dried out and frizzled like old corn husks, her arms mottled, though she couldn't be much older than thirty. Even her face had that brown animal look of something kicked about and smeared with a strange dusky color like cheap makeup, but it was simply her sunburned flesh. The couple ordered two pastis and downed them full force without adding the usual quotient of water. Nine o'clock in the morning with the whole day still ahead. Only craggy-faced alcoholics who passed their days in bars drank their pastis like that. When the woman ordered a second, the peanut seller tapped her on the shoulder. Without even looking at him, she reared back and let loose a stream of invective. *"Petit con! Emmerdeur!* Don't you tell me what to do!" When he tried to put his arm around her, she let off another vile sally.

All the patrons turned to look. One didn't generally hear that kind of language first thing in the morning, and certainly not from a woman. Didier's wife, Christine, never uttered anything stronger than *"mon Dieu!"* Like the rest, Didier was surprised by the foul, grinding speech of the wretched woman. As her man eased her backward past the bar, Didier got a whiff of her breath. She must have been up all night drinking. He noticed her dirty fingernails, her dust-covered sandals, but still he gave a sideways glance to the hard nipples that poked against her light shirt, the flat belly beneath. He imagined the tawny hair that would cover her sex and the way her slender legs would meet at the top. Didier ran his hand over his face. As he counted out the centimes to pay for his coffee, her curses echoed off the stone walls of the alley. Inside the café, Michel closed the doors as his clients silently waited to see what might happen next. Didier stood motionless there at the bar, falling into a trance as he listened and found himself taken back to a time when that sort of language, whispered rather than shouted, would pull him along as if he were attached to an unbreakable cord and the only thing he could think about was his own satisfaction. That day, the woman's shouts were palpable, laden with a perverse erotic promise, culminating for Didier in a soul-wrenching longing he hadn't felt in years. And he thought of Sabine, once so vibrant and alive, the married woman he'd made love to in secret when he was just an adolescent boy, the dream that had once been the center of his universe, now impossible to ever revisit or revive.

His coins clattered on the metal counter and he forced himself out into the street, moving rapidly in the opposite direction from the couple. He took a breath to calm himself, but his exhale ended in a drawn-out groan. He looked around to make sure no one had heard and mounted one of the narrow, less-traveled alleyways. His big feet moved unevenly over the steps of graduated cobbles and he felt as though his heart was being cut and abraded by the same sharp stones that he traversed.

He stopped in a shaded curve of a stairwell where he knew he would be alone. Cacti in full, golden bloom cascaded over the wall above him and he realized that it had been years since he'd had someone to love who loved him back. He suddenly laughed out loud at the ridiculousness of his thoughts and, looking down at the perfectly cut stones at his feet, knew that unlike them he would never fit into place in the perfect way they did. He didn't fit anywhere. And Didier suddenly found himself with the anguished thought that he'd never known even a remote intimacy with his wife, Christine. Didier would have enjoyed making love with her at dawn that morning when those lavender clouds hung over the horizon, but she'd been up before him, as she always was. At night, when it was pitch-black except for a brilliant, laughing star or two, she would turn away from him. And on the rare occasions when she did let him touch her, Didier sensed that it was just because she felt the weight of her own miserliness. The fact was, she wasn't attracted to him, maybe never had been. That's how it felt to him, her unyielding reaction to his appalling needs. He supposed she didn't ask for a divorce because she was a Catholic, or perhaps the appearance of happiness and normalcy was enough for her. In the shadow of the staircase, he let his wrist graze against himself, feeling his sex heavy and soft. His face suddenly clogged with emotion, and he wiped away what he could with a handkerchief, trying to get himself under control.

The sky was already shimmering white, the sun a burning opal at midmorning. Didier stumbled up to the top of the village, where the river-stone esplanade fanned outward from the church in a half-moon separated by lines of blue pebbles like some fantastic astrological map meant to interpret the heavens. Just beyond, a balustrade presented a vista over the entire valley, a view even better than the one from Didier's house because it was so much higher. And below hung the eternal clouds over the Rhône, a single file of pure white cavorting lambs. He knew that view so well, but that day it did not seem a part of him and he felt set adrift like one of the clouds.

Didier wished he could find some place where he could be by himself, but he knew that the church with its crenellated bell tower would be locked. There was no retreat. The white sun scalded his forehead. He tried to breathe normally but his chest felt like it might explode. Looking down, he saw the stands set up on the Place des Platanes, some with colored parasols or gaily striped awnings slanted over them. Christine and the girls would be down there somewhere selling his wine, charming the locals and the summer tourists. He pressed his fingers against his eyes until green and gold lights flashed against the darkness. Then he forced himself to move, descending rapidly through the casbah of winding streets and passageways that led beneath stone archways or by hidden gardens glimpsed through wrought-iron gates. He wandered up and down through the village for an hour or so, not speaking to anyone, just making his way silently through the maze of narrow alleys where only an occasional lost visitor might penetrate. Finally, there was nothing to do but return home. He found his elder daughter, Mimi, and his wife in the kitchen.

"Amélie said she'd take care of the stand this afternoon if *Maman* and I would make a cake for dinner tonight," fourteen-year-old Mimi informed him with a giggle. Christine appeared as gay as her daughter as she measured out sugar into a bowl. Didier wrapped his fingers lightly around her arm, but she shook him off as if confused by his touch. At lunch, Didier ate in silence, his head hanging above his plate.

He thought about taking his tractor for a promenade through his vines during the afternoon, but the heat was unbearable, the sun seeming to radiate right through the flesh into bone itself. So he kept up his ramblings in the shady areas of town, and finally, as the shadows lengthened, forced himself to visit his fellow *vignerons*, who were absorbed in selling their vintages. Usually he tasted with precision, rolling the wine over his tongue, breathing it in, and then using the spittoon that was always provided for serious oenophiles. But that day he didn't spit out a drop. Instead he drank the wines down and roared out his approval whether they pleased him or not. By the time he reached the fourth vintner, Antoine Moravec, his palate was so jaded that everything tasted just fine. Like the wine that had flowed down his gullet, his discernment was gone. Aware that his voice was getting louder and louder, he simply didn't care. His cries echoed in the stone rooms where the wine barrels lay on wooden pallets, and his body emanated an almighty heat even though the temperature of the *caves*, long ago chiseled by hand into the rocky mountainside, remained cool even on the worst summer days.

At six o'clock, an orchestra set up in the square under the sycamore trees, whose branches had been grafted together so they formed a leafy net that cast a profound, cooling shadow. Didier pulled one of the folding chairs near the bandstand and sang along with the old songs being played. People occasionally slapped him on the back and laughed at his booming voice that was slightly off-key. That night he was inebriated to the point that he didn't mind what anyone thought, he simply remained in his own private world, imbibing the delicious evening air and trying to stay steady on his rickety seat. Sometimes he would get up and sway to the music, watching the people going to and fro. To Didier, all the women in the square looked wonderful, the voluptuous ones with their low-cut blouses that revealed round, fleshy breasts, and the pert girlish ones who wore short skirts to show off their slender legs. All were equally fine as far as he was concerned. He looked them up and down and muttered to himself *"Ah, les gonzesses!"*—What dames!—with an approving nod.

The aroma of grilling meats began to waft from charcoal braziers. On the street below, spicy *merguez* sausage and kebabs on sticks were being served along with cardboard containers of *frites*. Didier felt hungry as he always did when he smelled or saw something good. But he continued to sit alone in the square watching the women. Once in a while two would dance together to the music of the orchestra and Didier could barely restrain himself from jumping up to join them, dreaming of pressing their pliant flesh beneath his fingers and holding them close. But drunk as he was, he knew he couldn't cross that line. If he'd been sober, he might have had his choice of dancing partners. Since he was fit and not bad-looking, he was attractive to a variety of the village women. But tonight they would shy from his touch, frightened by his red face and his rough farmer's hands. They might even laugh at him, and that would be unbearable.

Finally, the vendors began to close up for the night, pulling drapes of colored cloth over their stands. He looked up to see Antoine Moravec holding an open bottle of his unlabeled, personal stock. Moravec passed it to Didier, who took a swig.

"You make the best wine in the village," Didier said. "Apart from mine, of course."

Moravec laughed and said, "Didi, you're all alone tonight. Come on, let's get something to eat."

"I'm not hungry," said Didier, sitting up. Moravec's comment about his aloneness bothered him. He'd been careless getting drunk. Besides, he didn't particularly like the widower Moravec or his wines.

"Then have a drink at my house."

"Another time," said Didier firmly.

"All right, enjoy yourself," said Moravec, leaving him with the half-filled bottle.

When the vintner wandered off, Didier moved to the edge of the square and sat on the wide stone wall that formed the northwestern rampart of the town. At the end, the black windows of the tumbledown tower gaped. Just below, he could see his patch of vineyard where sunlight still slanted across the lush grape leaves. Above, in the shadow of the tower, stood Sabine's stone farmhouse. He remembered that once a luxuriant vine had grown up the side of the place, but now the wall was barren. Her front door was closed tight, as were the shutters on the street side. They would probably be closed on the other side as well, filtering out the light just the way she liked it, only one small, dim bulb left burning within to relieve the total darkness.

Didier remembered the shock of seeing the house blazing like a ship on a black sea the night her husband, Bruno, had been shot to death in a hunting accident. All these years later it was still whispered that he'd been murdered by a jealous husband, but no one really knew the truth. When Didier had entered with his mother the next day to pay their condolences, it had seemed like a different house from the one he knew, the shutters open wide and the brightly lit rooms quite the opposite of the dark interiors where he had spent hours in a miasma of blind, thoughtless sensation with Sabine.

As he peered over the rampart, no one loitered in the lanes below. The Dombasles never came to the fête. Manu didn't have any wine to sell since all his grapes went to the cooperative. Nor did Sabine participate. She had never cared about selling anything at a fair. She didn't knit or make pottery or crafts, but he remembered her cakes and the heavy aroma of spice that would occasionally greet him as he entered her dim vestibule. And then there was the luscious smell of her skin. If she could have sold that, Didier would have been happy to buy. But everything between them had ended with shock and mourning.

He sat feeling a little more sober. As the evening sun turned the olive groves in the distance from teal to gold, Didier slipped off the wall still holding the bottle of wine and walked to the edge of the square. The leaves above him were absolutely still. He looked at his watch. Christine wouldn't be expecting him for another hour or so. He wended his way around the rampart and then out through the gate and into the winding street below, a place he hadn't walked in years. Cement planters mounted along the stone balustrade were empty of blossoms, the earth inside them cracked and dry. This part of the village seemed uncared for, as if abandoned by its inhabitants. He sauntered down the steep street, well aware that what he was doing was bordering on the insane. And then he was at Sabine's door.

When she opened the house to him, it was as if nothing had changed. The darkened shadowy anteroom, the exterior shutters fastened tight in the salon, and the windows open to let in the evening air were all so familiar. Sabine glided back into a dark corner as Didier shut the door behind him. Standing still, he let his eyes get used to the half light. A familiar smell hung in the air, cinnamon with a hint of vanilla. Sabine was still straight, unbent by age, her face hidden in shadow even as his eyes adjusted. He put the wine bottle on the table.

"Have a drink," he told her. A tray of upturned glasses rested on the sideboard and she reached out, poured a half glass, took a sip, then drank it straight down. Didier stood very still and then he opened up his hands and lifted them toward her. Great heaving gasps racked his chest as if he was expelling the last of the air from a life that had turned into emptiness itself. Sabine slipped backward toward the kitchen door, where she removed a lace cloth from a small round table. She pulled it over her head and the tatted edges hung down over her face. For a moment, she looked to Didier like a strangely enshrouded bride. And then she spoke.

"Didi, you come here after all this time looking for me! But I don't exist any longer—not the way you wish me to."

Didier's hands fell to his sides. Sabine's voice had the same seductive sound, a little hollower perhaps, but with the exact cadence he'd once known by heart.

He stood there in the darkness trying to make out her face through the lacy disguise, knowing that if he touched her she would crumble like the scales of a dried-up fish whose flesh had been consumed long ago. But she had once been everything, her smooth arms and her breasts that he believed belonged to him alone, and that voice, that strong stream that washed over him, removing him from time and place, pulling him to her.

He could not speak. What might he express to her if he did? *Sabine, what you awoke in me is an unendurable torture that has ruined any semblance of happiness I might have had. I curse you for corrupting me, for abandoning me . . . for getting old!*

After a moment, Didier forced himself backward toward the front door. Sabine hadn't moved. She stood in the tenebrous corner watching him from beneath the web of lacy cloth. He grasped the doorknob. And as he did Sabine whispered, "You were my one true one! But I didn't dare hold on to you, Didi. You had a right to live life your own way."

The intensity of feeling that coursed through Didier kept him silent. After a moment, he turned to look at her. "Sabine" was the only word he could utter. He opened the door and peered into the empty street. Then, believing himself unseen, he slipped outside.

He had no intention of ever going back to Sabine's house. That Saturday of the fête, his inhabitual inebriation, and the roiling torment provoked by the street woman's curses had brought him to a level of baseness that shamed him. He tried to push the incident out of his mind. But afterward, his thoughts took on a depressing clarity that had previously been obscured. At night, Christine was always there to make his supper, his girls like twittering birds, either scampering up to their rooms or turning their backs on him as they went out the door to meet their friends. It was a semblance of life, but not real, and it had become abhorrent to him. He realized that he and Christine never went to people's houses together or entertained at home. She regularly went off in the evening to meetings at school, or out with Amélie and Mimi to concerts or the cinema, things that didn't interest Didier. And almost every night she visited her father in his big house in the neighboring town of Beaucastel. Christine's father, still a wealthy man, now suffered an impaired, arthritic dotage with servants hired to help with every aspect of his life. When Christine returned after her visits, there was no question of making love. She'd sigh or yawn, evidence of her exhaustion, and

Didier knew that if he simply caressed her arm or the nape of her neck, she would pull away.

For a long time, his evenings had ended with a small snifter of his own homemade *marc de Provence* that would send him straight into a deep slumber. But his nights alone had become increasingly burdensome to him. He no longer enjoyed the glassful of *marc*. It simply agitated and awakened him. Reading or listening to music wasn't entertaining and the television bored him. He thought of his youth and the final days at lycée when he and Berti Perra had grown close. But she was long gone with a new life in Scotland. There had been no chance for them, just a few happy moments that made his present existence seem so much worse. To ease his malaise, he began to take walks through his vineyards or up into the mountains after nightfall. But one night, stumbling along an unlit road, he felt the absurdity of his ramblings and the full weight of a profound alienation pressed upon him. His dreams of a lover who would accept him unconditionally were like fluttering wisps of ash over a hot fire. He would never find someone with whom he could feel free. And the emotion that had overcome him in Sabine's house began to recur with increasing intensity during his solitary walks.

Coming down from the mountainside one autumn night when a waning gibbous moon hung like a tilted silver coin, he smelled the sweet alcoholic perfume of grapes that had been left on the vines after harvest, grapes overlooked during the *vendange* or rejected because they had ripened too late. Didier found himself on the low road with a view upward to the village, the clutch of sycamore trees in the square, the twinkling windows of the stone houses that mounted willy-nilly up the rocky hillside to the medieval church and the fortified garrison at the top. He forced his eyes to bypass Sabine's house. Even so, he detected an evanescent light behind the shutters and felt an urge to mount the narrow road. But he couldn't allow that to happen again. The fantasy of finding in Sabine the woman who had once been such a delight to him was madness. It was still before midnight, so he ducked into the café, where the owner was drying glasses with a linen towel and placing them on the shelf behind the bar. Michel waved him in and said, "*Entre, mon vieux!* I'll buy you a drink." Didier had a quick cognac as Michel flipped the chairs upside down onto the tables and swept the floor, all the while complaining about the lack of clientele now that the summer was over.

After saying good night, Didier found himself outside again, fueled by the warmth of the now inhabitual alcohol. Knowing that he would have to walk it off before he could sleep, he took the road downward through a small copse of trees, then skirted the rocky embankment that brought him to the bridge spanning the Ouvèze River. It had rained for several nights and in the darkness the water ran black as oil rising up over the rocky banks and splashing against the cement stanchions beneath him. The moon was reflected in multiples in the unquiet water and appeared to jerk nervously like a fish on a line. Past the bridge lay the cement depot with its piles of sand, gravel, and hewn stone. A light glimmered dully from the encampment beyond where six or seven trailers housed a dozen souls. Some called that little clan of people Gypsies, but they weren't the Roma of

Didier's youth, who traveled in wooden caravans pulled by mules with an occasional stolen goat hitched at the back. Still, there was something unsavory about those temporary dwellings and he suspected that if an opportunity presented itself to rob a stranger, or make an easy break into an isolated house, it wouldn't be resisted. In fact, one of the inhabitants had been arrested just a month before for pickpocketing at the town market. The people who lived there seemed nothing more than worthless sludge, like the roiling muddy torrent that was plowing along beneath the bridge that night.

Didier looked at the sky, willing himself to think of nothing, not his family, not the little tribe living there in the wasteland down by the river, or anyone else. Instead, he began to whistle a tune through his teeth, a Spanish melody that was a staple in the Midi wherever there were gatherings of people who liked to dance the old-fashioned paso doble. The tune reminded him of the toreadors and running bulls and twirling black-haired women with clapping castanets that he'd seen at the ferias in Nîmes and Arles. And then, out of the corner of his eye, he noticed something coming toward the bridge. At first, he believed it to be a sand-colored dog trotting near the side of the river. He kept up his whistling and turned his face toward a sky that was filling with ashy clouds blotting out the moon. Another rainstorm on its way. When he looked over again, he saw that it wasn't an animal but a person coming toward him, a person walking in a kind of odd hop-skip. Didier made little drum sounds with his lips, remembering the rise in tempo that signaled dancing men to pull their partners close in a wild turn. And then the person was on the bridge and Didier continued his tune. The wind batted against him in its own percussive way as he recognized the khaki jeans and sandals and flapping cotton blouse, the same things she always wore. It was the peanut roaster's woman, the one whom he'd seen drunk in the early morning at the *fête du village*. She'd no doubt been at it again, as a wobble punctuated her bouncing step. Her eyes, wide and glimmering, observed him, whether with fear or interest he couldn't tell. He kept on whistling and humming, and it sounded to his own ears like a welcome, something that could never be considered sinister or frightening on an autumn night when there was no one else about.

"I know you," the woman said when she was close enough for him to hear her over the wind and water. Her deep, cracked voice was the sort that evolved only after quantities of cigarette smoke and alcohol had funneled through a person's throat. She bumped lightly against him, and as she looked up into his face Didier smelled the sweet gasoline smell of cheap liquor.

"You live up in the village there." She pointed in the direction of the illuminated ruin that stood on the highest peak above Serret. "You're Didi Falque!"

He didn't acknowledge his surprise, just kept to the low steady tune. She grabbed hold of the railing and lowered her head to look down at the turbulent waters. And then her eyes came back to Didier's with a slight squint as if she was pondering something. "I like to sing too!" She laughed and tapped her chest with her fingers. And then she grunted, "Tah-rumph!" which went along with the cadence of his song. She smiled up at him, her sun-darkened skin rendered into various shades of gray by the darkness. Between the fast-moving clouds, a hint of moonlight gave her mouth a wet, pinkish gleam. "And I like to dance!" She stepped in a surprisingly lithe twirling box step. No doubt she had the body of a girl, but Didier had seen her rough, worn face in the daylight.

"Tah-rumph!" Didier mimicked, and stuck out his foot as if he were a toreador about to enter the ring.

"Aha!" she said, placing her foot next to his and lifting her arms. He took one of her hands, and as her other hand curled around the back of his neck, he pulled her close and lifted her off her feet in a frantic whirl. She was so unexpectedly light, light and hard as a dry stick, that he almost lost his balance. Her clothes fluttered about her like dead leaves. When he put her down she clung to him, looking up into his face. "Yes, that's the way to dance," she said, giving him a wide smile. Behind her incisors were two gaps where teeth had once been.

Didier stepped back, but she was on him like a vine, her small feet on top of his boots. "More," she said like a child. And he danced again, galumphing roughly to the end of the bridge and then down onto the riverbank, where there was a cluster of wild boxwood between road and river. As he twirled her, they were raked by a pair of headlights from a passing car, and suddenly he found himself rolling on the ground with her. She didn't seem to mind and laughed as his big body vaulted over hers, she on top for a moment and then underneath again. When they stopped, he felt a wet kiss on his neck. As he sat back on his heels and started to get up, she grabbed at his crotch and Didier was surprised that instead of lust he felt only sadness mixed with compassion. He moved her hand away and stood. The wind came on so strong he almost lost his footing again on the muddy riverbank.

"I like you, Didi Falque," she said, lying there. She stretched her arms over the sparse tufts of grass. "I see you walking around at night. I see you and I wonder what you're looking for."

"There's nothing to look for," said Didier. "You should go home now."

"I don't want to. I'd prefer to stay with you." And then she rolled slowly over to her side, pulling her knees to her chest. Her clothes were damp with mud, and she sighed like a little girl. "I'm all wet and dirty!"

"I'm sorry," said Didier. He held out his hand to her. "Let me help you up." But she shook her head in a desultory way. Then, to his surprise, she fell immediately into a deep sleep right there on the muddy earth, perhaps knocked out by the alcohol and whatever else she might have consumed that evening.

Didier bent and gave her shoulder a shake, but she was dead asleep. He turned and looked across the bridge at the caravans. There were no lights. It wouldn't do to bring her back into that thieves' den. The wind blew hard and warm, bringing with it the odor of river water, rank and metallic. The stars and moon were hidden. It must be the filthy *vent du sud* that brought gray clouds, not the cold and cleansing mistral wind that cleared everything away. He looked back at the sleeping woman, thinking that same evil southern wind must have brought her to him. But then he stripped off his Windbreaker and tucked it around her. She'd be all right there on the high embankment until she woke up and found herself all alone.

He took the long way back to the village. When he got within the bounds of Serret, he was panting from the steep climb and every pore of his body exuded an icy sweat. The church tower tolled once. He stopped for a moment to catch his breath. His hands were brown with mud and the knees of his trousers were also coated. Christine would be certain to notice in the unlikely chance that she was still up. He decided to go straight through the village so he could stop by the fountain, where he could at least wash his hands and face and take a minute to compose himself. He quickened his pace as he passed Manu Dombasle's property and rounded the curve that led to Sabine's farmhouse above. Almost immediately came the first blessed drops of a cool rain bursting over him. Didier passed his hands over his face and neck and through his damp hair. And all at once something pulled him hard, causing him to stumble backward, and he thought that perhaps the peanut roaster's woman had somehow followed and grabbed hold of him. But as a blow fell against his shoulder blade, he pivoted and saw that it was Manu Dombasle. Before he could take a step back, a fist pounded into his belly. Didier doubled over and vomited a stream of cognac-tainted bile.

"*Fils de pute!*" Manu hissed in the darkness. "You bastard pervert! I know what you've been up to. Interfering with my mother! *Putain!*" Manu hauled back his thick forearm, ready to throw another punch, but Didier managed to deflect it and get out of the way. "I'm going to make you pay," said Manu. "I saw you leave *Maman's* house the night of the fête. She wouldn't say anything against you, not for months, but I finally forced it out of her. How dare you take advantage of an old woman! You can't disgrace the Dombasles! Your life in this village is over, Falque!" And as thunder cracked over their heads, Manu threw a roundhouse punch.

Didier wasn't sure if it was blood or rainwater that he wiped from his streaming cheeks. At home, he bathed his face in the kitchen sink and then lay silently down on the living room sofa while rain spattered madly against the glass awning on the terrace, keeping him awake for most of the night.

The rain continued as the commune slept. In the area of the Drôme, the Ouvèze River, swollen by overflowing brooks and streams, became a teeming floodwater. That night, the swell descended into the region in successive waves like an out-of-control oceanic tide that inundated riverside landings, washed away cars and roads, and in the end killed thirty-two people, including a mother and her newborn who were captured by the violent deluge. In Saint-Maxence, the Roman bridge withstood the onslaught, though in the nearby towns of Vau and Beaucastel, smaller bridges were swept away along with everything constructed or parked in the vicinity of the great black roll of water whose destruction would take years to put right. It was reported that a group of caravans was pulled under by the raging torrent. All the bodies were eventually found, battered and waterlogged, some unidentifiable.

Only a few suspected that the woman who was washed

away with the others near the stone quarry hadn't been with her companions that night. Someone mentioned seeing Didier Falque down by the river before the floodwaters raged, but this was never verified. And for most, the woman was considered just another unfortunate victim of that wild and unpredictable event.

6

The Names of Trees

The mistral swirled up the mountainside, shaking the cypress trees so their tops crooked like the backs of old men. Aurélien Pierrefeu watched from within the high garden walls that sheltered him from the wind's buffeting force. The iron-gated portal was open to the south, giving a view over the yellowed vineyards and a stunted but hardy peach tree that marked the edge of their two hectares. Beyond, low hills rolled down to the river valley. On the opposite side, a thin, tarred track mounted to the village of Serret, encircled with stone ramparts that had once served as a barricade against marauding hordes. Auri had been born in Serret and at the age of three months had been chosen to portray the infant Jesus in the Christmas pageant sung in Provençal, the language of the southern poets that his grandparents still spoke between themselves. Like most French people, Auri was not even faintly religious, yet he'd always been pleased whenever his parents described that winter day when he had been such an integral part of the town's festivities, swaddled in the straw-lined manger where he'd been surrounded by admiring shepherds and angels played by village boys and girls just a few years older than him.

That afternoon, sitting at the plank table his father, Jeannot, had built, Auri flipped desultorily through his history book. In November, it was too cold to eat meals outside in the garden anymore, so they ate in the kitchen, where his mother's peach, apricot, and blackberry jams decorated the open shelves like jeweled mosaics. But spending time with his family had recently ceased to be a pleasure. In fact, it was getting so that Auri was having trouble even being in the same room as his father.

That year, just after school had started, his friend Marcel had said, "My parents say your father is a *marginal.* Somebody who lives on the fringe."

Auri had squeezed his fingers into fists even though Marcel was a pal.

"My dad works," Auri had retorted. "He works all the time."

"I know, but always at different jobs. That's what they meant."

And it was true. His father wasn't out working that day, but instead was inside the house putting the final touches on a room with a separate bath that Auri would soon have to himself. For the present, the family was all lumped together upstairs, Auri in a tiny room at the end of the corridor, his younger sister and parents on the other side. But Auri didn't give a damn about the new bedroom downstairs, nor did he

care that he would no longer have to share the single bath-
room with the rest of them. He just wished to be lifted up
and spirited somewhere far, far away. The best he could do
at the moment was escape to the enclosed garden, where the
clematis that crept atop the iron gate rattled its dried-up
tendrils, the glowing magenta blooms that had graced it that
summer withered and forgotten.

His father, Jeannot, always said the mistral could drive
anyone crazy. The unrelenting *vent du nord* whirled down
the Rhône River, pounded maddeningly in one's ears, dis-
tributed dust and detritus under doorways, and endeavored
to flatten everything in its path. Auri felt disturbed by the
wind's evil mischief despite the fact that he was safe within
the garden walls constructed hundreds of years before,
when people knew the importance of sheltering themselves
from the violent sun and wind of the Midi. His open book
barely fluttered, but he felt the wind's creeping breath and
had the uncomfortable feeling that something was sneaking
up on him from behind. After a particularly fierce gust, he
began to distinguish the distant grind of a tractor as it drew
closer. The driver, their neighbor Manu Dombasle, was not
a friend despite the fact that he and Auri's father had known
each other since childhood. Dombasle owned a vineyard
that adjoined theirs, and Manu desperately wanted to add
Jeannot's two hectares of vines to his own, believing that
his former classmate should sell it to him for a song. But the
old *paysan* who had sold Auri's parents the house insisted
the vineyard remain attached to the property and Jeannot
had respected his wish and told Dombasle no.

The house had been practically a ruin when they'd first

moved in three years before. It sat on a mounded hill over-looking the valley. Everyone knew the place was a sacred spot because a temple had stood there when the Romans ruled Gaul. The idea of living amid such ancient stones had at first excited Auri. His father had showed him the carved capitals of once majestic columns, some of which had been used in the construction of their house. Jeannot explained that there were certain sites with spiritual power that just naturally attracted people to them, especially people who were in tune with the elements. After the Romans, the temple had been transformed into a chapel dedicated to Saint-Félicien. Eventually that had also fallen into ruin and for a period it was used as shelter by shepherds. But for Auri, the place had lost the charmed aspect that still captivated his father. The main room had been polluted by the absurd pottery tiles that Jeannot made for fun in the same kiln where he baked his large earthen pots and sculptures. Dancing bears, stinging scorpions, crowing roosters painted in black on the glazed ocher tiles that had been stuck up on the walls made the place look like a comic strip for infants, not a home where normal people lived.

The same crazy work made its appearance in his parents' bedroom that was up the stone staircase, a spare, white-washed space whose one window looked east. In there, tiles depicting ancient gods like Pan kicking up his hooves and Bacchus with his bunches of grapes and bulging stomach lined the walls. Auri used to admire the goddess Diana, with her bow and arrow and moon-shaped breasts, but now he simply found the motley assortment embarrassing. His father laughed and claimed his creations were his way of paying tribute to the ancient soul of the place. He was in the habit of doing a wild celebratory dance up and down the stairs of the house or in the garden, especially when the mistral was blowing its worst. His father always seemed to be in perpetual motion, making his pottery, doing all sorts of odd jobs, even going to Paris or Berlin to help his artist friends install their paintings in galleries where he would sometimes show his own work. And, of course, Jeannot was busy renovating their house.

Just after they moved in, while digging a trench for a water pipe, Jeannot had unearthed the stone-covered tomb of a chevalier, one of the twelfth-century crusaders who had returned from the Holy Land. He'd been buried with a metal lance that still rested against the dust of his breast. There weren't even bones left, just the corroded metal of the long saber and what might once have been armor made of chain mail. After the discovery, his father had heaved the great stone back over the grave site out of respect. "The dead have a right be in their own place," he'd told Auri. The warrior had been given a ritual burial. "You see," said Jeannot, pointing. "He faces east. They say Christ will come with the sunrise to raise the dead on the Day of Judgment. That's why they placed him that way, so he'd be ready."

The mistral gave a gust that shook the metal gate and made Auri start.

"Aurélien!" his father shouted from inside, "*S'il te plaît*, can you come here for a minute?" Auri pulled his long legs from under the table, but he did not stand. Now that he was fourteen he'd been growing in such steady spurts that he found himself, suddenly, surprisingly, taller than his father, who was a large man. He positioned himself on the edge of his seat and then took a breath, making sure not to move too quickly. His father could wait, and Auri would purposely make sure that he did. He rested his hands on his thighs. He might be tall, but he'd never look like his father. The circular glasses that he wore made his round head look like a *pétanque* ball and his snubbed nose was that of a clown. He'd once admired his father, but at times he found it amazing that Jeannot Pierrefeu had managed to catch and marry Mathilde, Auri's mother. He'd heard that Jeannot's friends Didier Falque as well as the artist Thierry had hoped to win the heart of the beautiful Mathilde. Auri didn't know how his rubber-faced father had managed to beat out the others. Of course, his father was intelligent, no denying that. Jeannot had gone to university and was able to converse about practically any subject, plus he could do anything with his hands. And he was funny, wickedly, hilariously funny. He kept Auri's sister, Ada, in stitches, but Auri didn't find his father's humor at all amusing anymore.

Auri remembered as a child looking with awe at Jeannot dressed head to toe in leather, ready to take him on his motorcycle for a ride up and down the hills and onto the rough tracks of mountain passes. On those miraculous afternoons, the vine rows had flipped by like the cards so skillfully dealt at his father's weekly game of belote, when friends would come to the house and his father would make everyone laugh with his droll jokes. How he'd longed then to be just like his father! But now being around Jeannot simply annoyed Auri and it was impossible to hide his disdain.

"Aurélien, *viens!*" Jeannot called again. And though Auri had been about to stand, he sat on for a minute or two longer, hoping he was provoking the same angry feeling in his father that he felt. He turned and looked at the vineyard, now bereft of grapes harvested by a family friend who in return supplied his father with a few cases of mediocre plonk, a ridiculous waste because his father knew how to make good wine, just as he knew how to do everything else. One autumn when Auri was twelve, he and his father had gone into the fields to do the *grapillage*, the late harvest, when vineyards are open to anyone who wants to gather the last bunches of grapes left on the vines. His father had an old crank press and they squeezed out the grape juice together and began the fermentation in a huge plastic *cuve*.

"These late grapes make a beautiful sweet wine that will last for years," his father told him. "I'm naming this one after you, Auri, since you made it. We'll open the first bottle to celebrate your sixteenth birthday! 'Château Aurélien' will go perfectly with your mother's chocolate cake!"

But Jeannot always seemed to give more than he got in return. If he'd sold the vineyards to Manu Dombasle, then perhaps Auri could be going skiing with his friends over school vacation. But his family never did the least extravagant thing because his father didn't have a regular salary. He was an artist, a mason, an *homme à tout faire* always on the run, unlike the parents of Auri's classmates, who had nine-to-five jobs and made sure to always escape somewhere wonderful during school holidays instead of remaining stuck at home like Auri's family always was. Jeannot's friends called him a *soixante-huitard* because he still believed in the revolutionary ideals of 1968, but he had been too young to actually participate in the demonstrations. Auri now thought his father was a royal phony, and Jeannot's lack of concern about money grated because it set them apart.

At last, he got up slowly on his slender stork's legs and went through the side door into the kitchen. The designs of black scorpions and chirping birds on the tiled wall jumped out at him, along with the eternal *cigale*, the insect whose loud, percussive whir symbolized hot summer days that were now long gone. An owl, a magpie, and a fat toad, all figments of his father's imagination, were stuck to the wall behind the stove, around the sink, and even on the old wooden beam above. A toad suited his father all right! He should make only toads, giant toads as big as he, because they looked just like him! Maybe they'd sell better than his pots and jars, *terre cuite* trays and vases that sat in his large studio, where the shiny metal chimney of the kiln reached like a signal higher than the tops of trees down on the plain by the river. The sign outside in the shape of a Greek amphora read: JEAN-NOËL PIERREFEU, POTIER.

Just beyond the open door of the back room, Auri's new room, Jeannot stood with one hand on his hip, a large metal hammer gripped in his other fist. He looked around when he heard the sound of Auri's footsteps. "Can you come give me a hand?" he said. "I can't hold this hatch open by myself." Auri didn't say a word, merely stepped forward, making it clear that it was an imposition on his usual Wednesday afternoon off from school when he should be allowed to do whatever he wanted. When his father lifted, Auri curled his fingers beneath the heavy hatch and Jeannot pulled through a coil of black-coated electric wires, running them swiftly around the floor edges to the places where plugs and light fixtures would be installed.

It was a cool day, but Auri's hands felt hot with the effort of holding up the heavy wooden door that must have once been used as an entrance for goats or sheep. His grandparents had told him what the place had been like in the old days, before the vineyards had been planted, back when the fertile plain was full of sunflowers, fields of swaying grain, and fruit trees that enrobed the valley and the rising hills with their springtime pinks and purples. Nothing of those days was left, except for the occasional apricot or cherry tree, or the old peach tree from which his mother made jam every year, even though the peaches, when perfectly ripe, were of an unequaled perfection, sun-warmed, right off the branch, sweet and deliquescent as a dripping honeycomb. *Deliquescent!* Auri felt angered that a word his father used had slipped so easily into his thoughts. He bent his knees and focused angrily on his numbing fingers. His father leaned forward, his body halfway through the hatch, and Auri imagined letting go. A grin creased his pale unlined face, but he continued to stand stockstill while his father hauled in another circlet of wire.

"If you like, I'll teach you how to run these electric lines so you can do it yourself one day," said Jeannot. "It's good for a person to know how to do a little of everything." That was another one of those oft-repeated phrases that made Aurélien roll his eyes. Most adults said the same things over and over, as if they had very small brains with only a few mundane thoughts that popped up at certain preordained moments. His father liked to use Provençal words too. "Did you know that in the Provençal language fruit trees are feminine, not masculine the way they are in French?" His father was always repeating things like that too. "*Pêchière, pommière, poirière*—after all, a tree that bears fruit should be female, no?" And they had their own *pêchière*, the peach tree that his father always touched with his fingertips when he passed, as if he were a druid honoring some local deity. Auri's grandparents were almost as bad with their Provençal sayings. They'd grown up speaking the dialect, but they were not within the perimeter of Auri's wrath and their words didn't grate on him the way his father's did. Those two white heads were harmless, mostly tending their kitchen garden and taking long walks together up into the mountains. They were like a pair of fluffy goats. How could you be angry at a goat?

In response to his father, Auri made an effort to use his most bored and disgusted voice. "If I ever need electrical work, I'll hire someone." His own voice often shocked him, coming out as it sometimes did in a surprisingly deep, unruly growl. But this time it was nothing more than a mousy squeak that belied his insulting words. His voice was not to be relied on these days. His mother, Mathilde, predicted that by the following summer he'd have the low, constant tones of a man.

"It's good to be independent," Jeannot replied. "You don't want to get stuck having to hire someone for every little thing. You're free when you can do it yourself."

"Are we almost finished?" asked Auri.

"One more minute." Jeannot pulled up another coil of

cable and just as it came through, Auri let the hatch fall full force on the rubber-coated wires.

"*Merde alors!*" Jeannot jumped up, his dark eyebrows knotted. Auri stepped back and held his chest high, but he felt no bigger than a cockerel. A month ago, his father had hit him for the first time, a quick hard slap on the cheek at the dinner table when Auri complained to his mother that he wanted a new mobile phone, the kind that most of his friends had. "Jeannot!" Mathilde had exclaimed as Auri sat back in shock, his hand pressed to his burning face. Neither of his parents had ever physically punished him or his sister, Ada. When his father apologized afterward and offered to shake hands, Auri's heart had given a painful twist, but he did not extend his hand in return. As far as he was concerned, a line had been drawn.

That afternoon, he stared into his father's face, breathing to himself, *I dare you!* Jeannot bent his head and said, "Your hands got tired. *Ça va.* I'll lift this time." He patted Auri on the shoulder before bracing himself and yanking up the hatch.

Aurélien didn't dare hesitate, but instead of bending to the task, he stuck his leg out and used his heel to drag the rest of the cable through the little doorway. He wouldn't bother using his hands, as that might make him look like he was a willing participant, or perhaps even apologetic.

"I want to finish wiring your room today because Thierry's having a show in Marseille this weekend. I'm going down to give him a hand."

Auri liked Thierry, a painter who was so massively muscled that he resembled one of the old cylindrical *poteaux*, the mounded stone well covers that still dotted the hillsides. With his long Fu Manchu mustache and his ribald stories, he always made Auri laugh.

"Are you bringing any of your sculptures?"

"No, I'm just helping out," said Jeannot. "I know how Thierry likes his *tableaux* displayed."

"Is he paying you?"

"Thierry is always generous."

That meant that his father was probably getting nothing. Jeannot had many friends and seemed to live day-to-day doing whatever presented itself. When the spirit moved him he made his pottery. In the summer, when the tourists came, he was often flush. But it was edging in on winter now. If only he had a father who was a shop owner or a businessman, everything would be so different!

Auri's mother, Mathilde, was also a potter, but she made small things in her own electric kiln. She also worked part-time at a horticultural store in town where she was paid the SMIC, minimum wage. Auri didn't like it when on market days she would go through the piles of used clothing that the ragman brought, picking out things for the whole family. His sister, Ada, didn't seem to mind. But Ada was only ten and didn't know any better. The idea of old clothes disgusted Auri. Now he refused to accompany his mother to the market that had once been so extremely entertaining with the buskers and the music, the man with the performing monkey, and the packages of hot, sugarcoated churros that had crunched delectably between his teeth.

With the hatch closed and slip-locked, his father sat down on a three-legged stool that they'd found in the small vaulted cave under the house. He'd stained and varnished it, and the wood shone dark amber.

Auri was surprised to see his father sitting in the middle of the day. Generally, Jeannot never stopped, always going here or there. But today he leaned his head on his hand for a moment and was very still. Then he yawned and stretched his hands up. "*Ouf!* I just had a *coup de fatigue.* Better have a coffee to wake me up. Would you care for a soda?" Auri would have liked one of the Oranginas that his mother had brought home as a special treat, but he shook his head. He didn't want to give his father the pleasure of his acceptance or have to sit down with him at the kitchen table and watch him drink his coffee.

"I'm going back outside. I have homework."

"When you've finished I'll run you into town and we'll pick up the gears to repair your bike." Auri shrugged. Bicycles were for little kids. His friends rode scooters now.

All at once something rumbled and a painful, squeaking crunch came from outside. His father leaped to the window. At the edge of their property, Manu Dombasle, dressed in his usual blue overalls and dusty boots, rode his tractor between the rows of grapevines. As Dombasle passed the corner of their terrain where the peach tree grew, his tractor swerved and he ground the side of it into the bark of the tree.

"Damn that *connard*!" said Jeannot. The last time Manu Dombasle and his father had spoken, Dombasle had made a stink, saying that vineyards should belong to vintners, not to those who knew nothing about them.

"Come on, Manu," Jeannot had cajoled him. "Maybe we

can come to an agreement—you could rent some of my vines." But Dombasle wanted to own the land, or nothing. For him, land was the only thing that counted.

"It's strange that he wants that bit of property," Auri's father had said. "He already sold off his best parcels and it's clear that he could care less about making good wines. What a waste!"

Auri watched as the tractor proceeded down the edge of the vineyard.

"He's trying to kill that tree out of spite," said Jeannot.

At the end of the row, Dombasle turned around and on his way back again jerked the tractor toward the tree. When the grinding noise came close, Jeannot threw open the window and hollered, "Manu! Are you blind? Watch where you're going!" Dombasle lifted his arm in an insulting manner and Jeannot muttered a curse. The tractor veered and regained its position in between the vines.

"Your mother's going to be furious if she sees what he's been up to," his father said.

Auri looked out at Dombasle, hunched atop his big machine. He had a head like a square peg covered in short, feltlike hair. Auri grudgingly admired the man, thinking if he himself were Manu Dombasle he might do the same, slam that peach tree each time just to let his dad know who was boss. He smiled and thought, *Allez, Manu!*

Auri skipped upstairs and grabbed the rest of his books. He wasn't a good student, but he had to do the minimum. His mother got upset when his grades were poor and he didn't like making her unhappy. When Auri left school he'd get a real job, something that paid a weekly salary so he could have a regular life like everybody else and his mother wouldn't have to buy her clothes out of bins.

Outside, the wind made the grape leaves flip and twist on their dry stems. The mistral blew colder now, but the sky was still blue. A few elongated clouds skimmed quickly by. The good thing about the mistral was that it pushed away rain and gray and kept the sky clear. Auri heard the clink of the espresso cup on the zinc-topped table as his father remained by himself inside. The afternoon seemed to have slowed down. Maybe his father was reading. He read a great deal at night, but generally not during the day.

Then a drill began its insect hum and in a moment Auri heard the rough pounding of the hammer making a trench in the plaster and stone so his father could run the electric wires up the walls. It wasn't easy work. Those old walls were strong and made of hard stone, not like the thin plasterboard in the new villas where most of his friends lived.

Auri tried to concentrate on his homework, but the hammering made his muscles tense. He stood up and slugged his fists into the air in front of him. When the hammer stopped, Auri sat back down. He fondled the pencil that he'd sharpened into a point with his penknife. At least the red Victorinox his father had given him the year before was good for something. Jeannot had said that a man could always make use of a well-made knife, and he'd felt Auri was old enough to have a fine one.

The infernal buzz of the drill mounted to a scream as once again his father pressed the reinforced steel bit into the stone. Auri knew Jeannot didn't like making holes in the old stones. He had too much respect for them. They should be left as they were, like he'd left the chevalier buried in the garden under his rude gravestone. Sacred stone. And then, the high, straining drill began its chorus anew. Auri covered his ears until he heard the unexpected clatter of the heavy tool crashing down against the cement floor. He imagined it broken, shattered on the hard surface. His father would be upset if it was damaged. Auri didn't run to help the way he would have just a year ago. He sat there, hands clenched together like a vise, not moving.

And then came a groaning cry from a deep unrecognizable voice, a voice as confusing as Auri's own strange peeps and croaks that changed every time he spoke. Perhaps his father had been on the ladder and fallen. Or maybe he'd driven the drill bit right through his hand. The scream resounded again, agonizing, rebelling against pain, inchoate, sending Auri to his feet. He meant to walk calmly, but instead he sprang through the doorway.

Inside, he found Jeannot on the floor, body twisted. His circular glasses lay nearby, the lenses cracked. And his father's wide blue eyes, set off by his reddened face, looked at him with horror. He'd ripped his own shirt open and one fist beat at the flesh of his breast in anguished, leaden strokes.

Auri hurled himself down next to his father on the hard floor. "*Papa! Papa!* What is it?" But his father only made a round O with his mouth as if he was trying to speak, trying to breathe, but couldn't. And then Auri heard the crunch of tires. It would be his mother with his little sister, Ada. He didn't even feel the ground as he flew through the room out into the garden and then beyond to their narrow, stony drive. As soon as his mother saw his face she said, "Darling! What's happened?" And Auri could only point.

There was nothing to be done. The firemen had come right away with their tanks of oxygen and boxes of emergency equipment used to start up a heart again. The ambulance took Jeannot to the hospital anyway, but any effort at resuscitation was useless.

And then they brought his father's body home. His grandparents helped Auri's mother wash and dress him and lay him out on the bed upstairs in the room whose window faced east. For five days his father lay there. Everyone in the village came to pay their respects and to say how sorry they were. Some mounted the staircase to gaze at their lost friend. "It looks like he's sleeping," they kept repeating. "It doesn't seem possible."

Auri stayed downstairs. He'd once glimpsed the body of a friend's grandmother laid out on a bier with a little frill framing her face so her head looked like some special dried fruit wrapped in a doily. There had been dry ice beneath to keep the body chilled, as it had been summertime. The thought of seeing anything like that or even being in the vicinity of his father's corpse was unbearable to Auri. He stayed outside until it was pitch-dark, and when he found himself nodding, he slept on a cot in his unfinished bedroom so his mother could have his bed upstairs. He did his best not to imagine his father laid out in his parents' room, his father who was always up on ladders or heaving long trays of molded pots into the fiery kiln, or pulling on his leather jacket so he could roar off on his motorcycle into the high reaches of the forest. Auri didn't want to think about Jeannot at all; the memory of his father belonged under an immense stone like the one that covered the chevalier.

Neither his grandfather Louis nor his grandmother Marie Rose cried, at least not that Auri saw. They seemed wedged together, each holding the other's forearms as if about to do a dance in tandem. "Jeannot looks so beautiful!" they said to each other when they came downstairs after visiting the body of their son, a thing that they did several times a day. They were like automatons responding to a clockwork spring, up and down the staircase.

"You should say good-bye to your father," his grandfather said. Auri shook his head, wishing he would never have to enter the house again.

"They're strong, your old folk," said Jeannot's friend Thierry when he came. Standing in the garden, he didn't tell Auri any jokes, though Auri wished he would. A good filthy joke might just do the trick. That would be the way to handle this. Instead, Thierry paced, smoking cigarette after cigarette, crushing them into a tin lid that had been left on the outdoor table. After a while, he went into a corner of the garden, pushed the wide blocks of his palms into his eye sockets, and stood alone. Finally, he came back and sat down next to Auri.

"Your father was unique, you know? That's the least of it. I never imagined living my life without Jeannot around. It's impossible." Auri tried not to think as Thierry went on. "Jeannot lived the way he wanted to. Most of us don't quite manage that."

"I thought you were down in Marseille," Auri said, hoping not to hear any more.

"I canceled the show."

"The gallery must be angry."

"They'll live."

After that, Thierry came back every day to exchange a few words with Mathilde and the rest of the family, but there was really nothing he could say or do.

When he could no longer keep his eyes open, Auri went into his new room. The wires that his father had inserted into the fissures looked like little black rivers running nowhere. There was no way he would ever go upstairs again, he told himself. Not to the room that faced east, not to the dancing gods painted on the ocher tiles, not to see his father who no longer existed, not anywhere.

He spent the days of mourning outside at the plank table. His cousin Cécile came every afternoon. She brought cards and games and they played them together. Cécile barely spoke, which suited Auri, who had no inclination for discussion of any sort. His mother, Mathilde, a pale shadow buffeted by the waves of people that took her back and forth from house to garden and up and down the staircase, was gone from him. And his sister, Ada, sent to a friend's house in order to spare her, made no appearance at all.

After three days, the mistral stopped blowing and the sky turned gray. That evening, his father's friend Didier Falque came by clutching his knitted cap. "I'm sorry, I just heard," he said to Auri. Didier bowed to Auri's mother and put his large hand on her shoulder, but he seemed too shocked to kiss her cheeks the way others did or say a word of condolence. He walked back to the table, where Cécile was dealing out cards, and looked down at the two young people with a blank expression, as if he knew neither of them. Auri looked up. He knew Didier had recently had some sort of trouble, there had been a scandal, but his father had never explained anything about it except to say that Didier had been unjustly accused. Auri knew that his father's friend wouldn't say the same silly phrases that most did. He certainly couldn't stand to hear any more empty words. A manly person like Didier probably wouldn't know what to say or even what to feel. Auri thought it would be good to be that way.

A thin moon shaped like a scythe rose in the darkening sky, bringing the evening full upon them. Auri's grandfather came out from the house with a bottle of wine. He opened it on the table where Auri and Cécile sat and poured a glass. He held it out to Didier, who took it without a word and stood waiting for him to pour another, or perhaps say something. But Louis simply stood there, hands by his side, looking off into the deepening night. There was no one else to pour for because all the other visitors were inside. Didier finally looked down at the glass in his hand as if seeing it for the first time. Auri's grandfather nodded and wandered back inside the house.

Didier stood there still as the night. Cécile had stopped dealing the cards. And then, without taking a sip from his wineglass, he leaned over Aurélien.

"Those vines," he said, moving his glass to indicate the property outside the walls of the enclosed garden. "Your father talked to me about them."

Auri stood, pleased that he towered over Didier Falque, even though the man had forearms that bulged formidably beneath his jacket. He excused himself to his cousin Cécile and motioned with his head for Didier to follow.

As they reached the gate Didier said, "I know Jeannot wanted no sale of land. But there's still money in the grapes. If I rent them from you, it will bring in a few hundred a year. Your father would have wanted you to have that."

Later, Auri told his mother about the offer, explaining that it wouldn't be a sale. Didier Falque would simply be paying for use of their vineyards.

In the months that followed, though Auri felt he didn't study any harder, he spent long hours poring over his books to keep other thoughts away, and his grades improved. Nothing was completed in his downstairs room at home, but he moved in. He ran an extension cord from the kitchen so he could have a lamp, and at night he left the door open so the heat from the wood stove could drift in as it might. When he lay down in his cot, his long legs felt heavy as metal rails and even his rib cage was cumbersome, so that when he was on his back he could hardly breathe and had to curl into a ball like a baby to get any rest. His mother busied herself with Ada's comings and goings. When she tried to comfort him, he gently nudged her away. But there was a little money now. His father surprised them by having some insurance, and his studio and large kiln with its spiraling chimney down by the river sold for a good sum to a young potter who had been looking for a place of her own.

The following autumn, Didier Falque harvested the grapes and paid Auri, who gave most of the money to his mother. With the remainder he was able to buy himself a scooter. Mathilde allowed him to ride it only on weekends. His greatest pleasure was taking the bike over the hills and up into the mountains, where the stands of pine trees sometimes opened up to reveal sunny glades. Sometimes he'd sit in their center and mound up a rocky cairn, or once, in a place where water sprang from between two old stones, he created a circular basin beneath. On rare occasions, he'd go down by the riverbed. From there he could see the top of what had been his father's workshop where the metal chimney glinted above the rough live-oak trees and the bushes of thorn and rosemary. It would be a long time of looking before he could gaze at that chimney without immense sadness.

Auri tried not to think about his father. When he did, he would get a severe ache as if his chest was compressed, and he would have to press his long forearms into himself to stop it. But it wasn't so bad when things would indirectly come to him, memories of carved stones or early sun in the eastern sky. Pictures of naked, dancing gods, and sometimes, even certain Provençal words—*pêchière, pommière, poirière*. The names of trees.

7

Homecoming

On a warm Sunday afternoon in October, Gilberte Perra MacLean arrived at her parents' house driven in a chauffeured limousine. At the sight of the gigantic car with its chrome fixtures and enormous white-walled tires, passersby began to gather in front of Domaine Petitjean's arched gateway. For years, the townspeople had referred to Gilberte as *"l'étrangère"* because she had departed for Scotland as a teenager and had never really returned. Her childhood friends still spoke of her fondly, and sometimes even saw her on her brief visits home, but they had no idea that she had planned this particular voyage. Gilberte's sons, William and Timothy, had occasionally come along on her rare stays, though as they grew older they balked at visiting due to the fact that they couldn't say a word to their grandparents or anyone else in the village because they could not speak French. Their Scottish father was rumored to be difficult, though in what way no one really knew, as he had never once shown his face.

Gilberte's parents, Liliane and Clément Perra, still resided on the perimeter of the village of Beaucastel in a manor house with a capacious garden and a Renaissance outbuilding with a wide, arched doorway that had once served as the *cave* where Domaine Petitjean wines were made. Over the years, as the vineyard's production expanded, the vinification and bottling of the *cépages* had been transferred to what Gilberte had always considered an unattractive cinderblock hangar constructed on the flat plain by the river. She was aware that the grape harvest had been completed the previous month, so there would be no frenzy of work upon her arrival, and she hoped to be greeted by her parents and possibly even her brothers, Philippe and Marco, and Philippe's wife, Marie-France. They all lived nearby, and they knew, after all, that this was to be a permanent homecoming for Gilberte. But as the chauffeur slowly rolled the car up the stony drive, the front door of the house remained obstinately closed. No one peered out from the tall windows on the ground floor or shouted a greeting from a balcony above, so she found herself climbing the front steps and hammering the iron knocker, whose echoing thuds resounded within.

As she waited, the afternoon sun shone on her ebony hair, warming her arms and shoulders and submerging her in a golden glow that reminded her of the constancy and strength of the Provençal sunshine, so different from the gray and rain of Edinburgh. A pot of spiky verbena on the landing emitted a perfume of citrus and she bent to pick a leaf, holding it to her nose and breathing in its lemony essence. She could hear the burble of water spilling into the stone *lavoir* just around the corner, the same fountain where many of the Arab women who resided in the village did their daily laundry. Unlike most vineyard owners, her father never hired Arabs for fieldwork or anything else. His family had owned property in Algeria, but after Algerian independence, they had lost everything. However, once in France, Clément had landed quite providentially on his feet. He'd successfully courted and married Liliane Petitjean, an only child and heiress to the large but not terribly profitable Petitjean vineyard that Clément made certain to take full credit for transforming into one of the more prosperous domaines in the area.

Gilberte knocked again on the front door. She was certain that her mother would be waiting, her darling mother, Liliane, the one person she had truly missed during all her years abroad. Finally, she let go of the knocker and turned around to see an elderly neighbor, Louis Pierrefeu, standing just outside the gates amid the curious bystanders gathered there. He lifted his hat and called out, "It's you there, Berti, isn't it?" A warm feeling arose in Gilberte at the sound of her childhood name. She'd always been fond of Louis Pierrefeu. When she gave him a friendly wave and replied in the affirmative, he continued, "You aren't au courant? An ambulance took your mother to the hospital in Saint-Maxence and hour or so ago!"

"Oh!" Gilberte lifted her hands to her face. "What happened?"

"*Je ne sais pas!*" He lifted his shoulders and gave an unhappy shake of his head.

As she turned to descend the steps, the interior bolt made a familiar creaking rasp and the front door jerked open. Her father's heavily lined face appeared and she approached to greet him. His frizzy gray hair in need of a cut stood straight out from his head like fiberglass, giving him a slightly deranged look. Yet, he was dressed in his Sunday best, a light twill jacket and a starched blue shirt and tie. Now that he had grown older, his skin had a purplish cast rather than the ruddy hue usually associated with farmers in the Midi. He could have been Greek or perhaps even Arab with those violet lips and dark, slightly bloodshot eyes.

"*Ma foi*, Gilberte, it's you!" he said, without giving her so much as a kiss on the cheek or even a friendly smile. "I forgot you were coming today. Your mother's had an accident!"

"Yes, Monsieur Pierrefeu was telling me. What happened?"

Her father glared at the small group ogling the fancy automobile and then said, "The silly goose fell and apparently broke her leg. Your brother just telephoned from the hospital. They're planning to operate tomorrow."

"I'll get the car unloaded and we'll drive over there right away!" exclaimed Gilberte.

The chauffeur approached the foot of the front steps and tipped his visored hat, oblivious to the crisis. "Where would you like me to put your luggage, madame?"

"Right here in the front hall, please."

As the chauffeur hefted a trunk fastened with a leather strap, her father stepped back, nearly losing his balance.

"You're not planning to move in here!" he exclaimed. Gilberte reached out to steady him and was shocked to find that his muscular forearm, normally firm as an ox shank, had turned to putty that slipped loosely over thin bone.

"*Papa*, I told you before, I've rented an apartment over in Serret in a house built into the rampart. The road is too narrow for this big car, so I'm temporarily dropping my things here until Marco can come to help me move in."

As Gilberte entered the cooling shadow of the hallway, the savory smell of her mother's *daube de boeuf*, long-simmered beef in a particular combination of wine and herbs, enveloped her. The aroma was something she had rarely encountered during her years in Scotland, and she was flooded with memories of the leisurely Sunday lunches of her childhood where course followed upon course, always ending with her mother's almond *tartelettes* and the ubiquitous cherries preserved in glass jars of eau-de-vie for those adults who dared to partake.

"*Maman* must have left dinner in the oven. I better turn it off."

"It's probably burned by now," her father replied. But when she ran to check, Gilberte found the daube perfectly cooked. Pearl onions and olives floated in the rich sauce. When she gave it a stir, a slice of orange peel surfaced. Returning to the hallway, she found her father angrily hovering as the chauffeur piled up the rest of her luggage.

"What possessed you to come back here in that ridiculous automobile?" he asked.

"Oh, *Papa*! The MacLeans had business in Brazil, so they kindly offered me their private plane and they arranged for a car to pick me up when I arrived in Nîmes. I couldn't have boarded a commercial flight with so much luggage."

"Those monsters must be thrilled to finally see the last of you! No wonder they were eager to send you off in their airplane!"

She didn't argue. It was true that her former parents-in-law had been implacable during her divorce from their son. The MacLeans had been furious that she was leaving Simon, largely because responsibility for their errant son would once again fall upon them. But that had all happened years before, and Gilberte had done her best to put any lingering resentments behind her.

Opening the double door to her parents' salon, she saw that nothing had changed since her last visit three years ago. Her father's chair, the only comfortable piece of furniture in the room, still stood in front of the fireplace, a leather ottoman placed in front of it. As usual, the heavy green drapes had been pulled closed against the western sun, leaving the darkened room hot and airless. Perhaps that's why her father seemed unsteady. Gilberte also felt a creeping fatigue. Her mouth was dry and she realized she hadn't had anything to drink since early that morning.

When she heard the chauffeur come back into the front hall, she folded a generous wad of euros into her palm, but as she tried to give it to him he smiled and waved her hand away. Then he tipped his hat and wished her good luck for her return to France.

Inside the salon, she found her father ensconced in the

high-backed chair, his crepe-soled heels resting on the tiled floor. She bent down, saying, "You haven't kissed me hello yet, *Papa.*"

But he ignored her proffered cheek and simply replied, "I don't understand what you mean by coming back here. Why didn't you simply remarry and stay put in Edinburgh?" He leaned forward and clutched the carved mahogany lion's paws of his armchair as if he wished to squeeze out of them the truth of what his youngest daughter's reappearance really meant. Gilberte took a step back, knowing that even though he was getting on in years, her irascible father wouldn't hesitate to reach out and cuff her if he got annoyed. That aspect of his personality had never changed. Growing up, she and her sisters had gotten used to being dragged bodily to their rooms and locked up for hours whenever they were unlucky enough to spark their father's volatile temper. Once he'd even tied her eldest sister, Marguerite, to a chair, and there had been worse punishments. But their father's lack of restraint had been just as bad with regard to their brother Philippe. None of them would ever forget the blue-black eyes and bloody lip meted out by Clément when, as a teenager, Philippe had left one of the tractors on an incline and it had slipped backward, breaking through several rows of newly planted vines. Marco, the youngest, learned early on to flee if he detected the slightest trace of anger in his father's voice and was the only one to escape the physical chastisements that the rest of them considered to be the normal course of things.

Despite their seeming resignation while living under their father's roof, the three Perra girls had not lingered long in the household. Marguerite was the first to go, before she was even eighteen. Gilberte's sister Pati had left home too, and Gilberte had followed in their footsteps, finding a job in Scotland, a place that had seemed to her impossibly foreign. At the end of her first summer in Edinburgh, she became affianced to a young Scotsman and definitively left her old life behind.

Gilberte sat down on the ottoman facing her father and repeated the same information that she'd already given several times by telephone. "I've told you, *Papa*, I'm back because I was tired of living abroad. My boys are grown and living their own lives. As you know, I'd been a French teacher for many years, not the most fascinating career, and so I've begun to think about doing something completely different."

"You acted as a babysitter for that crazy husband of yours for years, and got nothing whatsoever out of it! The MacLeans should have been down on their knees to you!"

Gilberte stopped listening. Talking about her former in-laws held no appeal. They lived in the lavish manner of nouveaux riches because of investments in North Sea oil. During the years of her marriage, she had visited their houses on three continents and accepted expensive gifts along with unlimited credit-card accounts that were automatically paid for at the end of every month. All that had been intoxicating for a young girl brought up in a conservative agricultural family where extra funds were used either for the purchase of land or to replant vines, never for frivolous expenditures. But Gilberte's father was correct that there had been problems. With no money worries and no business or employment to which her husband had to attend, there was rarely any restraint where alcohol, drugs, or eventually, other women were concerned. The wild nights that stretched into weekends and then weeks soon palled for Gilberte, especially after her two sons were born. But when they divorced, her husband had relinquished custody of Will and Tim, which was all she wanted. She never asked for any money beyond basic child support. In the end, she had remained on neutral terms with the MacLeans. She was all too aware of her ex-husband's problems, but they were no longer hers to cope with, and she had been simply too happy with her new freedom to bother casting any blame. *Comprendre est pardonner*—the phrase inscribed in gold letters above the church's altarpiece in Beaucastel had always made sense to her. It was better to forgive and forget. Afterward, Gilberte had enrolled at university and gotten a teaching degree. She'd made a modest living as a French instructor at a private boys' school in Edinburgh, but in the end, her three-bedroom flat in a tony area of Stockbridge, the one valuable asset she'd retained after the divorce, had become too expensive to maintain.

"Your harebrained idea of coming back here makes no sense. And I certainly hope you don't expect any sort of financial support from me at this point in your life!" Her father leaned back and closed his eyes in an effort to shut Gilberte out.

Her shoulders ached from the long journey, and even though it was only midafternoon, she wished she could go straight to her new place rather than try to explain what even to her was unexplainable. Not wanting to prevaricate, she said softly, "I have my own money, *Papa*. I want simply to take the time to see if I might be happy here."

"But that's ridiculous. How can you expect to reclaim something from a life that was over and done with decades ago?" Clément squeezed the armchair's wooden paws again and laughed. "Unless, *ma chère*, the truth is you've come home in order to await our finish!" He gave her that thin-lipped, mocking smile that he mustered when he wished to mask something that disturbed him. "Your mother and I are in good form, you know," he declared. And then added, "At least I am!"

Gilberte noticed that even the fine cut of his clothes couldn't hide the fact that her father was much diminished. He had always been a man of the earth, a person who could fit a harness to a recalcitrant horse or seal up tiles on a leaky roof, and who still occasionally pulled on his Gauloise-blue overalls to work in the vines. Despite his vigor, he had always remained mulish and intransigent. During all the years she was away, her father never wrote or came to visit, declaring Scotland an inhospitable place inconveniently located across a frigid body of water that had nothing to do with the Mediterranean.

"You are no doubt aware that your mother and I are well taken care of," he said, crossing one slender leg over the other. "Philippe is in charge of the vineyards, with my direction, of course. And Marco comes by every day." Her father cupped a hand by his mouth and with a sly grin quipped, "The truth is, Marco chiefly comes here to be fed." Gilberte remembered her younger brother as a child, tall for his age and painfully thin with wide bony cheekbones. Marco silently wolfed down his food at the dinner table each evening, always wiping up the last of the sauce with a crust of bread before telling his parents that he had homework to finish and wished to be excused early, his way of avoiding the eagle eye of Clément. Though Marco was still slender, he had grown into the stark geometry of his face, and the last time Gilberte saw him, she felt he had become quite handsome except for the slight stoop that cramped his elegant frame. Whether or not he was still afraid of their father, Clément, she did not know.

"Marco won't ever marry, I'm afraid," said her father in a bored tone. "Too moody. But he's useful just the same. He cemented down those *tomettes* that clicked like castanets on the dining room floor. A month ago your mother tripped on one while holding a tureen of hot soup and it slopped right down the front of her dress." He let out a jolly snort. Though her parents had been together for more than half a century, she and her siblings were aware that for years now each parent had taken an unseemly pleasure in the sufferings of the other. Gilberte wondered how her mother had fallen that morning and if her father once again had been amused. She found herself perspiring in the close, darkened salon and wished to be outside once again in the warm embrace of the southern sun.

"Shall we go to the hospital to see *Maman* now?" she asked.

Clément shook his head. "I'm not going. Philippe telephoned to say he is handling everything. This evening we'll discuss what's to be done."

"Well then, I'll see you later," said Gilberte. Her father gave her a cold stare as she stood up from the ottoman.

Before leaving, she drank two glasses of water from the

kitchen tap and then brought one to her father, who said nothing in response. She found her mother's gray Peugeot in the garage, and as she came down the hill from the village, the wide blue sky filled up all the space before her and she opened the window. The air batted pleasantly through her hair. Her own rental car wouldn't be available until the following week. She had taken a six-month lease so she could remain flexible in the event that her decision to move back to Provence turned out to be the wrong one.

"Don't let all this frighten you," the nurse told Gilberte when she entered Liliane's room and saw the small inert figure surrounded by tubes and monitors. "Your mother is fine for now. The doctor gave her a sedative, so she'll sleep until morning."

Gilberte sat down beside the bed. Even in sleep, Liliane Perra's prominent nose and delicate bones gave her the patrician look of landed gentry. Liliane's parents had been the tail end of what was long ago a wealthy and aristocratic family. Though the Petitjeans were impoverished, they'd retained the fierceness of their ancestors, who considered land to be sacrosanct and had never sold a hectare of their property even in times of dire need. Their only child, Liliane, possessed that same attachment to her family heritage and had never been afraid to stand up to her husband regarding the running of the vineyard. Indeed, the family domaine had gone from producing what had been a barely drinkable table wine to wide acclaim for a variety of prize-winning vintages. In addition, Liliane Perra was a great favorite around the village, a sort of queen bee, capable and efficient, and when she flirted and joked with her fellow vintners, almost exclusively men, it had caused Gilberte and her sisters to suspect that some among them might have at one time been in love with their mother, whether before or after her marriage they did not know.

As she caressed Liliane's hand, Gilberte wondered what her own life would have been like if she'd stayed bound up in the warp and weft of the small wine village instead of choosing the near anonymity of a city where, in the end, she hadn't had much success or happiness. A sound of footsteps in the hospital corridor made her turn, and the bronzed face of her brother Philippe peered into the room.

"Well, if it isn't the prodigal daughter!" he said, coming through the doorway. His wife, Marie-France, followed. Gilberte couldn't help but stare at her sister-in-law, dressed in a well-cut suit with a strand of black pearls cinched at her neck. Her hair was dyed the purplish henna that so many women in the south found attractive. She saw Marie-France hesitate for a second, and then, probably realizing it would be bad form not to embrace Gilberte, her sister-in-law advanced to give her three kisses, the Provençal *bise*.

"We're not sure how *Maman* did this to herself," Philippe said. "She must have tripped coming down the back staircase. The doctors say it's serious."

"Liliane must have been in a rush getting ready for your arrival," Marie-France added quickly, as if she had rehearsed what she would say in advance. "*En plus*, she's very nervous about your coming back here, Gilberte. Both parents have been on edge since you announced your plans!" She hesitated and then added, "You should be aware that they find your decision to return here very odd. And now, due to this accident caused by the stress of it all, your poor mother will be in the hospital for months!"

Gilberte managed to maintain a professional distance of the sort that she had employed as a teacher in conference with an irritable parent. "I'm sorry this has happened," she said. "I don't believe my mother's accident was caused by my return. But now that I'm here, I'll be glad to be of help in any way that I can."

"You have to excuse us, Gilberte." Philippe's face colored slightly. "We've been dealing with doctors all afternoon. We're both pleased that you've come. Somebody's going to have to be around to see to *Papa* while our mother recovers."

"What do you mean? Can't *Papa* live on his own?"

"He hasn't been himself lately. But we don't have to decide anything right now. I'm glad that we can count on you." He turned to look at his wife. "We'd better go. May we drop you back home, Gilberte?"

"Thank you. I prefer to stay here a bit longer."

Marie-France looked as if she was poised to make another remark, but Philippe took her by the arm and escorted her out the door.

When they were gone, Gilberte laid her head down on the edge of her mother's bed and closed her eyes. Her sister-in-law was certainly no longer the sweet, simple girl who had grown up above the appliance store that her parents ran on the edge of town. Philippe would eventually be the head of Domaine Petitjean and Marie-France had scrapped her jeans and T-shirts for apparel befitting her new station in life. She had also obviously adopted the hauteur she deemed appropriate to a woman married to a well-known and prosperous *vigneron*.

The walls of the dimly lit room glowed pale celadon. It was the same shadowy green of the park that Gilberte used to gaze at from the balcony of her flat near Dean Terrace when the twilight turned the trees slowly from emerald to gray. The beauty of those occasional, clear spring evenings in Scotland always reminded her of a natural world with which she was rarely in contact. Sitting out there in the calm of the evening, she had found herself conceiving of a future that had nothing to do with the citified life she'd been living. It became clear that she'd been so fixated on raising her sons and then working toward her degree that she had habitually denied herself simple pleasures like going to the cinema, dining out, or even having a glass of wine. When she thought of the last time she'd had sex, she realized it had been several years. She'd had a brief affair with a Londoner who had been quite taken with her. But when she sensed that he wished to make their relationship a more permanent one, she feared that her hard-won independence might evanesce and she'd once again be locked into the same sort of suffocating relationship she'd suffered through with her former husband, so she'd broken things off. Gilberte didn't feel like a spinster, not yet, but all at once she'd begun to feel the sensation of time's inevitable passage.

She must have dozed there next to her mother, because she was in the midst of a deep dream of mountains and blossoming trees when she found herself being gently patted awake. Then someone leaned down and kissed her on the temple.

"*Ma chère* Berti! It's so wonderful to see you!" said Marco. Tears came to Gilberte's eyes at the sound of her childhood name and she smiled up at her younger brother. "Come on, I'll take you home," he told her, taking her hand.

"I drove here in Mother's car."

"All right, then, let's go get a drink together. We have plenty of time. Our father always takes a siesta before dinner anyway."

The café in town was at the edge of a square where a fountain reflected the cloudless sky in its circular basin. Marco ordered a demi and Gilberte chose syrup of red raspberries mixed with sparkling water, which she immediately gulped down, surprised again at how thirsty she was.

Marco rolled a cigarette, and then reached over to tug one of her black curls. "You're looking pretty, Berti. Are you back here to find a man?"

She laughed. "Not at the moment. What about you? Do you have a girlfriend?"

"No one interesting."

"Maybe you have to go farther afield to find someone nice. When was the last time you took a holiday?" Marco sold heavy farm machinery on the outskirts of Carpentras and made a decent living, but he rarely traveled.

"Now doesn't seem like the right time, given the circumstances." His lips pursed in a pained half smile. Above them the canvas awning luffed as the evening breeze began to rise.

"Dear *Maman*," Gilberte replied. "At least now that I'm home I can help more. But I'm afraid that Marie-France and Philippe are not particularly pleased to see me."

"They're probably afraid you'll take charge in some way that they won't like." Marco puffed his cigarette and then picked a fleck of tobacco off his tongue. "However, if they can maneuver you into behaving like their servant, then they'll be quite content."

Gilberte remembered Philippe's words about taking care of their father. But she decided against bringing it up for the moment. Instead she asked, "What's new around here? Anything that I've missed?"

"Not too much. Your old friend Eva got a big job at Domaine du Chermon, so she and Sébastien can finally afford to buy a house. That's about it. Oh, but there was one thing." Marco leaned forward and lowered his voice. "Didier Falque and his wife, Christine, had a nasty divorce."

"Really? I thought they were happy."

Marco shrugged. "Who knows! But Manu Dombasle accused Didier of sexually harassing his mother—you know, Sabine—who must be in her seventies by now! I doubt Didi ever did anything to the old lady, but it became a public scandal and he didn't refute it. Of course, that's all anyone talked about for a while. Then came the divorce. Now he lives somewhere up around Mont Ventoux."

Gilberte remembered her classmate with his mat of untamable hair. He'd been awkward as a young bull during their years at lycée, yet she'd always known that at heart Didier was a gentle person and she'd been quite fond of him. Once or twice on her brief returns home, she'd crossed his path and found that his formerly unrefined virility had transformed into something subtler and more attractive. Many women would consider Didier Falque a *bel homme*.

She wondered what the truth could be about her former schoolmate's relationship with Sabine Dombasle, a person old enough to be his mother.

"Does he still own his vineyards?" she asked.

"Yes, I see him there on his tractor," Marco replied. "But he never comes into the village anymore."

Gilberte didn't want to hear anything further. It was true that in the Midi everyone knew everyone else's business, and part of the pleasure of small-town living was discussing the peccadilloes of others. Yet Gilberte had always felt that due to the success and prestige of Domaine Petitjean, the Perra name had been beyond reproach, and she, by association, had been immune to the sort of cruel innuendo and mocking sidelong glances that were reserved for the more vulnerable. Still, she was aware that she'd been the victim of gossip herself, including wild speculations of what her life had been like in Scotland, especially when she'd been married to the wealthy Simon MacLean. But she had always felt that these silly rumors were unimportant and they touched her not at all. That night, however, she was upset to hear about the sufferings of her former friend and was sorry that Didier's troubles had been the object of amused insouciance.

By the time she and Marco left the café, the sky had turned a clear sea color and two bright stars were visible straight above like illuminated clock hands pointing to the hour. When they arrived at Domaine Petitjean, Philippe and Marie-France were already there. Compared to her sister-in-law in her silks and jewels, Gilberte felt underdressed in her loose trousers and light cotton shirt. When she'd first arrived in Edinburgh, she'd dressed *à la fran-çaise*, showing off her rounded hips and full breasts, aware that she drew appreciative glances. But when Simon began to harp on what he termed her inappropriate seductiveness, even though it was *he* having the affairs, she'd taken to covering everything up, telling herself that in the British Isles people generally dressed for comfort and that she was simply making an effort to fit in. But that night she decided that now that she was back in Provence, it might be nice to again wear clothes that flattered.

During dinner, Philippe barely mentioned their mother and instead talked steadily to Clément about the new vintages and what would be sold for export. When the main course was finished he and Marie-France surprised Gilberte by getting up and saying their good-byes. In general, no one ever left the table before a meal was complete, which meant a cheese course, dessert, and at the end, a demitasse of coffee. Gilberte had seen six pear tarts on a baking pan in the kitchen, but she didn't mention them. Without her mother to orchestrate things, the proprieties of dinner had been obliterated.

From the hallway window she saw Marie-France stop for a moment on the outside steps to light a cigarette. Philippe stood just beneath, his hand on her hip. They were still as sphinxes. Gilberte sensed that in some way they found her return problematic. But they needn't worry; she hadn't returned for any personal gain, or to await the demise of her parents, as her father had intimated. In fact, money meant very little to her. The only thing she hoped for was a chance to begin life afresh. The truth was that though her time in Scotland had at first been new and dif-

ferent, and then had afforded her the chance at further education and a career, over the years she had begun to think
wistfully of her youth spent outdoors on warm summer
nights with her contemporaries, and the long walks on the
clear chill days of winter when the mistral chased all the
clouds away, leaving the sky a pure celestial blue. As a girl,
she'd be off with friends up to the mountains, where wild
chamois roamed and kestrels soared in the wide expanse of
blue far above her. She found herself dreaming of her life as
it had been when she'd known everyone in the village and
there was always something new and pleasant to discover.
In Edinburgh, her days had consisted of a dull back-and-
forth to work in the rainy darkness of early morning and
the lonely return on tenebrous evenings where no stars
shone in a cloud-obscured sky.

"I'm taking Berti up to her new home," Marco told their
father after he and Gilberte had cleared the table and done
the dishes.

"Will you be all right, *Papa*?" asked Gilberte.

"Of course, I'm fine. What do you think?" Clément
waved her away, and she wondered what Philippe had
meant about their father not being himself. His personality
certainly had not changed. But when she looked down at his
bony, splayed hands, they appeared to her held together by
musty cobwebs instead of flesh.

Marco could barely fit Gilberte's luggage into his tiny
car, but he folded the backseats forward and managed to
jam in the trunks. On the short drive, Gilberte fell silent,
thinking of the odd, unwelcoming household to which she
had returned. Yet as soon as they got to the tiny road that

skirted the ramparts of the neighboring village of Serret, the crenellations of the tower where she was to live loomed up in the darkness and her spirits brightened. Instead of the ruin it had once been, the structure was now perfectly restored, the stones clean and gleaming in the light of a streetlamp that hung from the ancient parapet like a jeweled pendant on a necklace.

The two furnished rooms she'd rented turned out to be clean and pleasant, with a tiny kitchen and living area painted pastel peach and the bedroom pale violet, colors that were rarely used in Provence, where rough whitewashed plaster walls were practically ubiquitous. She opened the windows to the warm night and the valley spread out below her, the vineyards and orchards and the smudge of an olive grove above the Ouvèze River, for the moment a narrow, silent stream that ran desultorily between two heaped banks of boulders meant to quell the rare floodwaters that had caused such havoc and death only a few years before.

Marco hefted her trunks up the two flights of stairs. For someone so thin, he had a strength that amazed her. When he'd finished, her brother descended the winding stone staircase. She followed him out through the front gate onto the street and watched him roll another cigarette. The keys that her landlord had sent clinked against each other on their steel ring as the two walked side by side. At the juncture of two roads, one coming up from the fields, the other running down along the edge of the ramparts, a simple stone fountain fed by an underground spring chortled its melodious song. Gilberte dipped her hand into the cool water then put her lips beneath the metal spout and drank.

The sweet scent of rotting grapes that remained in the fields after harvest mixed pleasantly with occasional whiffs of her brother's tobacco smoke. As a teenager, she'd puffed cigarettes on Saturday nights with friends in the village parking lot. Life had seemed so full of promise. The boys in her group each had their own special attractiveness and she'd felt a little snap of electricity whenever Jeannot took her hand or Didier Falque pulled her close for a dance at the local discotheque. She could have gone off with any of those boys, even married any one of them, but at that point, despite her attachment to her mother, she couldn't imagine remaining near her father for long. *Caractériel*, they called men like Clément, unpredictable and disturbingly moody. So Gilberte had been very careful not to get involved with any of the young men orbiting around her. She had simply bided her time until the moment when she could go off and create her own life.

Marco pulled the cigarette from his lips and came to stand next to her.

"We should talk about *Papa*," Gilberte said.

"All right, Berti," he replied. "If you really want to know, he has difficulty even organizing the paperwork now. Philippe would like to get his hands on the bank accounts, but our father is determined not to allow that to happen. Up until recently, our mother had done the lion's share. But over the past weeks, by the time I arrive in the evening she's so exhausted she can barely speak. They both seem to be hanging by a worn thread."

"Their insurance would pay for someone to come help them at home, wouldn't it?" she asked.

"Of course, but Philippe and Marie-France don't want anyone involved. That's where I come in." He took a last drag on his cigarette, then tossed the butt to the ground. In the light of the streetlamp Gilberte saw that his fingers were stained ocher.

"They expect you to come by every day? They're taking advantage of you, Marco."

She remembered her brother talking about going out on his own, maybe even traveling around the world. Instead he'd moved to Fenasque, an ugly little town just down the road. It had a Roman arch overgrown with ivy and a section of aqueduct still standing on the dank square where young men sat together at night hoping something would happen. The main road came right through town, causing car exhaust to blacken buildings that had never been handsome in the first place. It was one of those lost places, sinister in its way, and completely dead.

But Marco wasn't dead. His hair was dark as the grenache grapes that went into the Petitjean wines. The fact that he was tall, taller than anyone else in the family, which tended toward squatness in the men and petite but attractive athleticism in the women, was also to his advantage. His stature and gentle personality certainly would have been enough to attract one of the local girls. Gilberte didn't understand why he didn't have someone. She'd never thought of him as moody, the word her father had used.

"Maybe we both should stay away," Gilberte continued. "Let the others be the responsible ones."

And then Marco's telephone rang.

Gilberte was astonished to find herself sleeping that night not in her Rapunzel tower with its cozy atmosphere, but in the cavernous bedroom of her childhood. Philippe had telephoned after finding their father wandering around in the garden, confused and anxious.

"Get Gilberte over here!" was the first thing he said to Marco. "It's the least she can do."

Gilberte's old bed felt like cement and smelled of camphor with a damp, fishy undertone even though she'd put on fresh linens. She was used to the eternal dampness of Scotland, but even in dry Provence, rot and mildew encroached when rooms were uninhabited. Without life, things deteriorated. Could her parents be on that same trajectory? That night, in his pajamas, undisguised by his tailored jacket, her father had looked shrunken, a dark-faced waif with wild hair, but he'd snapped to when he saw Gilberte and had gone immediately to bed. She rolled to her side on the unforgiving mattress, bringing her knees to her chest as she had done when she was a child, taking slow breaths in the hope of inducing a relaxed, meditative state. Across the room stood the bed that had been her sister Marguerite's. A strange shape, probably just a folded duvet, gave the impression of a person. And in the silence of the night, Gilberte remembered Marguerite sobbing, and a scene long buried sprang to life and began to play itself out before her. She could practically see her father standing over Marguerite with the end of his belt wound tightly around his knuckles. His face had a purplish glow and he was not an emaciated and rattled old man, but a person in the full strength of active middle age. He was holding Marguerite against her mattress, his hand over her mouth, and he began to whip her as if he was beating a farm animal. Gilberte had been too frightened to move. She'd barely drawn a breath as she heard her father say, "Vincent Charavin told me he saw you walking through his orchard with an Arab boy." Once again the belt snapped. "No daughter of mine will be seen with one of those dirty Maghrébins, not ever! Do you understand?" And then he'd lifted his hand from Marguerite's face and left the room.

The memory was enough to jolt Gilberte out of bed. In recent years, she had rarely thought of Marguerite, the sister who had disappeared so long ago. But at that moment she recalled that within days of the beating, Marguerite had left their childhood home forever.

It was as if a curtain had been drawn aside. Finally, though her whole body was tingling, Gilberte lay back down on the musty bed and breathed steadily and deeply for a long time until she relaxed enough to get some sleep before the lavender dawn crept across the windowpanes.

As soon as she rose the next morning, she flung open all the windows in her room to let in fresh air. She remembered a particular village fête when her father had lashed out at all of them, even slapping her mother across the face when she had come to their defense. Their father's public displays of violence were not uncommon and certainly must have been remarked upon by their neighbors. She realized that whatever pride she'd had in being a part of the Perra family, owners of the eminent Domaine Petitjean, had been nothing more than an illusion.

That morning, Gilberte found her father sitting downstairs at the red Formica breakfast table. He glanced up at her, but said nothing and she did not bend to kiss him. She spoke not a word as he drank his café au lait and crunched his way through a toasted baguette as if he was one of those innocent old saints that one saw so often in Provençal churches carved out of fruitwood and perched by the side of an altar.

She neither ate nor drank, but stood by the window as the eastern light filtered through the curtains her mother had embroidered with red rosettes. Her father finally gave her a piercing look. Though his frizzy hair had been combed and flattened, the light brought out the fine wrinkles in his cheeks, and the sagging of his chin weighed down his face, deforming it. But the fact that Clément Perra had grown old and frail meant very little to Gilberte now that she was aware of the truth. It had become all too clear that her father had terrorized them all and was responsible for driving Marguerite so violently from the house those many years ago.

Comprendre est pardonner. She had thought those words so full of meaning, but they had inverted themselves the way the twisted form of a serpent could symbolize wisdom or evil. Now that she finally understood, she felt that she could never forgive. Instead she sat down across from her father, folded her hands before her, and said, "I was thinking of Marguerite last night. She's been gone so long. I wonder why she left with barely a good-bye, and then never, ever came back. Do you know?"

Clément waved his hand and looked out the window without responding.

"My lovely big sister. I still miss her." Gilberte made a motion of cleaning up the crumbs on the table, brushing them into her hand. "By the way, how did *Maman* fall and hurt herself so badly yesterday?" Clément looked up, his black eyes wide. For a brief second his nostrils flared, but he clenched his teeth and said nothing.

In the living room, Gilberte used the telephone to arrange for an *aide à domicile* to come the following day to look after her father. Then she drove to the hospital. Her mother's operation had been a difficult one and the doctors told her and her brothers to expect a long rehabilitation.

The next morning the *aide* arrived, a young woman named Blandine whose husband was a cheesemaker. The couple raised goats on a farm in the hills near Villemain. Blandine was a firm, capable person used to handling livestock. That seemed to Gilberte just what was called for, as her sympathy for her father now extended about as far as it would for an old and ailing dog.

When she introduced Blandine to him, her father shouted, "What do you take me for, some sort of doddering invalid?" He threw his coffee spoon at Gilberte, but she calmly responded that she was going to the weekly market and would bring home groceries so that Blandine could make his lunch.

The sun shimmered in a cloudless sky as she drove to town. She pulled into the sandy lot behind the armory and found a spot right away, happy to find that some things hadn't changed. That was where the locals parked, a place eschewed by the tourists because they feared getting trapped in the narrow cul-de-sac.

Coming toward the entrance of the market, she felt a sudden faintness along with a terrible thirst and she remembered she'd had nothing to eat or drink that morning. She passed a workingman's café that was also a PMU betting parlor, aware that a respectable Provençal woman could never be seen in a place like that. It would be impossible for her even to stop in to ask for a glass of water. Though she felt quite ill, she knew that if she was seen in there she'd be accused of having forgotten the strict codes of what was done in the Midi and what was not. It would have been easier for her if she'd been a tourist, or simply retained her Scottish ways and paid no attention to the mores that had ruled her life as a girl and were again encroaching upon her freedom.

Once she found herself beneath the shady canvas awnings of the covered market stalls, Gilberte began to feel better. She spotted people she knew and occasionally stopped to chat for a moment and admit that yes she would be permanently living here now. She was careful to exaggerate her Provençal accent so people would know that Gilberte Perra still had her heart and soul in the Midi and, even after all those years away, had not been transformed into a foreigner.

Passing down the narrow alleys, she admired the usual stands of fresh and dried herbs, bouquets of lavender, jars of honey, and a display of heliotrope-colored bars of *savon de Marseille* emitting their subtle perfume. At the fishmonger, whom Gilberte had known since she was a child, she made a purchase of several small gilt-headed *daurades* then continued on through the center of the market where the usual autumnal profusion of mushrooms, including cèpes, cut open to reveal their creamy interiors, were piled high in wooden flats. Near the central square she came upon a merchant selling a variety of olives in large glazed bowls. At the end of the display, standing in full sunlight, Didier Falque stood conversing with the olive seller. The *vendange* had been over for nearly a month, and though the fermenting of the new wine was in full swing, most vintners now had some free time after the intense labor of the harvest. She didn't remember ever running into Didier at the outdoor market before. Looking at him standing there, his weight on one leg as he purchased a bag of green picholines, he reminded Gilberte of the beautifully proportioned sculpture of a Greek boxer that she'd once seen displayed in a museum. The statue was of a bearded man, but Didier was clean-shaven and he wore his hair short, the wiry mass tamed now, the color of earth.

When he looked over and saw her, a grin creased his tanned face. "Is that you, Berti?" Once again, the sound of her childhood name gave her a little stab of pleasure. But she recalled the sordid gossip Marco had passed on about Didier and she found herself standing stiffly as he kissed her four times, twice on each cheek, in the manner of Provençal adolescents.

"What are you doing here?" he asked.

"I've rented a house in Serret."

"For a little vacation?"

"No, permanently," she replied. "At least I hope so." He frowned at her as if unsettled by the news. Then he looked

around and for a moment Gilberte wondered if he was concerned about the possibility of someone seeing them standing there together. Perhaps he understood that it wouldn't
do for her to be taken for his friend, or something more,
given the fact of the scandal that had attached itself to him
like tar.

"I don't live in Serret anymore," he told her. "Our house
was sold after Christine and I divorced." He looked at her
steadily. "Of course, you must have heard all about that. I
have a place in Sault now. It's better for me up there in the
mountains with the stags and the wild boar." He laughed,
but there was no joy in it. "I'd lived in Serret too long."

Just ahead, a woman paused and gestured at Gilberte,
but her eyes widened as they darted over to Didier, and
instead of coming to say hello, she proceeded on through
the crowd. When Gilberte began to move as well, Didier
suddenly reached out and took her arm. "I'll see something
of you now that you're really home, Berti. *D'accord?*" Gilberte nodded, certain that despite his firm grip on her elbow,
he understood that she could never be linked with him in
any way. At the same time, she felt a sadness and regret,
aware that these unwritten rules of behavior, particularly
strict for women, were outdated and irrational and put a
subtle stranglehold on the new life that she had hoped
would be, at last, happy and free.

After saying good-bye, she pushed through the crowd
toward one of the multiple cafés on the square, where she
was pleased to put down her heavy shopping bag and order
a glass of water and a café noisette. The encounter with
Didier had made her feel a bit off balance.

It was surprising that all these years later people in Provence would still so ignorantly shun a person for something that may or may not have even been true. Perhaps he and Sabine Dombasle had something between them and Didier felt duty bound not to reveal it in order to protect her. As Berti sat in the cool shade of the terrace, it became clear that she'd have to come to terms with this life that had cast her back amid the terrible snares of provincial propriety. Surely there must be some way for her to circumvent them; if not, she might be forced to move somewhere else entirely, or simply turn her back on the unbearable constrictions of an old-fashioned and outdated way of life.

8

Ma Chère Amie

A February cold snap caused frosty swaths of ice to form on sidewalks and turned tree branches into brittle, lifeless bones. Euphémie could feel the chill as she made her daily rounds in the glassed-in turret that surrounded the top floor of the locked ward of the *maison de repos*. Outside, the friendly auto mechanics, now huddled in hats and heavy jackets, no longer looked up at her to smile and wave hello. On Sundays, the churchgoers waddled to their automobiles with heads bowed, preoccupied with avoiding the treacherous slippery patches. People from the Midi hated the cold, and the continuing gray skies made them retreat into themselves like captured escargots. Even the white heron had departed from his rock in the river, perhaps escaping to the Côte d'Azur or some other more clement place.

Euphémie found herself feeling particularly isolated that afternoon as she walked around and around the enclosed hallway. When a nurse suddenly blocked her path, at first she was startled to see another human presence, as others rarely came there.

"What are you doing out here?" The nurse looked Euphémie over as if she were something unpleasant that needed to be swept up and disposed of.

"I'm taking my exercise, as I do every day," she replied. "You must have seen me here before."

"We don't want you disappearing on us." The nurse frowned. "Your daughter told us you enjoy flying up into the hills where nobody can find you. That kind of behavior is dangerous for you now, madame."

"I assure you that I never fly." Euphémie gave a wry grin. "Though, of course, I would vastly prefer to be outside."

"Perhaps we'll take you for a walk through town when it warms up. It's not a prison here, you know. People can go freely in and out."

Euphémie pressed her lips together. The nurses and visitors do, she thought, but never the patients.

When the nurse left her to herself, Euphémie increased her pace. She tried not to spend her days like the other inmates, lying in bed for hours or sitting in front of a television that blared idiotic drivel. Magazines fanned out in an orderly fashion on a hall table were years out of date. She had requested a newspaper or anything at all that was more current, but her entreaties to the staff were to no avail. She began to feel invisible. Everyone she had cared about was lost to her. Her dear friend Hamidou, with whom she'd eaten lunch on the mountain nearly every day, was just a memory. No one came to visit, not even her daughter, Flo, the person who should have loved her best, but did not. Euphémie found herself with the strange feeling that she was reliving the past when World War II had raged and she'd had no freedom. Now the polyester whites of the nurses evoked the same feeling as the evilly curved helmets and heavy uniforms of the German occupiers. Both represented forces pitted against her.

She comforted herself with the thought that, at seventy-eight, she was still healthy and very much alive. But the reality was that even before being institutionalized, she'd been forced to relinquish control of her life. It had been a winter day like this when her daughter, Florence, had come down from Lyon with her husband, Victor. Euphémie had arrived home from a delightful spree on her favorite mountain path, returning just as the sun turned into a crimson-eyed flame. To her surprise, Flo had yanked open Euphémie's front door, her cheeks flushed and her red hair in wild disorder.

"Where have you been?" she'd demanded. "Your neighbor Monsieur Charavin says you are out at all hours of the day and night like a madwoman! Perhaps you *are* mad!" Then Florence had run her fingers over the hall tabletop and flicked off the feltlike dust in disgust. "Do you see the filth you are living in, *Maman*? Plus I see that your checking account appears to be overdrawn!"

Euphémie sat down on a wooden stool in the entryway. There was no other place to go since Flo's wide body blocked her entrance into the house proper. "That's impossible," she replied. "You know that I've always been careful about my finances." Her checkbooks and papers were carefully arranged on her desk, the only place that was well dusted because she used it daily. But it was all too true that her house was neglected for the simple reason that she preferred to spend her days exploring in the hills rather than vacuuming and cleaning the two large parlors downstairs and the numerous bedrooms that lined the upstairs corridor.

Before Euphémie could defend herself, Flo's husband, Victor, had stepped forward, lacing his pallid fingers together into something that resembled a strangely entwined tuber. "It would be much more practical if Florence and I took charge of your affairs, Euphémie. That way you'll be free to do what you like and you won't have to concern yourself with these trivial annoyances." Victor's black suit and narrow puce tie didn't flatter a complexion white and shiny as a slice of raw potato. In her effort to placate them, Euphémie failed to see the darkness mustering itself against her.

As she tried to gather her thoughts, Flo began to shout again about Euphémie's transgressions. "To top it all off, Monsieur Charavin mentioned that you have been seen walking with an Arab man. An Arab! What can you possibly be thinking of, *Maman*? They're fieldworkers, not friends!"

"Darling! You must be talking about Hamidou, whom I've known for quite a while now. Such a dear man!" Euphémie stood up and reached out to caress her daughter's face in order to calm her, but Florence veered away. Then, like a dance with prescribed movements, one step following another, Victor removed a folded paper from his inside pocket, smoothed it down, and held it out to her.

"We've felt for a while that you needed special looking after, Euphémie. I took the liberty of having this drawn up." He put his waxen finger on the bottom, where her signature would go. "We'll go to the notary together in the morning and have everything put in order."

At first, she'd convinced herself it would be pleasant not to have to deal with the monthly bills. Everything was sent automatically to Lyon. The rental income from her house in Saint-Tropez that had kept her afloat for years now went directly into Florence and Victor's bank account. And the allowance they gave her—which Victor had groaned was more generous than they could really afford—didn't last out the month, no matter how she scrimped. Euphémie found herself reduced to her last sou by the third week and could only dream about the fine cuts of meat to which she used occasionally to treat herself, and her weekly indulgence of a Paris-Brest, a pastry filled with nutted cream, had now become an extravagance. For the first time since the war she felt hungry.

At least here in the rest home she got plenty to eat, even though the institutional food was not to her taste. That day she had been served a dispiriting lunch of rice with flavorless creamed mushrooms. But she'd gained weight since her arrival, which was a good thing. She certainly felt a lot stronger and was no longer famished.

On her way back to her room that afternoon, the elevator doors slid open and Florence stepped into the hallway. On her arm she carried a gleaming handbag marked with the double *C* of Chanel, but sadly her clothes were dowdy. Flo had never developed the style that most women who lived in big cities like Lyon seemed to achieve by osmosis. Even her beautiful orange hair was pulled back tight with a plain plastic clip.

"Hello, *Maman*, I've brought you a few things." Flo held up a canvas tote.

"Oh, you darling!" Euphémie took her arm. "I'm so glad to see you!"

In Euphémie's room, Florence drew out some magazines. "I brought along a little sweater too in case you're chilly, though it's really quite stifling up here!" Florence stripped off her coat and scarf and threw them onto the bed. It was true that the heat on the top floor was cranked way up. Like hothouse flowers, the deranged and infirm required unusual warmth.

Florence flopped down onto the single chair. "How have you been?"

"I've never been better, but the nurses don't believe me when I say I'm just fine."

"Well, you're not fine." Florence sat up straight. "The doctor said your condition just hasn't manifested itself yet. You're only in the first stages, but you could be subject to a debilitating dementia overnight! That's why you're here. You need to be protected!"

"But how could he possibly know what might happen? That doctor only examined me once."

"Physicians are well informed concerning these sorts of maladies."

"But being put away like this seems so, well, so definitive. Even if one day I'll be disabled, I'm not now!"

Florence stood up and pulled her scarf back around her

neck. "Listen, *Maman*, I'm doing this for you. It's ridiculous to argue, so that's that. Oh, by the way, at the front desk they told me that Arab man of yours has passed by several times inquiring about you. At least the idiots down there had the sense to turn him away. I told them under no circumstances is he to be allowed up here."

"Oh! But why not?" Euphémie cried. "It would be so lovely to see Hamidou again!"

"Please, *Maman*! It wouldn't do to have you sitting up here having a tête-à-tête with a Muslim. Who knows what sort of man he really is. Why, he might even be a jihadist!" Florence gave a dismissive shake of her head as if Euphémie was too thick to comprehend.

After Flo left, Euphémie stayed alone in her room. The rest of the afternoon stretched before her. She didn't feel like returning to the turret, where she was beginning to feel like a pet mouse darting senselessly through the same plastic tube. Instead, she stared out the window at the river that rose up in peaked whitecaps and crashed against the protruding rocks at its center.

Euphémie couldn't help but sigh. She and Florence had been at cross-purposes for years. When Florence was just thirteen, Euphémie's husband, Dominique, had gone off hunting in the mountains one day and never returned. Euphémie's regular walks turned into desperate searches even after the police had given up, but a body was never found. She never knew whether Dominique had fallen to his death in a ravine, committed suicide, or simply slipped away to begin a new life somewhere else.

After her husband's disappearance, she found that the

estate she'd inherited from her parents had been badly mismanaged. Only the big house and a dilapidated property in Saint-Tropez were left. Euphémie scraped together enough money to renovate the place in Saint-Tropez so she could earn some income renting it. But Flo, whom Euphémie did her best to love and take care of, became a high-strung, snobbish teenager, desperately clutching on to their titled name of de Laubry as if it were a life raft. When she enrolled at university, she quickly latched on to Victor, a person whose family owned a textile business in Lyon. Florence married him and fit right in with the bourgeoisie in La Croix-Rousse, making sure to set herself well apart from her mother. Euphémie blamed herself for the estrangement just as she had blamed herself for her husband Dominique's disappearance and his unkindness to her during their marriage.

Euphémie's truest guilt stemmed from the flood of relief she'd felt when she'd finally determined that Dominique was gone for good. He'd always been cold, something she put down to a formality that she at first believed was a virtue rather than a defect, having been used to her father's polite reserve, which in Augustin's case veiled a warm and humorous equanimity. But Dominique was not warm. In fact, he had a cruel streak, and being ten years older, he enjoyed making Euphémie feel inferior and ill educated. His treatment of her was degrading, but she'd dutifully put up with it during the years of their marriage. When he was declared legally dead, Euphémie determined she would never remarry. There was no need to put herself in harm's way ever again.

The only thing she and Dominique ever had in common had been their long treks through the mountains. When they'd first moved to her family home, her professorial husband had been willing to walk many kilometers with her, but for him, the passion was the hunt. He fired wildly at anything, indifferent to the natural beauty of the woodland and its inhabitants.

"Please, Dominique," she would say, trying to deflect the barrel of his rifle when she saw him aiming at some bird or beast whose heart was pulsing with life. It pained her to see him kill. During their walks, her husband appreciated neither the intoxicating scent of yellow broom in June nor the sienna leaf of autumn; only the challenge of the rocky path before him and the lust for blood drove him onward. He always kept his rifle with him, even bringing it into their bedroom at night and leaning it against the headboard within easy grasp. When Euphémie protested, Dominique told her that he'd gotten used to having a gun around during the war. She'd tried to be understanding, not wanting to imagine what her husband might have gone through during those difficult years, and assuming that, like her, the experiences he'd had were too painful ever to be discussed.

During the long nights locked on the top floor of the rest home, Euphémie began to wonder if she had been imprisoned for her sins. She had failed to truly love her husband. She'd lost the love of her daughter. And long ago she had even ceased being a churchgoer, turning into a simple pagan who preferred to commune with trees and follow the cries of songbirds rather than attend religious services. Perhaps that's why she was being punished, and perhaps she de-served it.

She thought of her last day of freedom, when she'd been drawn to the mountain as usual. On the path ahead of her, about halfway up, were two men, one a slight teenager wearing a Windbreaker made of bright turquoise material. The other man was stockier and dressed in a practical can-vas jacket. When he turned his head, she saw a beard streaked white like a badger's pelt. Whenever the two made an about-face to look at the view, Euphémie stepped behind one of the overgrown boxwood hedges that lined the rocky path. She didn't want to converse with strangers and pre-ferred to remain discreetly hidden. But when they reached a crest and turned again, Euphémie's heel rolled on a stone and she nearly fell. The men trotted down toward her.

"Why, it's Madame de Laubry," said the bearded man. She recognized him at once, her neighbor Gaston Prost, whose family had lived for generations in the *gentilhomme-rie* up behind the ruined garrison. He had been a charming boy, the one child who made Euphémie wish she had also had a son. Gaston lived in Paris now, only using his natal house during vacations. It was May and the celebration of the feasts of the Ascension and of Pentecost meant long weekends when Parisians descended en famille to their country homes. Sure enough, after taking her by the elbow, Gaston introduced his son, Séverin, whom she also remem-bered.

"Madame de Laubry, what a pleasure!" Séverin said, giving her a winsome smile. "I remember being invited to your house one Christmas Eve, everything decorated with holly and mistletoe hanging from the beams, just like a fairy's bower! You had all kinds of fascinating objects too—wasps' nests on the sideboard and a huge red glass vase filled with thousands of seashells."

"Oh yes," said Euphémie, "I used to collect those at our place in Saint-Tropez."

Then Gaston asked, "Are you sure you're all right? We can help you walk back down if you like."

"Oh no, really, I'm perfectly fine," Euphémie affirmed. Before saying good-bye, Gaston told her that she must come for lunch soon and that his wife would telephone.

But when they departed, Euphémie recalled that she'd been invited to the Prosts the summer before, and in an act of sheer unthinking selfishness, she had stolen a small box of candy that had been displayed on the coffee table, sequestering it in her purse. That had been during one of those hungry end-of-the-months when her allowance from Flo and Victor had not been enough to pay for her meals. She had pushed that inadmissible deed out of her mind, but now the petty theft came back to her magnified into an egregious crime. She toiled on up to the crest of the hill and then found herself careening rapidly off into the forest in an effort to outrun her shame. Beneath the shadows of the great trees, she noticed the sky itself grow darker and soon a light rain began to fall that quickly grew heavy. She sheltered herself under a pine tree whose layered branches made a low roof just over her head. As she waited, she thought of the sweetness of Gaston and his son. Feeling quite positive that the Prosts would never invite her to anything ever again, she found herself weeping silently as the rain turned to hail that danced across the rocky ground. The hailstones expanded in size and began to pelt her right through the protection of the overhanging branches. Flashes of lightning and hideous-sounding thunder rolled like grim laughter over the hills. *Never again at the Prosts!* it seemed to say. The air turned chill, and Euphémie, who had only brought along a light sweater, realized she would have to make the effort to get down the path and home despite the terrible weather. When she emerged from beneath the tree, an outsized hailstone hit the back of her head and nearly knocked her down. She stumbled toward the path and all at once one of those detested black Range Rovers that had no business on mountain paths ground to a halt in front of her. She held up her arm to protect her face from the juddering, pelting hail as a man exited from the car and lifted her bodily inside.

"What is the meaning of this?" she stammered, and was answered by a familiar voice.

"*Chère madame*, I realized that you must still be up here on the mountain." It was Gaston Prost, busy tucking a blanket around her. "I came to find you and take you home. And not a moment too soon!"

Despite his kindness, Gaston's actions had been the beginning of the end for Euphémie. When she'd developed a fever, Gaston had telephoned her daughter, Florence. From then on she saw her liberty begin to dwindle, until finally, after Florence brought her to see a strange doctor who made the startling diagnosis of her impending madness, Euphémie wound up in her current abode, a locked ward of patients who were for the most part non compos mentis.

It had been more than half a year since she'd arrived

there, and that afternoon Euphémie almost wished for the onslaught of the predicted dementia. Maybe it would hit her suddenly. Perhaps her ravaged brain would recall everything from her past as if it was happening all over again. Maybe in this new life she'd have a second chance to change things for the better.

During the days that followed Florence's visit, Euphémie tried to stay out of her room as much as possible. She spent her time beneath the fluorescent lights of the hallway eagerly reading the magazines Flo had brought. Sometimes she sat back and dreamed of the plants and flowers she used to gather on the mountainside, wild orchids and miniature irises, tiny wild leeks and skinny asparagus that popped up in profusion from dark, ferny leaves.

One day, as her mind drifted, the elevator opened and Gaston Prost, looking distinguished in a dark suit, stepped into the hallway with his son, Séverin. "Madame de Laubry!" he greeted her. "When we heard you were here, we didn't believe it!"

Looking at the two of them, Euphémie remembered that spring day when she'd met them on the mountain path, a day that had promised to be so beautiful, and then everything had turned out so very badly. When her eyes filled with tears, Gaston and Séverin looked at each other. Gaston held out his hand. "Let's find a more cheerful place where we can sit down and have a chat."

Pushing three chairs together in the common room, away from the flickering television set, Gaston spoke to her in his friendly way, so pleasant and informal that she felt just like a girl whom a handsome man was endeavoring to cheer with his light banter. His son, Séverin, was very like him. He had the same humor and joy, and that perfectly exquisite smile that acted like a dose of oxygen for Euphémie. Toward the end of the visit, Gaston said, "We heard that you'd had a stroke, or worse, but you seem perfectly alert, perfectly coherent. There must be some mistake." Séverin nodded in agreement, giving Euphémie another of his intoxicating smiles. Then Gaston leaned toward her and touched her hand. "You seem to be a person capable of facing things as they are. Do you mind if I speak frankly?" Euphémie made a vague motion with her head, fearful that he might address the very thing that she had so stalwartly managed to push out of her mind during her tenancy in the ward.

"If a family member is ill," Gaston continued, "then it's normal that those closest might wish to make sure that person is in a safe place where she will receive the care and comfort she needs. That goes without saying. But I have heard of times when relatives take legal steps—or what they say are legal steps—to obtain certain goods or an inheritance, an act that deprives the original owner of his or her rights. I don't want to overstep, Madame de Laubry, but have you ever considered that this might be true in your case?"

Euphémie's chest constricted in a painful way and she clasped her hands to her breast. Before responding, she had to wait a few moments so her voice wouldn't betray her. Then she said to Gaston, "Florence says the disease I have will come on suddenly. She believes that she is doing the right thing. I can't possibly go against her wishes."

"But you have a right to live freely," Gaston told her.

"It would be a terrible battle," said Euphémie with a sigh. "And it's my mistake. I signed papers relinquishing everything. It's finished."

Gaston sat back and smoothed his beard. "I'd be willing to predict that with one or two telephone calls we could get you out of here in very short order."

Euphémie sat very still. She could imagine those phone calls and what would be said. It was her own fault that she'd lost her property along with her rights. She'd just have to bear the consequences even if it meant being locked away for the rest of her life. She shook her head no.

"If you change your mind about this, a conclusion to which I believe you may come, you know where to find me," Gaston told her. Then he stood and kissed her hand in the old-fashioned manner and Séverin kissed her once on each cheek, his face smooth as a child's even though he was a young man of nineteen.

That night the mistral blew so hard that the metal windows in Euphémie's room made a strange whooshing sound like an airplane taking off, and though she was fatigued from the emotion of Gaston's visit, she couldn't sleep. Her thoughts flitted from one thing to another, but they always returned to what Gaston had said about her right to be free.

The winter continued unabated, the sky a peculiar gray, and when Euphémie counted the months she'd been in that place on her fingers she realized that soon she wouldn't be able to keep it to just ten. Soon it would be a year, and then more than a year.

In March, it began to rain. Great pools formed in the turret where she took her daily walks because the plate-glass windows were badly sealed. Euphémie began to forgo her exercise and instead sat in the hallway with the other patients. There was nothing to do, nothing at all to read, so she watched the occasional visitor drift by and the inmates bobbing to and fro like flowers blown by the wind.

One evening at about eight thirty, two nurses glided out of the elevator wheeling a gurney that held someone stretched out beneath white blankets. Usually a new admission was accompanied by one or two family members chirping brightly about how nice everything was, secretly relieved to be ridding themselves of an inconvenient burden. But this patient was alone. The nurses maneuvered the gurney into an empty room and Euphémie watched as one of them slipped a name card into the slot on the doorway. When they left, she crept over to take a look. Neatly typed was the name Charles-Henri Le Lièvre. Her heart leaped. *Her old school friend Lapin!* Though he lived in her village, she rarely saw him, as he only left his isolated house to cash his monthly retirement benefit at the Poste. She turned the door handle and, finding it unlocked, entered the room and bent over the inert form. It was Lapin all right. His head was still round as a baby's, but his hair was thin and completely white. When they'd been in primary school together, she had loved running her fingers through his fine blond hair, often leaving her small fist affectionately clenched at the nape of his neck.

As she stood over him, Lapin opened his eyes and, when he smiled, revealed the same absurdly crossed front teeth.

"*Ma chère amie,*" he said to her as if they were back in their old classroom.

"Lapin!" She touched the hand that lay unmoving on top of the white sheet.

"Yes, it's me."

"What's happened? How did you come to be here?" Euphémie asked.

"I suppose I've simply grown old. But my heart is warm with the pleasure of seeing you."

Could he be mistaking me for someone else? Euphémie wondered. For years everyone had talked about Lapin like he was a deranged eccentric, but she remembered the American pilot who had been shot down during the war and how Lapin had taken charge of everything. Very few people could have done what he did. Neither of them had ever talked about that day. When the war ended no one wanted to reminisce, and Euphémie certainly did not go looking for Lapin to find out any details. Like so many others, she'd just wanted to forget about everything to do with the war, the brutal death of the young flier, the killing of the German soldier who had assaulted her, and the terror concerning the possibility of her father being shot as a reprisal for a murder in which she had been involved.

Lapin coughed, a straitened, rasping sound. She pulled the pillow beneath his shoulders to prop him up, guessing he might have pneumonia, or worse.

"Sweet Euphémie," said Lapin. "I heard you were here, but I didn't know how to help you." He coughed again, but not as severely.

Glistening tears fell out of the corners of his eyes and

Euphémie gently wiped them away. Poor Lapin must be delirious. She saw that his fragile skin was embedded with a mass of wrinkles as if a fine net had been pressed onto his face.

The door opened and a nurse peered in. "What's going on in here?" She eyed Euphémie with a grimace.

"Monsieur Le Lièvre is an old friend of mine," Euphémie replied, affecting her most dignified tone.

"Be that as it may, you cannot remain," said the nurse opening the door farther.

"Why is my friend in this place?"

"He was found lying in a field. He's a mental deficient, so he was sent here."

"But that's ridiculous," said Euphémie. "If he's ill he should be in a hospital. You can't help him here."

The nurse made a rapid motion with her hand. "It's time for you to leave this room!" Knowing the consequences of disobedience, Euphémie exited, but not before she had stroked Lapin's head once more and bid him good night.

The next morning she was up with the dawn. Without bothering to dress, she tiptoed toward her friend's room. She found Lapin awake, but his face was even whiter and his lips bloodless.

"Can I get anything for you?" she whispered, bending over him.

"Oh no," he gasped, reaching up to touch the collar of her dressing gown. "Just stay with me. There are things I want to say."

It was impossible that anything needed to be said, thought Euphémie, particularly if it dealt with the distant past. All that was dead and gone like her poor mother in 1940, then her father a few years later, and finally, dear Agnes, who had helped to raise her.

"Don't tire yourself," she said. "It's just nice to be together again, the way we were in school. Do you remember Father lending you books?"

"Yes, I remember your wonderful father," Lapin panted. "But I never liked your husband." She was silent. What could Lapin know about Dominique? "You never knew that my father was with the Resistance," Lapin continued. "After the war, there were reprisals, secret killings of those who had betrayed our country . . ." Euphémie touched her hand to his lips. She could guess what was coming. She remembered how Dominique had been, whether they were walking in the woods or lying in bed at night, his rifle always within reach. He feared something and now it all became clear. He'd no doubt been clandestinely at work for the Nazis when they had occupied France, and Euphémie was well aware of what happened to certain collaborators after the war was over.

"Don't speak," she said to Lapin. "I understand. But it doesn't matter anymore."

"But it does because I caused you pain. You never knew what had happened. I hid him too well, just the way I had hidden the German soldier."

Euphémie turned away to raise the window shade that blocked the violet-blue of the morning light. The truth seemed too much to take in. But somehow it was a relief. Now she knew what had really happened to Dominique. When she returned to his side, Lapin's head was turned away and he appeared to be in a deep sleep. She tiptoed out of his room. When she returned an hour later, she found that he was no longer there. He had died shortly after her visit that morning and his body had been swiftly removed from the ward.

Though Euphémie remained profoundly shocked for several weeks, it was as if Lapin's death had tolled the end of winter. Spring came almost immediately, but the delicate pink and white flowers of the fruit trees blooming outside the cathedral might as well have been made of plastic because Euphémie remained interred where no soft breezes or perfumed air could penetrate. On the hillsides, wild thyme and rosemary would be bursting with purple buds issuing their pungent, savory scent. Her fingertips conjured up the feel of their rough stems as she rested in the afternoon sun that streamed through the plate-glass windows of the corridor. She was stronger than ever, but the ennui of the place was sapping her energy. Euphémie was waiting for something to happen and wondered if perhaps it was her own death that she was actually waiting for.

Before lunch one day, she recognized an elderly visitor who often came to see his wife, one of those white-gowned figures who spent her days in an armchair in the lounge, her face vacuous. As the man made his way to the elevator after his visit, a nurse repeated some numbers and laughed. "Fourteen-seven. How ironic! That's the date of the storming of the Bastille!" The gentleman chuckled at her little joke. Euphémie watched as he pressed the numbers and the elevator doors opened and then closed behind him.

She waited until the nurses were occupied with getting

the patients into the refectory at lunchtime. When there was no one around, Euphémie carefully pushed the three digits on the numbered panel by the elevator. The doors seemed to whisper *Open sesame!* as they slid apart—as if in a fairy tale! In the lobby, the desk was unmanned at lunchtime and she walked out into the warmth of the tarred parking lot. She knew the way to go. Past the cemetery at the edge of town, a narrow path took her up into the hills. It would only take an hour or so by foot and she knew all the shortcuts.

Euphémie had been used to walking on the flat tiles of the terrace and her heart ached with pleasure as her feet turned this way and that on the stony road. The redolence of wild herbs and spring flowers surrounded her as she scaled the first long hill and found that her legs were just as strong as ever. At the fork marked by wooden arrows, she followed the road to the left instead of the one that led to her village. No one saw her and no one passed. She skirted the fire road and kept to the narrow path where cars couldn't go, breathing the cool air in the dappled shade of the dense forest. She felt in her core that she was not some separate creature passing through glade or woodland by rocky cliffs, or the little springs that emerged between banks of flowering mosses and blooming bulbs, but that she was an integral part of all that surrounded her. What she breathed was absorbed like nourishment into her lungs, her rib cage, her thin, capable legs, still so sturdy and dependable.

Finally, she turned off and descended a long slope. At the bottom she half slid through a thatch of tender mountain holly. Across the road was a small house. Hamidou was sitting outside it on a metal chair pouring tea into a gold-rimmed glass. When he looked up and saw her, his fox-colored eyes widened with a start, but then a smile crossed his face and became a grin that revealed his large yellow teeth.

"*Madame!*" he said, standing up. "They let you out!"

"Yes, Hamidou, I'm free." Euphémie laughed. She clasped his hands in hers.

"But, madame, where will you go? Your house has been sold!"

Euphémie stood very still and thought about that for a few moments, not particularly surprised. Gaston Prost had indicated that something other than an impending illness was behind her incarceration. Hamidou pulled another chair up to the small table. Euphémie sat down and thirstily drank the sweet mint tea that he served her.

Of course, it was the property that Florence had wanted so badly. The place in Saint-Tropez had probably been sold as well. The money would raise Florence and Victor's status in Lyon, though it was common knowledge that he was rather a failure. Euphémie found that she wasn't angry or particularly upset. Only the thought of Florence's cold heart gave her any pain.

When they had finished the pot of tea, she looked at Hamidou and said, "The sale of my home is not a tragedy. It was too much for me anyway. Much too big!" Hamidou drew his large brown hand over his weathered face and stared at her without speaking. "Still, I'll have to find a place to live," she said. "Just one or two rooms would be sufficient."

Her friend continued to gaze at her. After a moment, he stood up and excused himself. He went into his small house and came back almost immediately. Then he sat down next to Euphémie and said, "My neighbor Madame Bonnefoie moved away to live with her daughter in Toulouse. The family wants to rent the place." Euphémie turned and looked with pleasure into her friend's fiery amber eyes. "Madame Euphémie, they have been looking for someone just like you!"

Hamidou reached into his pocket and withdrew something that Euphémie at first took to be a squirming yellow snake, but as he placed it in her hand she saw that it was a golden necklace. "This belonged to my wife, Rachida," he said. "It will help you pay the rent. She would have wanted me to do that for you."

The authorities didn't find Euphémie for three days. The first night, the staff didn't miss her until dinnertime. When the director was informed, he took a drive around the town and then, later in the evening, he called the police, who explored a larger area with no success. Florence wasn't informed until the following day, and it took her until that evening to arrive from Lyon with her husband since only the very last train of the day had tickets available. They had to stay in a cheap and insalubrious hotel since the good places were all taken. The chief of police took it upon himself to drop in on his childhood friend Gaston Prost, who he knew was vacationing in Serret. At an unconscionably early hour the next morning, the policeman drove to the meager hotel and awakened Florence and her husband, who made it clear they were not pleased to see him. Nor were they thrilled when Gaston appeared in the breakfast room just as they were finishing their cafés au lait.

Oddly, it was Florence's husband who capitulated first. Victor knew the law, but was also acutely aware that small-town gossip with even the tiniest grain of truth could destroy a person's reputation even in a big town like Lyon. Gaston was insistent on several points. He appeared quite different from the mild, humorous young man Florence had once admired in her youth. Despite her efforts to interrupt and disagree, she was forced to be quiet as Gaston stated the facts. In the end, Florence and Victor agreed to everything, promising to pay the monthly charges on Euphémie's new house and to give her a generous allowance; the amount was suggested by Gaston, who also recommended a reliable woman who could come in to cook and clean several times a week. At the end, Gaston politely shook their hands with the air of someone who realizes that, though it's rare, some things in life can quite naturally fall into place if the right pressure is judiciously applied.

Euphémie began her days early, taking whatever road presented itself up into the mountains, unafraid of the people she might encounter. She bought herself a pair of comfortable sneakers and a silky sky-blue jacket that was waterproof and reminded her of a dress she'd once worn to a party. To add to the pleasure of it all, she carried a light but powerful pair of binoculars on a strap. Birds of all sorts fascinated her. As she watched them, she imagined their little hearts beating, the tiny muscles pumping bright red blood to keep them flying, flying ever onward and upward through the summer sky.

9

Mont Ventoux

I t was a rainy night in February and from Berti's high window a swirling mist obscured the view of the valley below. She moved a lamp onto the kitchen table, pleased to be inside her stone tower, where the walls were a meter thick and the place well heated by an electric radiator that glowed a comforting red-orange behind its metal grate. A gust of wind pounded like a flat hand, spattering drops against the windowpanes as she began to iron a pair of linen pillowcases embroidered with the family's initials, the double *P* for Petitjean-Perra, that had once belonged to her mother. Every once in a while she sprinkled drops of perfumed water onto the linen, and as she pressed down a whiff of scented steam filtered through the air, evoking memories of summer walks through fields of blooming lavender.

Her mother, Liliane Perra, had died of pneumonia just before Christmas despite intravenous antibiotics and other eleventh-hour measures taken by the hospital staff. The family realized it was a blessing, since Liliane's femur had been so badly shattered that her doctors feared she would never walk again. Liliane's husband, Clément, had not attended the funeral. Whenever Berti went to see her father now, he turned his face away from her and she wondered if he was ashamed of his malignant behavior as a husband and a father, or if he simply no longer wanted to deal with his daughter who knew too much.

The deep haze that night reminded her of winters in Edinburgh. Her new life in Provence, which had at first held such promise, was becoming increasingly complicated. After her mother's death, Grégoire Dieulefit, the local notary responsible for the settlement of estates, had called Berti in for a discussion. She'd known Grégoire for years. The notary knew everything about her family, just as he knew everyone else's business, since he was responsible for any and all transactions regarding property.

"Your mother was certainly a strong-minded woman," Grégoire said, opening the enormous dossier marked *Perra-Petitjean*. "We don't usually see this kind of thing, especially in the days when your parents married, but she insisted on a *séparation des biens*. In other words, she kept sole ownership of the vineyard along with the rest of the property, and that includes your parents' *manoir* as well as your grandparents' house in which your brother Philippe now lives. Obviously, your father has the right to stay in the family home until his death, but the property was your mother's and will be divided equally among you children."

"Divide up Domaine Petitjean?" Berti exclaimed. "But

the vineyard has been in mother's family for several hundred years. The thought of breaking it up is unbearable!"

"Don't worry, we're not going to make any hasty decisions, Berti. I'll be speaking to each of you and then we can determine what's to be done. I imagine it will be close to impossible to locate your elder sister, Marguerite."

"We haven't heard from her for thirty years."

"That's what I've understood." Grégoire turned over a sheet of paper. "In the short term, the best solution might be for Philippe to run the vineyard while paying the rest of you a portion of the yearly earnings. We'll have to see if that would be agreeable to everyone. But certainly the grandparents' house should be sold and the proceeds divided, unless Philippe is willing to purchase it."

Berti now understood why her brother and his wife, Marie-France, had initially been so hostile toward the idea of her return to the Midi. She had always assumed that Philippe, being the eldest son, would inherit the vineyard. It was difficult to believe her mother would ever have conceived the idea of splitting up Domaine Petitjean. In any case, Berti was grateful that Grégoire Dieulefit, like most *notaires*, moved with glacial slowness. They hadn't even had a family meeting yet, so she wasn't sure what her sister Pati in Belgium would say, or Marco, for that matter. She tried not to think about what might ultimately transpire, but the possibility of selling off her mother's vineyard to strangers was out of the question.

However, Berti had other things on her mind. She was considering returning to school, since her only option for a career seemed to be teaching French to tourists, something that held little interest for her. However, now that the domaine was in peril, perhaps learning about the cultivation of wine would be something to contemplate, especially if in lieu of selling, she became responsible for a portion of it. In the meantime, she'd started a part-time job at the *mairie* in Serret where the pay was decent. For the moment, her bank account was holding steady and she told herself that at least her first few months back in the region of her birth had not been stagnant.

That stormy night, the globe of the streetlight hung like a mist-ringed moon in the square frame of her window. Berti folded her mother's pillowcases into quarters and was unplugging the iron when her intercom sounded its electronic chime. It was already past nine o'clock and she certainly wasn't expecting anyone. She hesitated before lifting the receiver. As she put it to her ear, the pelting rain made the sound of disjointed static, and before she could even say hello, a masculine voice said, "*Allô*, Berti? It's Didier!"

Without thinking she blurted, "What are you doing out on a night like this?"

"I came to invite you for a drink."

Berti didn't like the idea of Didier at her door. She'd seen him briefly at her mother's funeral, but they hadn't spoken more than a sentence or two. What might people think if they saw him standing there in the street like a wet hound? Didier Falque, of all people, with his strange secrets that had been so publicly exposed and were still gossiped about with a nasty snicker.

"You should have telephoned," she replied.

"I don't have your number."

A torrent of water gushed from the galvanized pipe at the edge of the roof. Maybe she should simply go downstairs, but it would be even more awkward standing face-to-face with Didier in the teeming rain.

"Wait a moment." She tried to think, but came up with no plausible plan, and so she pressed the black button that released the latch on the downstairs gate.

Didier must have taken the stone steps two by two because when she opened the door he was already on the landing wearing a green mackintosh and no hat. His thick, wiry hair, impermeable as his slick coat, glistened with raindrops. He gave her a strange look, as if taken aback at seeing her dressed in a sweater and blue jeans with nothing but thick socks on her feet, and she was reminded of the shy boy who used to approach her in the schoolyard of their lycée. Instead of giving her the usual *bise*, he simply leaned forward and pressed his cheek against hers. His hot wet face with its scratch of beard was disconcerting, and she stepped backward.

"Perhaps this isn't the time to invite you anywhere, Berti. It's so miserable out." He sniffed the air as he entered the room and asked, "What's that perfume?"

"*Eau de lavande*. I was ironing."

"We have fields and fields of lavender up by Sault, but I didn't expect to encounter that on a cold winter night!" He took off his coat, leaving droplets of water on the tile floor. "Sorry if I interrupted you. I was nearby and remembered you were living here."

"You're not interrupting," she replied. "I was making plans for my life. I keep making new ones, then changing them as I go along."

"A change of plans doesn't mean you're quitting us, I hope?"

Berti shook her head. "It's too early to make that decision. Please." She held out her hand to take his wet coat and motioned to the small sofa that stood against one wall. That and a dining table with four rickety chairs were the only furniture in the minuscule living space. Up two steps through a narrow entry was her bedroom. She closed the door that led to it.

"What can I offer you?"

"*Un petit cognac?*"

"I'm sorry." She shook her head. "I have coffee or tea. Or there might be a bottle of wine that my brother brought."

"A daughter of Domaine Petitjean who isn't sure if she has a bottle of wine?" He laughed. "Your family should be more generous."

"I really don't need it. I only serve wine when I have company." She realized that sounded as if she never saw anyone, so she masked it by adding, "I rarely drink wine myself."

He leaned forward, his elbows on his knees. "Tell me about your plans."

"I'm simply considering my options. I'd like to do something different from what I've been doing."

"I always admired that about you, Berti, your courage and the fact that you had the nerve to go away and begin a whole new life. Are you enjoying it here now that you've returned?"

She nodded, thinking of the way she was greeted each morning by neighbors and acquaintances. It was a pleasure to stop and converse, something she'd rarely done in Edinburgh, where she'd found herself becoming more and more anonymous after her boys moved away.

"I'm amazed how attached I am—have always been—to this place," she said. "I love it even when it's like this!" As the wind made a violent pass over the roof, they both turned to glance at the streaming raindrops that glittered like topaz in the streetlight. Then Berti entered the small galley kitchen and drew out a bottle of red wine from the cabinet beneath the sink. She rifled through a drawer for a corkscrew and found the kind that vintners use, with a little knife attached. Her landlord had obviously furnished the place with a tourist in mind, a tourist who would enjoy trying all the famous appellations of the region. But she wasn't a tourist who was just passing through. She brought the bottle to the table and handed the little corkscrew to Didier. Then she brought him a glass.

He withdrew the cork with a gentle pop. "Won't you join me?" he asked. She shook her head and pulled out a kitchen chair, not wanting to sit too close to Didier, who took up most of the room on the narrow couch. "I remember you used to like wine," he said. "That summer before you left, we used to drink together at the Burrus."

"Yes, in those days I drank plenty of wine so I could convince myself that I was full of confidence about leaving home. But that wasn't really the truth."

Didier slid the open bottle onto the table without pouring it and looked over at her. "You know, Berti, you are still the same honest, good-natured girl you were at school, always so kind—even to a brute like me!" Berti looked down, wishing he wouldn't say such personal things, but he seemed oblivious to her embarrassment. "When I saw you at the market and you told me you'd rented a place and were permanently back here, I thought something really wonderful had happened. It's so strange to find you living here again after all this time." He stood up and walked over to the window. Her ironing board was still propped open and he ran his hand over the folded linens and then looked out into the night.

When he returned, he stood next to her for a moment. Then he leaned down and took her hand. As Berti felt his touch it was obvious that his youthful ineptness had disappeared. She considered asking him to leave right then and there. Instead, she felt a kind of languor come over her as he gazed down at her in silence. Then he lifted her hand and she felt his warm breath on the inside of her wrist. The tips of her fingers naturally curled to touch the sandpapery cheek that somehow felt just as pleasurable to her as his kiss. But she managed to take hold of herself and gently extricate her hand.

"This can't happen." Berti stood up. "We'd never have any peace. Everyone would know about us in two minutes. Just you appearing like this tonight—"

But Didier cut her off. "I couldn't care less what people think. We're not children anymore, Berti! Or is it my reputation that's bothering you? You're afraid you'll be seen associating with a pervert?"

She shook her head, not knowing what to say. But it was true that she didn't want her life poisoned by vicious, small-town gossip. Harassment of an elderly woman, a neighbor, was what Didier had been accused of. And the victim was Sabine Dombasle, whom he'd known all his life.

Didier's hands dropped to his sides and he walked back to the window, where the streetlamp emitted its citrine glow. She could smell the aroma of the strong red wine and felt somehow intoxicated by it, knowing all the while that this was impossible. The electric radiator hummed and she felt her face grow red. She wanted to turn it off, but she didn't dare draw closer to Didier.

"I'd like to tell you what happened, Berti," Didier finally said. "It's important to me that you know. Will you listen?" She fixed her gaze on the glowing window. He must have taken her stillness for an affirmation because he went on talking in a low voice. "Remember when we used to take the school bus together in the morning? We were still just kids with another whole year or two of lycée ahead of us. It was then, that spring, that Sabine Dombasle started something up with me. It was my first experience with sex and it was exciting. I won't tell you it wasn't. Sabine took the lead and I was more than ready for all of it. But when her husband was shot to death in that hunting accident, it all came to an end. I never saw her again except when I'd spot her from afar. Our relationship was over just like that, as if it had never happened."

Didier slowly passed his hand over his forehead with a sigh. Then he continued. "One night a couple of years ago, I'd had too much to drink at the *fête du village* and something reminded me of Sabine—the Sabine of *then*. So I went to her house as I had as a boy. That night she'd seemed strangely like her old self, even acting as if she'd been expecting me.

"Of course, I didn't touch her. She's an old woman. There was no denying that fact even in my drunken state. But I was shaken, standing there in her presence again, hearing her voice and remembering how she'd once been. When I left Sabine that evening, her son, Manu, must have seen me go and eventually forced some sort of false confession out of her. I have no idea what she told him. It's not important. Afterward, Christine divorced me. I come back to the village only to work the vines and see my daughters. If not for those things, I would never have shown my face in Serret again."

Berti kept her eyes on Didier. They faced each other in silence for quite a while. Finally, she heard him say, "I still don't understand what drove me to Sabine's that night. Perhaps I was hoping to pull the world down on top of my head." And then he moved away from the window. "I better go," he told her. The streetlight flashed like boiling glass as he drew close to her. Didier cupped her face in his large, rough hand. Then he took his coat and left.

In March, an unseasonable hot spell caused blossoms to suddenly sprout forth on the fruit trees. Berti was aware that warm weather in early spring didn't come without risk. A frost could easily ruin an early-budding orchard. Wine-growers also became concerned when the sun's rays became too strong too early, and fragile, canary-colored leaves pushed out of the brown papery bark of the vines. Still, Berti felt grateful for the blue skies, a sign that spring was on its way, bringing with it change.

It was eight o'clock when she went down the stone staircase to the street, thinking that she'd have time to stop at the village café before going to work at the *mairie*. The air was cool first thing in the morning and she'd wound a heavy scarf around her neck. The café owner, Michel, automatically made her what she always had: a noisette, strong espresso with a dash of milk. But that morning instead of his usual friendly greeting he scowled and said, "It's not even the season yet and I'm already sick of the tourists. When they're not here I make no money, but when they are, the place is bursting at the seams and I can't stand it! I've decided that at the end of the summer I'm going to sell this place and move up to the mountains, where the real people live, to a village where one can expect regulars all year round!"

"We'll all be very sad if you do that," said Berti, stirring a lump of sugar into her coffee. "Maybe you'll change your mind."

He shook his head. "I've had it up to here with the traffic, the boutiques, the fancy restaurants—all just to attract more tourists!" Berti kept her mouth shut. Part of her job at the *mairie* was to promote tourism. All the villages that made their money from wine were eager to attract visitors. But perhaps Michel was right; there were just too many of them.

It was still early and Berti decided that instead of driving to work she would walk, taking the long way around the village. As she descended through the stone portal, the closely pruned vineyards looked like ordered patchwork. The first thing she passed on the road was Sabine Dom-

basle's house. Berti had spotted Sabine at the weekly market just before Christmas, dressed in an old black coat.
She'd been turning over orange rutabagas at a vegetable
stand. Perhaps she had been planning a Christmas dinner
for Manu. Berti imagined them huddled over a table together, eating silently. She wondered if Sabine ever felt
guilty about betraying Didier, the person with whom she'd
obviously once been so enthralled.

When she reached a dip in the road, she saw one of Didier's vineyards spread across the hillside. Here the expo-
sure to the sun was different from the other vineyards. No
burgeoning buds were showing on the vines, so if another
frost came, his grapes wouldn't suffer any harm. She found
herself emitting a sigh. She hadn't seen Didier since that
rainy night a month or so before and the thought of him
made her uncomfortable and a little sad. She tried to concentrate on the beauty around her and the warm sunshine
that felt like a soft hand caressing her hair, but that made her
remember Didier's touch and she picked up her pace.

Her favorite part of the walk was through a sandy gully
where brambles and small overhanging bushes made an
archway overhead. Even without leaves the branches were
so thick that they turned the air around her blue. A swampy
odor ascended from the dank sand. She'd played there as a
child, hiding in the undergrowth during games of *cache-
cache* and then breathlessly clambering up the steep chalky
sides of the slope where tree roots were the only purchase.
A great fear had always overwhelmed her as she fled to a
hiding place. Even though she was playing with friends, the
image of her father bearing down upon her, his teeth

clenched in anger, always arose before her. Sometimes, in her panic to get away, she tore her flesh on thorns, causing beads of blood to form upon her arms and wrists as she bounded into the sheltering woods beyond. She never felt the pain of the scratches until later because the terror of the moment had been so intense. But then came the thrill of getting away scot-free.

At Easter time, Berti was given a week's vacation. She had made no particular plans, having instead spent all her free time the month before filling out forms in order to gain entry into a program at the University of Montpellier. One of her old school friends, a vintner named Rémi Faraud, told her that he and a dozen other winemakers had plans to open a shop that would sell their wines right there in the village. They all thought Berti would be perfect to run the place since she knew the region so well and would be able to speak English to the tourists. At Montpellier she signed up for several courses that had to do with the cultivation of wine. She had begun to think she might rent a tiny apartment there in the autumn, or simply move out of her tower in Serret for good. After all, Montpellier was a big town, where she'd make a lot of connections in the business. If the local vintners actually got their wine store up and running, she could always move back to the vicinity.

Berti decided to spend part of her Easter holiday at the sulfur springs in Mondraque, a village up beyond Mont Ventoux, where she could relax alone at the spa there. She threw her things into the backseat of her Clio and took the road to Saint-Maxence, passing by its Roman bridge and on up into the region of the Drôme, where the Toulourenc flowed in a deep crevasse below the steep mountain road-side. All along the way the river glittered like a silver ribbon under a sapphire sky. Wild fruit trees were in full bloom on the slopes, and Berti's heart lifted at the sight of the tiny purple and white blossoms on the gnarled plum and apple trees. The imposing Mont Ventoux loomed on the other side of the gorge. There was still snow on the summit, which, from her angle, appeared elongated, like a white cat stretched upon a pillow. She remembered going up there as a girl with friends one Saturday, hoping to spot wild chamois on the high slopes. But they'd all been shocked not only by the excruciating gusts, a mistral so strong that they could hardly keep their footing, but also by the intemperate chill, even though it had been the month of May. At a particularly precipitous point where she had not taken account of how perilously the gravel rolled beneath her feet, she'd lost purchase and begun to slide down the rocky cliff, beneath which there was nothing to halt her fall. Just as she'd opened her mouth to scream, a strong hand had grabbed her arm and pulled her back. For a moment, she couldn't move or speak, she'd been in such a state of panic.

"*Ça va?*" a voice behind her had softly whispered. And she'd realized it was her friend Didier who had reached out just in time.

Berti found herself speeding and slowed the car. The road upward curved in tight switchbacks, making the wheels careen as if they were on ball bearings. She passed through familiar mountain hamlets with signs advertising home-made sausage and millefleur honey. Farther on she came by a fenced-in trout farm that had been there since she was a child. Its huge stone basins, larger than swimming pools, were filled with glittering gray-pink hatchlings that swam in synchrony like birds. Finally, she descended to the village of Savoillans, whose plowed fields and single lane of houses bordered the Toulourenc. The sober village church stood just past a stone bridge that arched over the river, and on a whim Berti drove across it and pulled up next to the bell tower. Across the way, a solitary horse with a round, muscular chest looked up at her from a field where newly sprouted grass gleamed a verdant chartreuse. She remembered that there was a fountain on the main *place*, fed from a mountain spring. Feeling suddenly thirsty, she rounded the corner and drank deeply from the iron spout.

Afterward, she returned to where the horse was grazing and followed the path to an adjacent field. Feeling the ground warm beneath her feet, she lay down upon it and gazed up into the branches of a linden tree. On the other side of the field stood a line of poplars barely budded, their shoots shimmering like lemon drops in the morning light. Berti put her hands beneath her head and stared up at the cloudless sky. Nothing's going to drive me away from here for long, she thought as she lay in the warm patch of grass. She felt her body relax and conform to the shape of the earth, and in her repose she realized how stressed she had been between money concerns, getting used to her work at the *mairie*, and dealing with the red tape that entrance into the university entailed. On the cushioned ground she breathed in the scent of wild honeysuckle and a feeling of peace settled within her. Behind her, the horse made a contented snuffling noise.

When she turned her mind to what the afternoon at the spa in Mondraque would offer, the pleasurable sensation dissipated. The fountains there spurted sulfurous waters that were considered revivifying to bathe in and to drink. Her nostrils flared at the thought of the water's aroma of rotten eggs and the hot briny taste. Inside the spa was a good-sized swimming pool, but Berti didn't enjoy jumping in because no sun entered through the tinted windows and the water was cold. She decided that she would avoid the pool and perhaps sunbathe on the little terrace with a view over the town and then have a massage. But she remembered the salt rub a fleshy Eastern European masseuse had given her the previous visit that had caused red welts like little cuts to appear on her skin.

Berti gazed at the cerulean sky against which the branches of the linden moved to and fro. Finally, she decided she'd better go. She walked slowly back to her car, contemplating the way light and shade shifted on the speckled ground. Leaving the village, she bumped back over the steep bridge that traversed the river. After only a few kilometers, she came to a crossroads where she pulled over and stopped her car. A sign pointing to the left indicated Mondraque and its spa. To the right, three other signs listed the high mountain villages of Banon, Simiane-la-Rotonde, and Sault. Berti remembered what a lovely drive it was up there, especially in summer when the lavender fields were in full bloom. She'd done it often as a girl and had even once taken her sons there for a picnic and a leisurely promenade through the ordered lines of purple and gray lavender.

No cars were on the road behind her. She thought of the spa again and the rather sad town of Mondraque, where there was no nice place to eat. But she'd be drinking sulfur water that would probably kill her appetite anyway, so the quality of the food wouldn't matter. She thought of the masseuses with their pale muscular arms who trod across the white tiles of the underground area where the sauna and the steam rooms emitted their hot vapors.

Berti looked up at the road signs once more. And then she started the car and put on her directional signal even though there was still no one behind her. Then she turned, not to the left toward Mondraque, but to the right, in the direction of the three villages. As the road before her ascended, rocky promontories on either side hemmed her in. Then all at once the vista opened up and she found herself above vast, airy fields with the wide, cloudless sky overhead. Just opposite loomed majestic Mont Ventoux, the mountain that had been the stable, unwavering point during the whole of her young life. As she gazed around her Berti felt that even though she'd taken that route many times, she was in the midst of a journey to someplace new.

When she arrived in the town of Sault, she parked along the ramparts. The café stood on a promontory overlooking the fertile valley. Its cheerful green-and-white awning luffed in the breeze. She decided she would stop for a coffee there if she didn't find what she was looking for. In the meantime, she made her way along the *grande rue*, which was in actuality not much more than a lane with a newsstand that sold postcards and a *quincaillerie* whose baskets, brooms, and other household goods were hung on hooks outside the doorway.

And then she saw the shop she'd hoped to find. The head of an antlered stag was stenciled on the front window with the words LE CERF: BOUCHERIE TRAITEUR inscribed in a circle around it. When she pushed open the door, a small bell on a metal coil jingled. The salty-sweet smell of hams and a hint of black truffle pervaded the air along with the honeyed perfume of caramelized fruit. From the timbered ceiling hung dried sausages and cured legs of boar wrapped in a plethora of dried herbs. Inside a glass counter were crusted meat pies and terrines displayed on white paper doilies. A rack attached to the stone wall held mountain liquors made from juniper and wild herbs. Berti smiled when she saw a bottle of Domaine des Amouriers, a wine made by a vintner who had been a close friend of her mother's, displayed in a wicker basket. For the first time in ages she felt that it would be nice to drink a glass of wine.

The owner came in from the back dressed in a white apron tied over one shoulder. He was a fit man of about forty with a short black beard that stuck straight out from his face like boar bristles. When he greeted her she suddenly remembered his name was Laurent.

"It's been a while since you passed by here, madame," he said.

"Yes, several years, I'm afraid," Berti replied.

"Well, welcome back. What would you like today?"

Berti leaned over the glass case. She chose a pâté of pheasant and several slices of *jambon fumé*. "I would like one more thing to round out the meal," she told him. "What do you suggest?"

Laurent pointed to a mushroom terrine. "This would go well. And there's something else you should try. This morning my wife made *petites tartes* with wild strawberries. Would you like one?"

"I'll take two, please," said Berti. "And a bottle of Les Amouriers as well."

Laurent wrapped everything in packages of wax paper stamped with the same image of the buck pictured on the front window. He put the tarts in a pastry box that he tied with a crimson ribbon. Everything went into the straw basket Berti had brought with her.

She thanked him and then said, "A friend of mine moved here a while ago, but I'm not sure where he lives. Perhaps you know him. Didier Falque."

"Of course I know Didi. He lives over behind the church." Laurent gave her a smile and indicated that she should simply follow the street into the central *place* and then up a curving passageway.

Berti thanked him and closed the shop door behind her to the sound of the clinking bell. It was already noon and the sun was shining brightly overhead. It had occurred to her that Didier might have gone down to Serret to tend to his vines that day. In that case, she would return to the café and read the morning papers. In the meantime, she was curious to see the house where he was living. She passed the central square, where there were half a dozen ancient sycamore trees, some nearly hollow but still viable, as new leaves were already poking out like tiny fans from the thick branches. Restaurant tables with yellow wicker chairs around them lined the sidewalk. Farther on was a cobble-stoned alley that climbed gently upward. As she followed the curve of the stone wall she caught a glimpse of the church spire ahead and then spied an iron gate behind which several ornamental pomegranate bushes were in full flower, the fleshy petals gleaming a glossy golden red. Just inside, a man was bent over a rough wooden table, work-ing with an adz. He had a strong body and was dressed in blue jeans, a work shirt, and leather boots with thick soles. At the sight of him, Berti suddenly felt unsteady. Her heart clenched and she gripped her shopping basket to her chest with both hands. In a sickening rush she realized that she might not be welcome there. After all, Didier was a prosperous vintner, an attractive-looking man, and he was free. He might be involved, or even living with someone else. A sort of agony coursed through her. There was no reason why she might be the only woman in the region who would interest a man like Didier. She hesitated, think-ing that perhaps she could get away unseen and return to Mondraque and its sulfurous waters instead of being dis-covered there in the middle of an alleyway like a desperate cat. But as she was about to take a step backward, Didier turned. He gazed at her, his eyes at first inquiring and very dark, but almost immediately his mouth spread in a wide smile and his eyes gleamed as he strode toward her. When he reached her, he closed his mouth and then opened it again, unable to stop grinning.

"What on earth are you doing here?" he asked.

"I asked Laurent the butcher where you lived, but I was afraid you might not be home," she blurted. "I brought something to eat." She held out the basket to him.

A stone house with a red tile roof stood just beyond the blooming garden. On a flagstone terrace a round wooden table with two chairs was bathed in soft sunlight. Didier clasped her hand and led her through the gate.

Acknowledgments

I wish to thank Dee Ratterree for her unwavering faith, friendship, and brilliance, and my friend Gail Hochman for her time and encouragement. Thanks also to Trish Todd, David Jauss, Abby Frucht, and Ellen Lesser. And to Katharine Beebe for her perceptive questions about life in France.

CONSTANCE LEISURE began her career as a magazine editor in New York before moving to Paris with her husband and two young children, who were raised and educated there. While living in Paris she began writing both fiction and nonfiction about daily life in France. For the past twenty-five years she and her family have traveled to virtually every corner of the country. Early on, while on a trip to Provence to fill up the trunk of the family car with wine, they stumbled upon and purchased an old farmhouse with an enchanted garden in a small wine village in the Vaucluse. Little by little, the house in Provence became the center of her family life and her creative imagination.

Simon & Schuster Paperbacks
Reading Group Guide

Amour Provence

Constance Leisure

For Discussion

1. *Amour Provence* features a varied cast of characters. Which one's story resonated with you most? Why?

2. Share your thoughts on the novel's structure. What did you like or dislike about the way the story unfolded? In what ways did the unconventional narrative challenge you as a reader?

3. What long-term repercussions does Didier face because of his youthful affair with Sabine? Why are people so quick to believe Manu's accusation that Didier took sexual advantage of Sabine? Why do you suppose Sabine would permit her son to make such a claim and not refute it?

4. What do you make of Didier's encounter on the bridge with the peanut roaster's woman? What does this scene reveal about Didier?

5. Talk about the instances of bigotry in the novel. Were you surprised at the level of animosity directed toward the North African immigrants, Rachida and Mohammed

among them, living and working in the community? Why or why not? What are your thoughts on how Mohammed advises Rachida to handle the cultural differences they encounter?

6. Compare Rachida's life in Morocco to her life in France, where she has greater freedoms but is subject to racial abuse. In which place would you rather live if you were her?

7. Jeannot is introduced in the first chapter along with Berti and Didier. When he reappears in chapter six, why do you think the author chose to present him through the perspective of his teenage son, Auri, rather than in the third person? Why does Auri wish his father, whom he once admired, was a different sort of man?

8. "My parents say your father is a *marginal*. Somebody who lives on the fringe," Auri's friend remarks to him about Jeannot. How does the area's social and economic hierarchy impact its residents? On which characters does it have the greatest effects, positive or negative?

9. Lapin is considered a deranged eccentric by many of the townspeople. Is this reputation deserved? Why do Euphémie, Rachida, and Berti have a different view of Lapin than most everyone else?

10. Why does being confined to a psychiatric hospital remind Euphémie of the war years and trigger long-buried memories? Why does she feel that "perhaps she deserved" to be

confined against her will in the rest home? Why does Euphémie turn down Gaston's initial offer to help get her get out?

11. Why does Berti return to Provence after so many years living abroad? How is her homecoming different from the way she envisioned it would be? Is she content with the decision she made? What does she see differently now about the area, especially in regard to how provincial proprieties affect women?

12. Berti suddenly remembers witnessing her father viciously beat her sister Marguerite, one of the frequent acts of violence he committed against his children. How does this recollection alter Berti's perception of her family? Why is she unwilling to apply the adage "forgive and forget" to her father and all he has done?

13. Why is Berti reluctant not only to become romantically involved with Didier but even to be seen with him in public? Why does she later change her mind and seek out Didier? What are her intentions when she goes to his house with a picnic? What do you suppose the future holds for Didier and Berti?

14. Discuss how marriage is portrayed in the novel, from Rachida and Mohammed's arranged marriage to Clément and Liliane's volatile partnership to Euphémie's union, which ended under mysterious circumstances. What is the significance of Liliane's bequest to her children?

15. What did you know about Provence prior to reading this novel? Has your perception of it changed? If so, how? What is unique about the villages that serve as the story's setting, and what universalities do they share with other small towns?

A Conversation with
Constance Leisure

Tell us about your connection to Provence. When did you first visit the area?

When my husband and I moved in Paris we took our children down to Provence one autumn during the Toussaint vacation. While there, we spotted an advertisement in a local magazine for a farmhouse for sale near where we were staying. We visited the place with a real estate agent who stood in the garden eating grapes off the vines that were attached to arbors. There was something magical about the place, but we felt it wasn't sensible to act on a whim. When we returned the following spring, the house was still for sale and the asking price was much lower. Fate had intervened on our side. Now, making grape jelly from those fruited vines has become a ritual that I perform with joy each year.

What prompted the idea to set a novel in the region?

We had been living in Provence on and off for twenty years when I began to write about the region. The landscape and climate of the Midi—the rolling hills; the high mountains; the river valleys; the vineyards; the hot, dry summers; the smell of springtime herbs and flowers—had always touched me. The character of the people who live there reflects the landscape: sometimes harsh, sometimes sweet and mild. The Provençal are proud, love to talk and enjoy themselves, and above all have an enthusiastic willingness to throw themselves into life whether times are good or bad.

As an American living in Provence, that would have been a natural angle for you to take in a novel. Why did you decide not to go that route?

It is the French who interest me. I didn't have any desire to tell a story about an ex-patriate. I wanted to tell a story from the point of view of the people who grew up in the Midi, who have lived whole lives there. I hoped to give a special insight into how the Provençal think and feel.

Had you wanted to write a novel for some time, or was it a spontaneous decision to do so?

While I was living in France, I began several novels that took place in the US. But after a while I felt I was losing touch with my home country. I didn't have my finger on the pulse of American life anymore. When I began writing about France there was an immediate surge of life and I knew I was on the right track.

Why did you choose to structure *Amour Provence* the way that you did? What challenges, if any, did this present while you were writing the book?

I began writing first about individual characters, and then I realized that these people were not only close neighbors, but that their lives were intimately intertwined. Even though some of these characters had wildly different stories and experiences, the *terroir* (the special location they live in), as the French call it, held them together—and held the novel together. All of them have a deep attachment to the land they come from, their French patrimony.

Which of the many compelling characters in the novel came to you first? Which one was the most interesting to create?
I loved Didier right from the beginning though he changed a lot as I wrote. At first, I thought he was a very discontented person who had a certain penchant for violence, but then I realized he was a much more evolved, and evolving, person than that. I also am extremely fond of Euphémie, who is so much a creature of the natural world. She reminds me of one of those Turgenev characters who romp through forests and don't really have a home. And I have a special feeling for Aurélien. I had three younger brothers, so teenaged boys have always been something I find interesting to write about.

One of the most gripping and poignant parts of the novel is Euphémie's recollection of events that took place during World War II when she was a teenager. How did you go about researching this aspect of the story?
I have been interested in World War II for a long time, especially the Holocaust. I'd read several nonfiction books about what happened in Provence during the war. And I'd heard a lot of stories from our neighbors. When a friend took me to a memorial erected for several young American pilots who had been shot down in 1944 in a vineyard near my house, I scribbled down their names in my notebook and began to

ruminate about how I might eventually incorporate that incident into a story. One of the young fliers was named Harry.

The book's epigraph is a lovely passage by poet Guillaume Apollinaire. Why did you choose this particular verse, and what does it reflect about *Amour Provence*? What is the *amour*, or love, referenced in the title?
I felt those verses by Apollinaire reflected a certain longing for life and love that several of the main characters evince. I didn't realize while I was writing the novel that many of the stories are about love: platonic love; love of a parent for a child; marital love; a sort of distant, watchful, undemanding love like Lapin's love for Euphémie; and, of course, passionate sexual love.

Weather plays a significant role in the story and affects the characters' lives and livelihoods, including the mistral, a fierce wind that according to Jeannot "could drive anyone crazy." Have you experienced the intense weather extremes in Provence firsthand?
Oh, yes! Anyone who lives in Provence has been nearly blown over by the mistral when it is at its fiercest—and there's nothing colder than a mid-winter mistral. Conversely, in the summer the sun can be so bright that it burns right into skin and bone. The locals rise early in order to get chores done, and they make sure to take a siesta during the midday hours to spare themselves that intense heat.

You previously worked in book and magazine publishing. What is it like being on the other side of the process now? What was your path to publication like?

It took me several years to write this novel, so that was quite different from fast-paced magazine publishing where we'd be churning out issues every month. But as an editor, I still remember the excitement I would feel when I picked up a manuscript and began reading something that I thought was really good. There's a magic to that. I hope my readers will feel it for *Amour Provence*.

What would you most like readers to know about *Amour Provence*?

I wanted to impart a genuine feeling for what life is really like in Provence, its special atmosphere, the food, the people, the markets, the weather, the attitude toward life, the life of a small village, and sometimes the hard choices people have to make, choices that can sometimes enrich a life even when they are not easily made.

Enhance Your Book Club

1. Winemaking is the livelihood of the Falque and Perra families and for many others in Provence as well. Tour a local vineyard to learn about the process, visit a local wineshop, or host your own tasting and uncork several different varieties of French wine.

2. Follow Berti's lead and have a Provence-themed picnic, serving foods similar to those she selects to share with Didier, like pâté, mushroom terrine, *jambon fumé* (smoked ham), and strawberry tarts. Or make *daube de boeuf*, beef simmered in wine and herbs, a regional specialty that's cooking on the stove when Berti arrives at her parents' home. You can find recipes for the savory dish at epicurious.com and food.com.

3. Have each member bring a color image of Provence, such as ones depicting the region's iconic lavender fields, olive groves, mountains, historic towns, and châteaux. Create a collage of the images to help set the scene for your discussion of *Amour Provence*.

4. Author Constance Leisure lives in Provence part-time. Visit her website (constanceleisure.com) and blog (constanceleisure.wordpress.com) to learn more about her and to follow along on her adventures in the region and beyond.